The Latin Run

One Hell of a Ride

T.K. Harsen

For permissions, inquiries, or more information, please contact:

Bold Books Publishing

Lillith@boldbookspublishing.com

Credits

Cover Design by Elizabeth a Bold Books Exclusive Designer

Editing by Aimee Ferro Edits

Printed in the United States of America.

First edition, 2025.

PROLOGUE

Mexico was the one place on Earth I desperately never wanted to call home—at least not anytime soon. Exhaustion clung to me as I gazed across the open ocean and tried to comprehend how I had survived the past week. The sun cast its dying light over the endless waves of the ocean as the boat rocked gently beneath me, picking up speed.

I was lucky to be alive, but the memories—oh, the memories—they wouldn't leave me alone. The chaos I had endured still flooded my thoughts, causing me to question what the fuck I had been thinking when I decided to be a 'yes man.'

I never understood why people lived life safely, or how they found happiness in the mundane comforts of a small suburban home. That type of lifestyle had never been for me. I craved adventure, or at least, that was how I had always lived.

I took nothing for granted. Lived every moment as if it could be my last.

And after those past few weeks, that was precisely what I had done. The only positive thing that had come from all of it was the stack of cash I had stowed away in a hidden compartment under the sofa of my fifty-five-foot Sportfish yacht that made everything feel a lot better.

Well, that and I wasn't in a Mexican prison or worse—dead.

I lifted the bottle of my ice-cold Corona to my lips, and I couldn't help but smile.

"God damn... this is good."

As the sun cast its dying light over the endless waves, the boat rocked gently beneath me. I felt a strange mix of triumph and dread. The ocean's horizon stretched infinitely before me, a reminder that while I had escaped one storm, the vast unknown still lay ahead.

Chapter One

Two weeks earlier...

The heat from the afternoon sun had felt good against my skin, despite the beads of sweat that dripped off me, which reminded me of exactly where I was. Cozumel, Mexico. It had been good to me that year. I had waited what seemed like months to enjoy my part in the local Bill Fish tournament, and though first place had been stolen from me, I had made out pretty well.

I gazed across the bay from behind dark lenses and took in the sight of the other fishing vessels and the people who busied themselves with cleaning up after a long day out on the open water. Bill Fish wasn't like normal tournaments; it could take hours to bring one of those fish in. That was if you even hooked one to begin with. It was a dangerous sport... but a thrill I had loved.

I lifted the cold bottle of Corona to my lips and savored the delicious flavor mixed with lime as I wiped the sweat from my brow with my other hand. The warm breeze that came off the ocean had made the heat more manageable for sure, but it hadn't stopped the slight burn I had felt against the back of my neck.

"Time to get this shit taken care of." I placed the bottle down upon the decking before I reached for the hose. The soft spray of water brushed against the slick decking as I rid it of the salt displaced during my time out at sea.

There had always been something about the call of the open ocean that calmed my mind and set me at ease, and that day was no different. The fact I lost the money I had by not getting first place had pissed me off. Not that I had been hard on cash. It would have just been nice to have.

"¡Qué pasa, Tomas!" a familiar voice had called out.

The heavy footsteps on the deck turned my head as I peered down the dock to see Jeffryn Alejandro walking toward me. It had been some time since I had last seen him. Yet, no matter the distance or time between visits, it had always felt like we picked up right where we had left off.

We had met years ago when I was hired to captain an offshore supply boat in the Bay of Campeche. A friendship had quickly formed between us, and we worked side by side until I retired. He had come from a prominent family in Mexico, with strong political ties. At 38 years old, he had more connections to the world down there than I had cared to dive into. Not to mention a substantial amount of money—some earned through legitimate means, but most acquired through questionable methods. Regardless, the parties he hosted were always enjoyable.

I dropped the hose and jumped down off the deck onto the boardwalk, my arms open wide as he stepped into my embrace.

"Jeff, it's good to see you again, man!"

"It's good to see you as well, Cap," he replied, pulling back. "I heard you were in town. How are you? It's been too long."

I nodded and let my eyes drift to the boat before I pulled a rag from my back pocket to wipe my brow.

"Things have been busy, but I'm hanging in there," I replied before I glanced back at him. "I'm in town for the tournament. I was planning to look you up when it was all over. How have things been with you?"

"They are good," he replied softly before he looked back at the boat. "Is this your boat?"

"Yeah, man!" I exclaimed and stepped back with pride. "Come aboard, let me get you a beer and out of this heat."

Jeff hesitated, his eyes drifting down to his watch before he nodded. "Sure, I've got a few minutes."

The high sun shone down on us as I gestured for him to follow me until we both made it back to the deck of my boat. There was no way I was chatting with him outside. The heat had been enough for one day, and my body desperately sought the reprieve of cool air from the salon.

The moment we entered, my feet automatically made for the fridge as Jeff's low whistle from behind me caught my attention. "It looks clean, Cap. What year is this?"

I grabbed two beers, popped their tops and turned to face him. His dark eyes wandered over every inch of the varnished teak wood boat with eyes wide in amazement, as if it were the best-looking boat he had ever seen. Amusement filled me from his reaction.

"It was built in 2001, but I put some money in it."

"Very nice." He nodded as he stepped forward to take the beer from my outstretched hand. "It looks great, Cap."

A soft chuckle escaped my lips every time he affectionately referred to me as "Cap." Short for Captain, a title I had proudly held for many years. I still couldn't believe he had joined me as my first mate and translator all those years ago when I was hired to run an offshore supply boat in the Bay of Campeche. With his impressive background, he certainly hadn't needed to work, but it had been his love for the ocean and his skilled hands that had drawn him toward me. It felt like fate had brought us together as we quickly became inseparable friends and colleagues.

"Thanks," I replied. I had been used to seeing the boat the way it looked, and it often blew right past me how good of a job had been done in restoring it.

"Where did you get the woodwork done?"

I laughed. "Yours truly, man."

He raised a brow, his eyes widened in shock. "Seriously?"

"Yep, I put everything I had into her. So all the renovations are on me."

A moment of silence fell between us as I cleared my throat and walked toward the lush seating I had installed after the renovations. My body had been tired after being out on the open water all day.

"So, how are things with you... truly?"

Jeff had seemed hesitant again as he lifted the beer to his lips, the cold refreshing beverage going down slowly as he walked over to the seat across from me and sat down. "I've been working a lot. Haven't had much time for fishing or anything else for that matter."

"I'm sorry to hear that," I said as I lent forward on my knees. "I would have loved to have you out there fishing the tournament with me."

He let out a soft chuckle as he shrugged his shoulders. "I was supposed to be fishing it, but as usual, something came up, and I couldn't."

"That sucks, man. Maybe when you're free, we can take the boat out this week."

His smile grew at my offer, a light of excitement in his eyes as he nodded. "That would be great. I'm sure you could use some pointers."

The sarcastic comment had caused us both to laugh. The memories of our time together when I had still worked the shipping lines came back the longer we had spent together. "Hey, I did better in the tournament than most probably expected."

"Did you place?" he asked, his brows slightly knitted together.

"Yeah, I took third for six grand. I barely missed second for thirty-five. It would have been nice to get that kind of money."

He sat there silently and grinned at me with a goofy expression on his face that he used to always give me when I had done something stupid. It had only taken me a few seconds to realize why he was looking at me the way he was, a light bulb quickly went off in my head.

"Was that your boat that caught the one outside the pass in the last ten minutes?!"

He started laughing. "That was my crew; I was tending to some business in Honduras."

"Y'all took me for twenty-four grand, asshole!" I replied as I shook my head. However, my comment had only made him laugh as he shrugged his shoulders and looked toward the window.

The cue had been obvious as I stood to my feet and peered out the window to look across the marina. "Which boat is yours?"

"That's it at the fuel dock," he replied before he came to stand beside me, pointing to a beautiful sixty-five-foot Hatteras, 'obviously new' with all the bells and whistles, the name Maria on its stern.

"I see you named it after your sister."

His smile came back as he nodded. "Yeah, Tomas. She is still in Miami most of the time, but she will be back here tonight; she heard from someone that you were in town and sent me down here to check."

"Is that right?" I replied softly, thinking about the last time I had seen her. "Tell her I said hi when you call her with your report."

He didn't need to say much about her as he nodded, stood to his feet and downed the rest of his beer. "I have to get going. I have business to take care of. Do you want to take a ride with me?"

"I'd love to, man, but I have a few chores to do... we can meet up later if you want, though."

It had sucked that he had to leave already, but I knew how hectic his 'business' could be. And though I had ridden with him many times before, that day just wasn't the day for it.

"If you want beer, why don't you come up to my parents' old place. I'm having a party, and I'd love to have you."

Party. The thought of partying again with him was joy to my ears. God only knows what we could end up getting into, but it sure as hell felt like a good way to spend the rest of my time in Cozumel.

"Sure, I'll be there." I smiled. "What time?"

"Around seven... I'll see you then."

Once he was gone, I stood watching the sun descend closer toward the horizon. The mix of oranges and yellows that had cascaded across the sky had been a sight people would pay to see, and I had gotten to see it every day.

A million-dollar view and nothing but time on my hands.

At least until that night.

Chapter Two

As I finished the last of my tasks for the day, memories of the six years I spent working with Jeff flooded my mind. Our journey together had started in Mexico, where we were both hired to run a supply vessel. I was the Captain and Jeff was my first mate and translator. Even back then, it was clear that he came from a wealthy family, although he still lived at home with his parents.

From the moment we met, we hit it off. Jeff spoke perfect English and offered to teach me Spanish, which proved to be incredibly useful during our time in port. Whenever we docked, he would introduce me to his friends from other vessels and we would go bar hopping around town. The bond between them reminded me of life in a small town, where everyone looked out for each other and loyalty was highly valued. This was something I deeply respected, especially after dealing with people who had proven to be disloyal in my past experiences. At this point in my life, I wasn't sure if I could trust anyone.

I first met Jeff just before Christmas in 2004 when I asked him to show me around so I could do some shopping for gifts to send back home to my family. After making our purchases, we had seafood on the beach in Ciudad del Carmen. We stumbled upon a simple but charming palm-covered hut with plastic tables and chairs set up on the sand. They cooked over a large grease pit on an open fire and served the best fried fish in town. We ordered some beers and fried snapper.

As we sipped on our drinks and waited for our food, Jeff turned to me with a serious expression on his face and said, "Tomas, I want to talk to you about something. If you're not interested, just say the word and I won't bring it up again."

Intrigued by his tone and demeanor, I replied, "What is it?" That's when he brought up the topic of buying and selling diesel fuel for the Cartels, among other illegal activities.

Having some experience with this kind of business from my time in Nigeria, I asked Jeff to tell me more about how it was done in Mexico. He explained that the schemes they ran came from a Logistics branch of Pemex, the government-controlled oil company. "These programs direct the vessels to which platforms they should service and what cargo they should receive," he said. Jeff revealed that there was a separate division called Marine Control, which tracked all the vessels 24/7 on radar to ensure they were following their assigned programs. He also mentioned that he went to school with all the guys who worked in both divisions and everyone was involved in this scheme to avoid getting caught and going to jail.

I could still feel the nervous anticipation that coursed through my veins as I considered their offer. But after witnessing the strong bond and camaraderie among their group, I couldn't help but feel a sense of reassurance. It seemed like they had all their bases covered, and this type of operation was just another day in the life for them. With a deep breath, I agreed to give it a try.

Over the course of the next few years, we conducted a lot of business together. We would often jet off on cartel-owned private planes, indulging in extravagant trips to places like Belize for lunch or Honduras and Venezuela to set up deals. It was a lavish lifestyle, but one that came with a significant price tag: "While you were making millions for the Cartel, you were untouchable and living large!" However, there was also a dark underbelly to this world, as I soon found out.

As long as you were useful to the Cartel, you were safe. But if you ever became a liability, there was always the looming threat of disappearing without a trace. My partners in crime—Jeff, Ramon, and our band of merry pirates—continued on with the business for years until we hit a major roadblock. The Mexican Navy began cracking down on our operations, leading to impounded vessels and jail time for some unlucky individuals. Yet even those who avoided imprisonment were not spared from brutal punishments: "The lucky ones went to jail; others were shot and dismembered or dissolved in vats of acid."

It was in these dark times that I decided to leave the business behind. Sure, I had to pay a hefty fifty percent of my earnings from the past four years to get out alive, but it was worth it. After all, fifty percent of something is better than nothing—or worse yet, death. I still have a few friends who are involved in the business, but I keep my distance from most of them, knowing all too well the dangers and consequences that come with being a part of this world.

The sound of a horn blowing in the distance pulled me from my thoughts, and looking down at my watch, I noticed that time had ticked on farther than I'd expected. Turning off the hose, I stowed it away and went below to get ready. Jeff said the party was at seven and though it was only five-thirty now, I was never someone to be overly late for anything.

Especially in this society. Respect was everything.

Showered and freshly dressed, I ran a hand through my blonde shaggy hair and headed off the boat towards the tiki bar near the docks for a few drinks before heading out. It was a ritual I did every night, and though I had plans tonight, I wasn't planning on changing anything.

The tiki bar was a large pavilion, with a palm leaf roof, and a bar at one end facing the Marina. The part I enjoyed the most were the people who frequented it. It was typically a nice mixture of locals & tourists. The girls smelling like coconut oil coming in from the beach.

The moment I sat down, a dark-haired native beauty greeted me with a smile on her face that stretched from ear to ear. She wasn't the typical girl who worked the bar, but I wasn't going to complain. Especially when her busty rack peeked behind her low cut white top leaving nothing to the imagination.

"What can I get ya, hunny?" she asked, catching me completely off guard. Not only was her English really good, but her accent sounded familiar to the people I knew from south Texas. Something I wasn't expecting. And when she moved, I got the faintest hint of coconut.

"Your English is good."

She stared blankly at me before letting out a soft laugh. "Thanks... so what can I get for ya?"

"I'll take a Corona, please."

She didn't bother to keep the conversation with me as she spun around, grabbing a frosty Corona from the cooler and placing it on a coaster. The sight of her working made me slightly more curious as to why a girl like her was spending her time down here.

Before I had the chance to ask, she slid me a menu.

"Oh, no thanks. I won't be eating. I have plans tonight."

"You mean Jeffryn's party?" I paused slightly puzzled by her question as her smile widened. "Im not psychic, I saw you guys talking on the docks today. Are you guys friends?"

I wasn't used to people being in my business, but it quickly reminded me how in this place, someone was always watching you. Even if it wasn't intentional.

"Yeah, we worked together a few years ago," I replied. "My name's Tomas, but Jeff sometimes refers to me as a Gringo or Tomador."

Reaching across the bar, I offer her my hand which she gladly shakes. Though the puzzled look of amusement on her face makes me wonder what's currently going through her mind.

"Tomador?" she says slowly, as if it's a question she isn't sure she should be asking.

"It means drinker," I replied with a chuckle. Lifting my beer to my lips as I watch the amusement fill her face before she shakes her head.

"Do you drink a lot, Gringo?"

I shrug slightly. "It's an inside joke."

"I bet it is," she retorts, placing a hand upon her hip. "I'm Diana. I work for Jeffryn."

I knew that his parents owned a construction company years ago, but I didn't know that he had anything to do with the businesses at ports. My mind wondered if this is only a part time thing for her, and she works with him elsewhere.

"Oh right. So you work at the construction company?"

Her brows furrow before she laughs again, shaking her head. "No. I work right here, hunny."

"He owns the bar?" My question was more of disbelief as she nodded, staring at me like I was literally insane. For someone who's supposed to be friends with this man, I was sure out of the loop on what he had been doing the last few years.

"Yeah, his parents turned the construction company over to him and his sister a couple of years ago. Maria ended up buying Jeffryn's share and in turn, he bought the Marina."

My jaw all but dropped onto the bar at her words as utter disbelief filled me. I felt jealousy warm my face as I turned and glanced across the two hundred plus slips covering the small cove. "Holy shit. He owns the whole fucking marina now?"

"Down to the stool you're sitting on," she says pointedly. "Are you sure you know him?"

A smirk litters the corner of my lips as I shake my head. "I'll have to admit, it's been a long time since I've seen him. I knew his family had money, but I guess I underestimated that. It's good to see him doing so well."

Silence fills the space around us as she lays the rag she was using to clean down and glances around into the night air as if expecting someone to be watching her. "Well," she says softly, leaning across the bar in a whispered voice. "Don't say it came from me... but the word is that he has gotten himself in a bit of a spot."

"Is that right?"

She nods, standing upright once more. "Just hearsay."

I let the situation sink in, and with it, I can't help but wonder what else I'd missed out on since we used to last run together.

"What time are you heading up there?" she finally asks, bringing me back to reality.

Glancing down at my watch, I take in the time. "About fifteen minutes. Why?"

"If you want I'll ride up there with you. That way you don't get lost."

I didn't miss the faint bit of mischief on her lips as she spoke. And lifting the beer to my lips, I downed the rest of it before setting the empty beer on the bar. "Give me another one of these, and I'll wait for you."

It was an open invitation. One I wasn't sure she was going to accept, but who knew where the night would end up leading us.

One thing was for sure, I was going to have to see what was bothering my friend.

****

I hadn't expected her to come with me, but she did. Thirty minutes later, the two of us sat in the SUV that Jeff had lent me and headed up towards his parent's property with nothing on our minds but having a good time. I had to admit, when he said he was lending me a car to use, I wasn't expecting a black Range Rover to be sitting in the parking lot.

I'd half expected a Ford Explorer or something.

Not that I'm complaining. It's been a while since I rode in style.

"Where did you learn English?" I decided that small talk was better than silence. I glanced at her, her eyes lifting from her phone as she raised a questioning brow before a smile lined her face.

"Texas. My father is a Border Patrol agent on the U.S. side, and my mother is a teacher in Brownsville."

"Oh," the word left my lips as I slowly processed the information. "I thought you were a local girl or something."

She laughed. "Most people do. I was born in Matamoros but we immigrated to the states when my father was offered a job working for Border Patrol. I was only six at the time."

"That's amazing. It's great that your father was offered that kind of work."

My comment didn't seem to go over too well as she left out a heavy breath and turned her attention towards the window once more. "Yeah, it was an amazing offer. But something about Mexico kept bringing me back."

"Oh really? Is that why you're here now?"

"No." She laughed, shaking her head. Her eyes shifted to me once more. "I came down here on a cruise ship last year with a few friends. I met Jeffryn at a marina party and when we were getting ready to leave the next day, I overheard him complaining at the tiki bar about some bartender he fired for stealing from him. I told him that I didn't really want to leave and had experience bartending... he gave me the job on the spot."

"Really?"

She nodded again. "Yep."

"You don't have the desire to go back stateside then?"

She shrugged her shoulders as she contemplated my question. "I was only going to stay for a few months, but I never left. Almost a year and two months later and I'm still enjoying the life I have created here. Truth is, I love island life."

I couldn't deny what she was saying. I'd often thought about never leaving this place, but home always called me back and being in the Florida panhandle was a life I loved more than anything. Being with family was something I loved even more than anything.

"I relate to that." My admission was soft, my eyes stuck to the road as I navigated my way down deserted roads towards the direction of a home I'd spent much time in with Jeff.

"What about you?"

Once again, her voice brought me out of my thoughts. My eyes drifted to her for a split second before finding the road again. "What about me?"

"What's your story? I mean, how did you become Gringo Tomador?"

Laughter filled the space in the vehicle as I thought over what she was asking. It'd been sometime since someone had really asked me how I became who I was. And though I wasn't prepared to tell her everything, I could at least tell her something.

"I started working on fishing boats as a teenager and found my love for the sea. I eventually became a boat captain, and worked all over the world until landing a job in Mexico where I met Jeff and his sister, Maria."

"You know Maria?" she replied, her brows lifting slightly as her grin widened.

There's no way I could get around her curiosity as I nodded slowly and cleared my throat. "Yeah, we dated for a while."

"Oh, I see," she paused, as if contemplating her next move. "Was it serious?"

"No, not really," I replied, shaking my head. "We were pretty close for a while but she was going to school in Miami with the hopes of taking over the family business."

"What about Jeffryn?"

"He's not the office type," I said with a slight chuckle. "Kind of like me, but obviously, more successful."

She smiled at me, her eyes casting towards the window once more as she ran her fingers through a strand of her hair that rested upon her shoulder. "You seem to be doing alright; I've seen your boat at the Marina."

"My life savings I'm afraid." If she only knew how broke I was, she probably wouldn't be showing me as much interest. Not that she was that kind of girl or anything, but I've met the type who are. Quickly dismissing the thought from my head, I opened my mouth once more. "I took third place in the Bill Fish tournament today though. Won a little money, but I was hoping for at least second; it would have paid out thirty-five thousand."

Her head snapped toward me once more, eyes wide as her mouth dropped open. "Wow! What did third place pay out?"

"Only six thousand," I say tilting my head to the side before shrugging.

"That's still good!" she said excitedly. "Sure, it isn't thirty-five thousand. But it isn't like six is chump change either. That's still a lot."

Jeff's family home began to peak over the horizon, lights through every window lighting up against the dark sky that seemed to grow brighter the closer we got. As much as I've been enjoying the conversation with this lovely woman beside me, I'll be glad to see Jeff.

"Perhaps, but by the time I buy fuel and supplies… it doesn't leave much left. Maybe Jeff will have a job for me too."

Eventually, the vehicle came to a slow crawl as she pointed me down a road off to the right that led through a rod iron fence with a large gate that sat open to all brave enough to join in the festivities. I can't help but be taken back by how grand things already seem, from the security of the gate to the ceramic tile driveway that winds up and down through an expansive manicured lawn. Until it opens up to something far more spectacular.

"Wow, you weren't kidding," I said under my breath, but loud enough for her to hear me. My mind was completely blank as I took in what looked to be a massive three story building with large white pillars that reach far into the sky.

"Yeah, hunny" she said, placing her hand on my leg. "It's beautiful, but too much bling for me; I'm a simple girl."

I caught the drift of her comment, but decided against acknowledging it as the vehicle finally came to a slow stop outside the front of the building. Everywhere I looked, security guards in black uniforms carrying guns walked the property. I knew that his family was important, but didn't remember him having this much security back in the day.

Though I supposed by the look of the people lingering outside and making their way through the massive dark stained front door, these weren't the same type of people I was used to seeing when I saw Jeff years ago.

It's clear that times have changed.

And with it, so had Jeff.

CHAPTER THREE

THE MOMENT DIANA AND I stepped out of the car, the boisterous laughter of Jeff's guests floated towards my ears. As long as it's been since I've seen him, things really weren't any different. He always threw the best parties. I guess now, it was just that time had gotten the best of us both. That and he hit the jackpot when it came to money.

Gazing towards the front door of the home, I quickly spotted him. He stood with what looked like a few well-dressed business associates locked in casual conversation. Until he seemed to notice us, his eyes lighting up as he waved in our direction before excusing himself from the men he was with.

"What do you think, Tomas?!"

What do I think? Shit, this was more than I could have ever imagined.

"Holy shit, Jeff!" I exclaimed. "This is awesome, man; I need to work for you!"

My comment was said jokingly, but Jeff didn't seem to notice. Instead he pulled me into an excited brace. "Say the word, Tomas!"

"I feel underdressed," I admitted when we broke apart. I didn't miss the way his Brunico suit felt against me when he hugged me and glanced down at my own clothing, I was definitely underdressed for this occasion.

"Don't worry, Tomas, everyone is in shorts. And... I just got here. I'm actually going to change."

Glancing at his outfit once more, I didn't miss what appeared to be a thousand-dollar outfit, maybe even more. Though for him, it wasn't the right attire for the evening, which made me feel even more unsure about what I wore. I don't voice it. Instead, I watched his attention turn to Diana with nothing but affection.

"Diana," he muttered, pulling her into an embrace as he kissed her cheek. "You look as good as ever. Are you taking care of Tomas?" I agreed with him; she had changed from her bar clothes into a halter that showed off her flat stomach and a sarong, which did nothing to hide her plump ass.

"He appears to be one that can take care of himself," she retorts, her eyes drifting over me with a slick smirk on the corner of her lips before she moves forward into the house. "I'm going to find a drink."

Jeff nodded, glancing back at me. "This is true," he replied, putting his hand on my shoulder. "Come in, Tomas. Let me show you around."

Enormous double doors with Marlins carved into them graced the entrance of his home as I followed him, stepping into a massive foyer with vaulted ceilings and a sunken living room accented with a wall of windows that gazed out over the Caribbean. The view, breathtaking even in the dark, one can only imagine what it will look like in the daylight.

And if that wasn't enough, Jeff had brought in a damn Mariachi band to play music throughout the house as the guests enjoyed themselves.

"Diana," Jeff called out towards where she was caught in conversation with a dark-haired woman I've never seen before. "Can you show Tomas to the bar? I'm going to change."

Her eyes met mine before she turned her gaze on Jeff with a sickly sweet smile. "Sure thing... follow me."

She was a complete contrast to the woman I met out on the docks, the same woman I'd driven here with. Almost as if the moment we stepped into this place, she fell into her element. A woman far from high society, but still with all the regal qualities of a woman I'd find back in the states.

We crossed the room towards the bar just around the corner, but I couldn't help but pause in my steps. My brows furrowed slightly as I took in the bartender in a full penguin suit as if he was waiting on a five-star event, when everyone around him was in shorts or bathing suits.

"Margarita, please," Diana says, before turning to me. "What are you getting?"

"Uh—just give me a Jonnie Blue straight up."

As soon as the bartender got to work, my eyes drifted to the room once more. How in the hell was it that I've landed myself in a place like this? Especially during everything that had been going on since I left the states and came back here.

"It's a little overwhelming, isn't it?" Diana asked, pulling me from my thoughts.

"I guess you can say that," I mumbled in reply as I shook my head. I lifted the glass to my lips and took a sip, continuing to admire everything around me. "I see Jeff has a lot of friends these days."

She nodded, not seeming as impressed as I was. "It's the hottest party in town, hunny."

I could see why it was. Jeff was never someone to do something small, and to see how much it had grown didn't surprise me. Minutes later, Jeff walked around the corner looking more like the Jeff I remembered—standard board shorts and flip-flops, his mop of unruly black hair as wild as the day I met him.

That was the man I used to get into shit with.

"See Tomas—" he laughed, arms open wide as he approached me, "much better."

"You definitely look more like yourself now."

Grabbing a drink from the bar, he stepped towards me, eyes gazing around the room as a smile pulled at his lips. "What do you think?"

"About the party or the clientele?"

A deep chuckle reverberated from his chest as he shrugged his shoulders. "Both."

Taking in the gorgeous women clad in tight bikinis that left nothing to the imagination, I had to admit that it was one hell of a sight to behold. "The clientele has gotten much better."

"It has..." He quieted, eyes searching the sea of bodies that filled the room and overflowed to the patio outside. "There was another reason for me asking you to come out here, my friend."

"Oh?"

Our friendship over the years had always been a strange one, or so I'd been told. But the man was like a brother to me. He knew he could ask anything of me and I would be happy to help him in any way that I could. Usually, he was very direct and straightforward. He wasn't the kind of man to beat around the bush so for him to need something or have an ulterior motive and not come right out to tell me what he needed was a bit odd.

His eyes met mine, a tight smile playing at his lips before his hand touched the top part of my back. "I want to introduce you to someone."

"Who would that be?"

"Don Miguel and his brother Victor. Friends of mine."

Friends? What kind of friends?

"Sure, man. Lead the way."

Taking the lead, I followed behind Jeff through the crowd of people living their best life amongst the alcohol and music of Jeff's home. Our steps retraced the way we came in until two large men in cream-colored suits came into view, standing near the entrance to Jeff's home, looking out of place dressed as fancy as they were. It only took a moment for me to realize that they were the same two men Jeff had been speaking to when we pulled up outside.

"Don Miguel, Victor." Their deep brown eyes turned to meet our arrival. "I'd like you to meet Tomas."

Don Miguel, a large man well over six feet tall and close to two-hundred and fifty pounds stepped forward, eyes scanning over the length of me before holding out his hand. "You're the boat captain."

Clasping his hand into a quick shake, I nodded. My eyes drifted towards Victor, who was equally as big as his brother but stood more in the background, letting Don Miguel take the lead. "I am a boat captain."

"Jeffryn has told me a lot about you," he admitted. "You run big ships."

"Retired now," I replied with a nod. "But that's where I met Jeff. We worked together in the bay of Campeche."

The two men glanced at each other, silent communication passing between each of them before their eyes turned back to me. They didn't have to say anything at first for me to already have some sort of clue where this conversation was probably going to lead.

"He tells me that you understand how business works in Mexico."

I knew it.

Taking a sip of my drink, I hesitated to reply. I already knew damn well what he was referring to, but I needed to be sure.

"And what business would that be exactly?"

Knowing me as well as he did, Jeff could tell the conversation was bothering me, and shifted his weight from one foot to the other; maybe it was the vague sarcastic tone in my voice or the look in my eyes. "Don Miguel, this is a party, my friend," he said, placing his hand on his shoulder, "we can discuss business later, For now, let's just enjoy the evening."

Don Miguel looked straight at me, his intense eyes scanning up and down again, sizing me up and clearly irritated at best that he'd been interrupted.

"Very well," he conceded with a shrug, "bring Thomas with you tomorrow and we can have lunch in Merida."

I looked at Jeff with a hint of surprise in my expression. "Merida?" I inquired.

"I thought we could ride the bikes over," he suggested swiftly, "unless you have other plans?"

For a split second, I considered whether it would be wise for me to be unfortunately unavailable, especially given my intuition about Don Miguel's business. Giving Jeff's guest a momentary look, I decided against doing so.

"No, I'm game," I answered as I shook my head nonchalantly.

"Good," declared Don Miguel loudly, "Victor and I have some other business to attend to tonight, but we will see you tomorrow."

"I look forward to it," I added politely as we shook hands and with that they left.

Putting my serious face on, given I was certain I knew what kind of people Don Miguel and Victor were, I turned to Jeff and said, "If I didn't know better, I would say that was an interview, Jeff. You wanna tell me what's up or what's going on here?"

He placed his hand on my shoulder and smiled reassuringly. "Don't worry about it, Tomas. I promise we will talk about it later, but for now, shall we get back to the party and have another drink?"

As we stood at the bar and picked up another round of drunks, Jeff clearly saw that I was engrossed in my thoughts. "What's up, Tomas?" he questioned.

"To be honest, I was just thinking about Don Miguel and Victor," I replied. "I am not going to lie, those guys look shady and I am not ready, nor willing, to get mixed up in that sort of shit again."

He put his arm around me and smiled knowingly. "Don't worry, Tomas. You know how things are in Mexico, everyone with their hand out, seeing what they can get from you or what you can do for them."

"Yeah, I am more than aware," I replied as I took a swig of my scotch.

Chapter Four

I was lowering the glass from my lips when Diana's beautiful smiling face entered my view. "We haven't been here thirty minutes and you have already left me wandering around on my lonesome. Hey, Jeffryn, let's show Tomas the view!"

Without waiting for any sort of reply, she grabbed me by the arm and led me through the glass doors, and around the huge swimming pool that was illuminated with bright blue lights. They were almost as bright as the teeth on the massive bald guy walking toward us. His smile a little unsettling, but with the way Diana seemed to light up I didn't pay it too much attention.

"Cantrelle!" she shouted as she ran over and jumped into his arms. "When did you get back?"

"Just now," he answered in the same sort of Southern, Texas-like accent as hers.

He might have had a very friendly demeanor, someone who was both educated yet jovial, but he didn't look like the sort of guy you would want to mess with. He must have been at least 6'4" and upwards of 280 lbs, most of which appeared to be solid muscle.

Dressed in black, fitted trousers and a tight white shirt, his choice of dress merely emphasized the fact that he was built like a brick shithouse.

"Tomas, let me introduce you to Cantrelle; he is the Captain of my boat and also Head of Security."

Hesitating for a brief moment, I reached out and took his hand within mine. The strength of his grip felt like a vice closing around my fingers. "I guess it was you that kicked me out of second place in the tournament?"

He looked confused, then realized what tournament I was talking about and his smile quickly broadened. "Ah, no, afraid that wasn't me, Cap...I had to go to Miami with Maria. That was actually my deckhand who runs the boat when I can't."

I couldn't do anything else but roll my eyes and shake my head. "Great, that's even worse!"

Cantrelle's revelation that I was beaten by his backup prompted a laugh from everyone else.

"You said you were with Maria; is she here?" I asked, quickly changing the subject.

He nodded his head toward the glass door, my eyes following his gesture. "Yeah, Cap, she's in the house somewhere."

Straight away, nervousness filled my chest as my heart raced. Maria always had a way of prompting an emotional response from me. I was always fond of her and it didn't take much for us to realize we had a thing for each other. We ended up getting together and I always knew it would be nothing more than a fling, and yet it still stung when she broke it off to go to college a few years ago.

It was the type of relationship that came to mind thanks to the most random things—be it a scene in a film or a piece of music.

Sometimes it made me smile thinking of a silly moment, other times I genuinely felt hurt and missed her. However, it was a whole different ball game to be potentially coming face-to-face with her again.

I was jolted from my deep thoughts of the past when I heard the unmistakable, soft voice of Jeff's sister calling my name. Turning around, I was greeted by the image of her standing in front of me wearing a black sarong and bikini. Her whole body was tanned, which made her smile seem even brighter, and she still had long, black hair to the middle of her back. At 5'8" and with an athletic physique, she could easily have entered Miss America, but she was every bit as intelligent as she was beautiful and had forged an incredible career in business after she graduated from Miami University.

"How are you, Tomas?" she said elegantly. "It's been too long."

She stepped forward and gave me a long hug, and during the embrace I looked over her shoulder at the group that had moved toward the bar to give the two of us some space.

"It has indeed." I replied, trying to keep my composure.

Every time I'm around her, it takes everything in me not to let myself lose control. She isn't just beautiful, she's captivating. The kind of woman you can't keep your hands off of.

No matter how hard you might try.

"I heard from Jeff that you finally bought your boat," she stated with a warm smile as we pulled away from each other.

"You heard right. It's an older one but I'm fixing her up slowly."

"You will have to take me out on her sometime," she suggested with a sparkle in her eyes. The same sparkle that melted me on more than one occasion.

"For you… anytime," I confirmed, very happy at the thought of spending some time again. "I do have one question," I asked as I leaned in closer again, "Jeff mentioned he sent you down to the docks today… you're not keeping tabs on me, are you?"

Her cheeks instantly flushed at my question. "Always, Tomas."

I couldn't tell if she was teasing or whether the moment had just become awkward given our previous history as a couple; I certainly felt awkward, that's for sure, so I quickly changed the subject. "Jeff tells me your Mom and Dad are still in Mexico City and that you are running the business now?"

"Who is keeping tabs on whom, might I ask? Sounds like you've been keeping tabs as well," she playfully inquired. "As for my parents, yeah, they live there now. At least for the next four years or so. Dad is working for President Fox's administration."

My brows lifted at her comment as I gave an impressed nod before taking a sip from my drink. "I'm sure he's happy about that. I remember Jeff talking about how the ol' man had been after that post for a long time."

She hesitates in her response as her eyes gazed around the pool at the other guests before falling on me once more. "It's starting to get a little loud out here. Do you want to take a walk?"

Take a walk? Her sudden change of tune was a little out of character, but given how things had always been between us I brushed it aside with a nod of my head. "Sure."

Taking hold of my arm, Maria maneuvered me back inside the main part of the house. It was clear there was something on her mind. Granted, that could also just be wishful thinking on my part. Or perhaps a bit of hope that maybe there would be something to rekindle. The last thing I had expected when coming to Mexico and fishing in the tournament was seeing her again.

Hell, seeing any of them again.

But, here I was—back with the same people I'd ran with years ago.

The cool night air greeted us as we stepped outside. The two of us headed towards a long stairwell, which was illuminated from underneath by spotlights, before leading out toward a less populated part of the lawn.

"This place is really something," I enthused, attempting to make casual conversation to lighten the air. However, when a sigh escaped her it became clear she wasn't sharing in the same enthusiasm that I was.

"Oh yeah, it's something alright." She replied, as she glanced back at the house. It was hard to tell if she intended to sound rather unimpressed, so I pretended not to notice. Though my mind couldn't trail away from her puzzling attitude. Especially considering she was usually a rather vibrant person.

"I saw your parent's place up on the hill as I drove in," I continued, trying not to totally change the topic but at least move to something she might feel like engaging about. Which seemed to work for the moment as her gaze turned back to me with a teasing grin.

"I will have you know that is my place now," she replied in a mockingly stern tone. "I'll admit, I have been remodeling parts of it, but it's still pretty much the same as you remember it." Her gaze turned back to the building hosting our party. "You know what... I hate this place that Jeff has built. I don't know, it's all kinda cluttered and busy."

My lips parted at a loss for words as I glanced towards the house and then back to her. Taking hold of my arm, she seemed to shake off whatever thoughts she was having about Jeff, his home and the part as she led us down toward the beach, the lapping of the waves on the shore far more audible than visible.

"He might have changed much up here, but that little cove between here and my place on the hill is still the same as when we used to go down there."

The thought of our *private* times together was something I thought of often. Memories I held onto, no matter where I ended up.

"I remember, they were good times."

That comment seemed to perk her up, a smirk falling upon her face as she looked up at me. "You are a bad man, Tomas, taking advantage of lil ol' me like that!"

"Oh, please, I don't think you can lay that all on me." I replied, teasing her. "As I recall, I am not sure exactly who took advantage of whom that night."

A massive grin fell upon her lips as her eyes went wide. "I think you're getting old. Your memory must be playing tricks on you."

"Oh, my memory, huh?"

Rolling her eyes, she playfully swatted my shoulder. "Come on, let's go down there and I can show it to you again."

"Is that right?"

The grin upon her face twisted into a smirk of seduction as she gently shrugged her shoulder. "Up to you."

The teasing manner in which she had replied to me had my cock straining within my pants. Every part of me wanted her. To touch her, hold her... fuck her senseless. But it was hard to read her at times—to know if she was serious.

However, as she continued to walk I couldn't help but wonder if the Maria in front of me was the old Maria. The fun, light-hearted rebellious Maria. Or if this was simply a woman looking for something or someone to entertain herself with for the time being.

Regardless, as she moved—I followed.

"Other than more lights so you can actually see where you are going, it does look the same as I remember," I confirmed as we strolled arm-in-arm down to the small cove that cut into the cliff at the bottom.

"I had the jetty and docking slot at the water's edge rebuilt, but they are the same size and place as before." She added, taking in the scenery around her. "I also had a little gazebo built with a tanning platform. It's so nice to come down here and just relax in the sun."

It wasn't easy to see at first, but once she turned the spotlights on, everything became more visible. The way they glinted off the water was quite hypnotic. We strolled down the weather-worn planks that jutted out to the water. The drop-off once you hit the water was quite steep and as I stared out into the darkness, I knew that things were different below the surface.

Forcing myself from my thoughts, I took a moment to evaluate the current situation while taking in everything around us. "Is it me or is the beach bigger? There were more lava rocks and bushes over that side. In fact, I'm sure of it... I still have the scar on my foot!"

Soft laughter escaped her as she shrugged her shoulders once more. "Okay, yes, we expanded the beach a bit to make it more aesthetically pleasing to the eye."

The beauty of the changes they made are everywhere. But to Maria, they were just a memory of experiences she had already lived.

"Admit it, it's awesome down here, huh?" she boasted, her brown eyes sparkling as she looked proudly at her little sanctuary.

Nothing more was said as she wrapped her arm more tightly around mine and rested her head on my shoulder. We sat there silently looking out into the darkness. Any feeling of awkwardness had passed and had now been replaced with a serene calmness.

I didn't even think before I asked, "Are you seeing anyone at the moment?"

She shook her head slightly and then confirmed, "No, well, nothing serious, not that I'd have time even if I wanted to. I've been working pretty constantly since I took over the company after I graduated last year. I plan to change that very soon since I have my college roommate working for me and I plan to pass several responsibilities to her in the next few months."

I lifted my arm out of grasp and put it around her neck, resting my head on hers as I did so. "You know my motto—work to live, don't live to work!"

"Easier said than done. Oh, I do miss the simplicity of island life. I know we can't go back to times past, but even something similar would be nice."

She adjusted her position and moved her long hair to one side, exposing her neck. "I see you finally bought your boat. I have only seen it from a distance; tell me about her?"

"She's a 55-foot Viking. The new one was a bit too expensive and out of my price range, but she's nicely equipped."

"I was thrilled for you when I heard," she added enthusiastically, "I know you badly you wanted one. If money was an issue for the boat, I take it you are not still working in the oil fields?"

I turned up my nose and shook my head softly. "Nah, that is all in the rearview, or should I say to the stern. I pick up a variety of other jobs that pay for food, fuel, and beer."

"Oh, for the quiet life," she said reticently.

"Hey, it ain't all sunshine and rainbows, you know? It's not always easy, but I get by," I explained. "Looks like you and Jeff are doing alright, more than getting by?"

"Looks aren't always what they seem. You of all people should know that. I worry about Jeff, far more than he realizes." The amount of concern in her voice was instantly noticeable. "He's a massive party boy and is so quick and easy to trust people. There are always assholes, bad people and those out for what they can get around him, influencing him and persuading him to get involved in things he should steer well clear of."

I held my reply for a moment. I was sure I knew at least some of the people she was referring to, and yet I was unsure whether to take the conversation down that route. I care about both of them deeply, and I couldn't have lived with myself if Jeff ended up in serious trouble that I could have helped avoid had I just asked the question.

"Would I be right in thinking you are talking about Don Miguel and his brother?"

The question hung in the air, and I regretted raising the subject as the silence held.

"Is it that obvious? Yes, amongst a few others, but Don Miguel is the worst. Listen, be careful will you!" If I didn't know better,

I would say that it was genuine fear that tinged her every word. "I know Jeffryn was talking with you and Don Miguel, you really want to think twice before you get mixed up with them."

"You don't have to worry about me, I know the type and I have dealt with them before," I calmly reassured her.

She shook her head. "Of course, if someone threw you to the wolves, you'd come back a week later leading the pack," she declared with sarcasm making a mild entrance.

"And what does that mean?!" I replied in mock shock.

"You know what I mean. Jeff isn't like you, Tomas. He doesn't have your intuition, your instincts of self-preservation, your natural suspicion. He trusts everyone and walks blindly into trouble. You are good for Jeff and he really admires you, he'll listen to you if you show concern."

"I am here for a few weeks this time. I will see what he has in mind and I promise that I will drag him away, if necessary, if I don't like what I hear. Even when I am not here, you should know I am only a phone call away." Even though Maria knew this, I couldn't help but reiterate it to her–a reminder should she ever need it.

Maria tipped the remains of her drink into her mouth and then handed me the empty glass with a grin as she batted her eyelashes. "Tomas... would you be so kind as to get us both another while I relax down here?"

My eyes did their customary roll, and I shook my head. She always could wrap me around her little finger. "You do all this, import half the Sahara and yet you didn't think to install an icebox down here. Priorities, Miss, Priorities!" I said with a laugh.

As I started walking up the path, all I heard was her giggle behind me.

CHAPTER FIVE

IT SEEMED THE ATMOSPHERE wasn't so calm back at the house. I was walking around the pool deck toward the bar when I heard the sound of two male voices arguing in Spanish. Certain languages lend themselves to making even a mellow argument sound intense, German and Italian being two such examples, Spanish was another. From the far side of the pool, Jeff stood watching two apparently rather drunk guys arguing and pushing each other.

"Hey, Jeff, looks like everyone is getting on really well right now," I said, gesturing to the two men confronting each other.

"Every party, there's always one or two that start this shit. They just can't help themselves," he replied with a sigh.

Almost straight away, Cantrelle appeared through the glass doors and Jeff motioned to him and then pointed to the two guys. He walked briskly over and stood between them, at which point one of the guys shouting attempted to push Cantrelle out of the way. He failed to do so, and Cantrelle grabbed him in one swift maneuver with his massive arms and threw him straight into the pool. Everyone around the pool laughed at him as he swam over to the side.

"C'mon, man." Cantrelle reached down and helped him out. "It's time for you to go," he stated as he pointed to the main gate.

The guy put up no resistance and calmly followed Cantrelle away from the party. The momentary excitement didn't seem to dampen the party mood and within moments everyone was carrying on as if nothing had happened.

"You clearly still know how to throw a party," I said to Jeff as I raised my glass in his direction.

He grinned back at me knowingly. "I assume you and my sister have been getting reacquainted again?"

"She was just showing me the dock she fixed up behind your parent's old place," I answered, innocently enough.

"Yeah, yeah, and I play for the Mexican football team," he joked. "Now, if you will excuse me, I'm going to do some reacquainting of my own."

He stretched out his arm and this gorgeous, large-breasted woman with tanned skin and long black hair walked under it, kissed him, and whispered something in his ear.

"Seriously, it's not like that at all," I insisted, even if I was slightly embarrassed. "Honestly, we are just friends now."

"Whatever you say, my friend," he said in a sort of nudge-and-wink sort of way. "I will pick you up around noon tomorrow. If I don't see you, enjoy the rest of the night." With that, he walked away, woman in tow.

Fine by me, truthfully. I wasn't about to confess I still had strong feelings for Maria, but what did it matter as it couldn't even become anything serious.

I walked over to the bar to get our drinks and at one end, Cantrelle was sitting with Diana.

"I liked the way you dealt with our irritated guest just now. For a moment, I thought you were going to pummel the poor bastard."

"Nah, Cap," he replied with a shake of his head. "I just needed to cool him off."

"Mission accomplished," I said with a laugh.

I chatted with them for a few while the drinks were poured. It was easy to see why everyone liked Cantrelle. He might look like a brute, but he was always smiling and had a very likable personality.

"I hope you will both excuse me," I asked as I picked up the drinks, "there is a thirsty lady waiting for it."

I bid them farewell and headed back to the path and down to the dock. Maria saw me coming long before I reached where she was still sitting.

"I hope I wasn't gone so long you were dropping off?" I asked.

"Don't be silly. I was just remembering the last time we were down here," she answered as I handed her the drink and sat back down beside her.

"How could I forget?"

By this point, she had slid over to me and placed her hand on my leg.

"Careful, don't start something you don't intend to finish," I said with a Spock-like raised eyebrow.

The wicked smile she gave said more than any words ever could. After downing her drink, she stood up in front of me and dropped her sarong to the ground to reveal her delicious olive skin. I reached up and pulled her on top of me and began kissing her neck.

"Tomas, I have missed you," she told me as she wrapped her arms around my neck.

"Me too. I honestly never thought I would be back down here with you again," I told her.

She rolled over onto her back and pulled me on top of her. We both wanted each other, that much was clear, but we both also appeared to have a need to savor the moment. Like reunited lovers.

The next thing I knew, Maria was shaking my arm vibrantly and calling my name.

"Tomas, Tomas, wake up."

"Uhhh," I said groggily as I came around. "What happened?" I began to look at my watch.

"It's past 5 AM," she replied with a giggle, "we actually fell asleep. I think maybe we'd both had enough to drink."

"It's still early morning, I think we still have time to pick up where we left off," I suggested, half in jest but with some honesty.

"It might be alright for you, but I have an 8 AM flight to Miami," she replied, playfully slapping my bare ass.

"Oh, really?"

Disappointment filled me as I sat up. The cool breeze blowing in from the water hit me in the face, forcing a small smile to my lips.

"Are you going to be gone for long?" I asked, curious as to what her plans were.

"Only until the end of the week. Anyway, I don't think you need to worry too much. I'm sure Jeffryn has plans for you."

That was a given.

We both dressed and made ourselves presentable, before Maria suggested that we walk up to her house so she could fix us some breakfast before she got ready. The idea of spending a little more time with her did sound nice. It had been too long since I'd gotten the chance.

Much like the pathway from Jeffryn's house, on the far side of the cove there was another one that was still just about illuminated, even as the sun was beginning to rise. As we reached the top and strolled across the garden, the house came into view. From the outside, it still looked almost exactly as it used too.

There was a large covered patio that ran the length of the rear of the house, on the right, two large sliding glass doors led into the kitchen and dining area. On the second floor was the study and the living room, or at least it used to be.

I walked in behind Maria and took a moment to glance around the dining room. The family had always been into their art, and I noticed the array of expensive paintings on the wall; I even recognized a couple of them.

"I see some old paintings that used to be here but I see you have added to the collection. If I am not mistaken, I see you have a couple of Olga Guy's paintings?"

Her head snapped round quicker than usual with a look of genuine astonishment across her face. "How do you know her work; a Van Gogh I get you spotting, but an Olga Guy. You were never the artsy type before."

"I suppose I'm still not an artsy guy. I went to an art show with a lady friend in Panama City when we visited Florida and saw some of her paintings. People in the business told me that Olga is the hottest Latin artist since Frida Kahlo, and she is even becoming quite a muralist." " I saw one in Downtown Panama City, in amazing detail."

"Okay, not a conversation I ever thought I would have with you, but for what it's worth, it is true," she said as she picked some items from the refrigerator. "How about some Chilaquiles for an early breakfast?"

"Sounds good."

She busied herself, keeping with the conversation as pointed in the direction of one of the paintings on the far. "That one is called *Deep Green*, I bought it from a collector in Miami. It cost me one of Diego's, but I had to have it!"

"It's impressive, but then you always did have a fine taste."

"If you were to ask Mom or Dad, or even Jeffryn... I think they would suggest it was an expensive taste," she declared with a slick smirk to her lips.

She was expensive, everyone knew that.

"Hey, you said it, not me."

Maria whipped up the Chilaquiles, and before I knew it we were dining on them at the table before she ran off upstairs to have a shower and get ready for her trip. She was always last minute when it came to going somewhere, something that hadn't ever really changed with her.

As she charged around above me like some supercharged road-runner, I poured myself another cup of coffee and simply enjoyed being in her home. The property was beautiful, and as I took a seat at the table, I couldn't help but admire the water outside her dining-room window. The view was the kind that I eventually wanted to have. A bit of envy filled me but waking up on the San Blas and having coffee while I stared out to the Sea is hard to beat.

I thought about the first time Jeff invited me to his house. His family was very much like my own—very welcoming to strangers.

His dad was a prominent business man with a lot of political ties. He knew everyone, regardless of whether that was a good or bad thing.

His mom was an extremely strong-minded woman who seemed to hold everything together. She was old-fashioned in some ways, insisting that everyone sat at the table during meals and giving the kids chores.

Knowing them as I do, I suspect Jeffryn and Maria were a handful when it came to that. A little smile crept across my face as I thought of the first time we had dinner together.

It was an amazing meal and when everyone was finished, his mom gestured to Maria, who immediately turned to me and said, "Don't think you get out of it. I'll wash—you dry and Jeffryn can put everything away."

That provided everyone else with plenty of amusement as they laughed over their drinks while I was dragged to the sink with a pile of dishes in my hands. It made me feel totally at home and like a member of the family. Not unlike how I feel now. There was even an air of domestication in my mind. Living on a boat was a little different to living in a house, and with a cup in hand, it reminded me of that night.

"Were you actually just talking to yourself," Maria asked as she came downstairs dressed in a black business suit but with her hair still damp. "That's the first sign of madness, you know."

"No, I was just thinking about the first time we had dinner here, and how we ended up doing the dishes. It just made me smile."

"The look on your face when I told you that you were helping with the dishes... priceless. But unfortunately, I don't have time to go down memory lane with you. I'm already running late and really have to go." She replied, a frown forming her lips as I stood to my feet placing my cup on the table.

"That's okay, I know you're a busy woman."

"Sometimes...do you need a ride to your boat?" she asked as she rushed around grabbing her purse and carry-on suitcase.

"No, I'm all good. Jeff lent me the Range Rover. I can just walk back to his place and pick it up."

"Are you sure?" She asked, stopping in her tracks with hesitation. "I don't mind taking you."

Soft laughter escaped me as I shook my head. "No, I'm sure. You go ahead."

"Okay. Well, you know where the spare key is, lock up on your way out. I'll be back on Friday if you want to hang out." Rushing over to me, she placed a soft kiss to my cheek before turning on her heels and heading out the door.

The last thing I'd expected was to have a moment like this with her. Hell, to even be in the place I am now. But between her and her brother, I can't help but think it's for a reason.

It's just figuring out what that reason is.

Taking a moment, I lifted my cup to my lips once more as I turned my attention once again to the world outside the window. My thoughts turned from my interactions with them to my plans for the day.

The boat needed an oil change, but that could be put off for another day. I also needed to do some maintenance on the generator before it crapped out on me again, but there was no fun in that. I told myself I had patched, plugged, kicked, cursed and fixed that damn thing countless times. Yet, it brought me down a notch from the upbeat mood I had been in.

I decided against those and my attention turned to the suggestion Jeff had made. Maybe it would make me some money to fix things properly. Sure, he would lend me the money if I asked, but I wanted to make that a last resort. At the very least I could see what exactly he had in mind.

Washing my coffee cup, I headed out the door making sure that it was locked before placing the spare key back where it belonged. My feet once again took me down the path that headed back to Jeff's house.

There's no telling what kind of things he had planned for me.

But one thing is for sure... It's bound to be interesting.

CHAPTER SIX

Driving back to the marina was pure bliss. The sun slowly rose behind me, casting a golden glow over everything in its reach. Salty ocean air filled my nostrils as I drove with the window down, the sound of the engine intermingling with the faint cries of seagulls awakening for the day.

As I continued along the northern side of the island, I could see the marina coming into view. Boats bobbed gently in the water, their masts swaying slightly with the gentle waves. The rest of the ocean was calm and serene, offering a shimmering path towards the horizon. Morning had already bustled with activity, as people went about their daily tasks or headed to the beach just beyond the marina.

It was a routine that repeated itself every morning and late afternoon, as everyone sought refuge from the scorching midday heat. This was where the term "siesta" originated from - a Spanish word meaning rest or break in the afternoon

The gravel track leading to the parking lot behind the Tiki crunched beneath my tires as I pulled in. From the back door,

Cantrelle and Diana emerged, both sporting life jackets and piquing my interest as to what they were up to this morning.

"Where are you two off to?" I asked as I stepped out of my car. "Is there a ship going down?"

"We're going out on the wave runners," Diana replied with a mischievous glint in her eye. "Fancy joining us?"

"With pleasure," I answered, intrigued by their offer.

"There's plenty of room," Cantrelle replied.

"Just give me a minute to check on the boat and apply some sunscreen," I said, quickly heading down the jetty to my boat. I couldn't spend my entire time here focused on work. Jeff wasn't even at his place when I returned this morning. Might as well have some fun while I can.

However, as soon as I reached my boat, I hesitated. It was clear that someone had been on board in my absence. The shoe prints on the deck, belonging to someone with large feet, were a dead giveaway.

After ensuring that no one was still on board and everything was in its place, I pushed the thought aside. Maybe it was just a nosy harbormaster checking up on things. Who knows around these parts? Shrugging it off, I applied sunscreen and grabbed a bottle of water before making my way back to the beach.

Cantrelle and Diana were already pulling the wave runners into the water, or jet skis as they were more commonly called. Despite the busy waters, it was surprisingly peaceful.

"I've got you all set, Cap," Cantrelle declared with a grin. "We're taking a run around the east side of the island and should be back in an hour. Diana has shrimp to boil..."

I ran my hand over the sleek design of one of the wave runners, impressed by its craftsmanship. Cantrelle's chuckle brought me back to reality.

"You take that one, my friend," he said, gesturing towards the water. "But be careful... they're all supercharged and can really fly."

With a nod, I hopped on the wave runner and revved the engine, eager to feel the rush of speeding across the ocean.

"Lead the way!" I shouted to Cantrelle as he pushed off into the waves and took off at full throttle. I followed suit, feeling the exhilaration of gliding on top of the water at high speeds.

As we skipped and jumped over the gentle waves, Cantrelle pointed out a sleek sport fishing boat zooming towards the marina. Its wake churned up the water behind it, creating a perfect opportunity for us to jump from side to side in unison. The sound of our laughter echoed across the ocean as we followed the boat's path towards the east side of the island.

The water had calmed considerably by the time we reached our destination, appearing like a sparkling mirror reflecting the rays of sunlight dancing above. Running close to the shore, we could see the magnificent coral reef stretching out into the ocean before dramatically dropping off. A rainbow of colorful fish darted around us while graceful rays glided along the deeper edge of the reef.

As we continued to weave back and forth across the ocean, I couldn't help but steal glances at Jeff's lavish cliff-top house on the south side of the island. Despite reaching speeds of 50 mph, it stood out like a beacon against the blue sky. I couldn't help but wonder how much money he must have stashed away in such a luxurious abode.

My thoughts were interrupted by the realization that Jeff was likely planning to offer me a job in his line of work, which was most likely barely legal or even illegal. The allure of easy money tempted me as I raced across the water, but my past experiences in this line of work sent chills down my spine. I knew all too well that for all its wealth, there were just as many dangers and enemies lurking in this world.

My mind raced as I considered Jeff's offer. Sure, the money would be useful—I could finally fix my generator and maybe even build a tower - but at what cost? My abrupt departure from this business had not been well-received by some very powerful and dangerous individuals who would not hesitate to harm me if given the chance. The thought of risking everything again for a chance at wealth made me shudder as I continued to dart across the water, my mind torn between fear and temptation.

As we flew across the crystal blue waters, Cantrelle and Diana raced ahead. I revved my wave runner's engine and caught up to them just as we reached the Cancun side. We continued along the coast until it was Diana's turn to fall behind. We slowed down to let her catch up, taking sips from our water bottles in the scorching heat.

"Thanks for the invite Cantrelle"

"No problem, Captain," Cantrelle replied with a smile. "Usually we spend an entire day zipping around the keys, but today we're just going around one side and heading back. Time to turn around, so let's circle around the ferry."

We turned back the way we came, finishing in half the time since we didn't stop to play on any wakes or get lost in our thoughts. As we approached the beach, we hit the gas and rode our wave runners right onto the sand, engines shutting off simultaneously.

"That was awesome!" Diana shouted. "I gotta go start those shrimp."

She gave Cantrelle a kiss on the cheek before running up the beach in her white bikini. Cantrelle and I couldn't help but watch her trot away. We glanced at each other and smiled. Nothing needed to be said.

"Need help putting these away?" I asked Cantrelle.

"Nah, we got it," he said, gesturing towards a young Mexican boy walking towards us. "This is Jose, my deck hand. He was the one who drove the boat in yesterday's tournament."

"It's nice to meet you, Jose," I said, shaking his hand.

"You too. Are you a captain?" he asked.

"Yeah, I have the Cape San Blas moored in the harbor behind Tiki." I pointed at my boat and Jose smirked before high-fiving Cantrelle.

"Cap, you almost won the tournament yesterday...until we caught that last big one just outside the reef," he boasted with confidence. He was a cocky little shit, but there was something about him that I liked.

"Win some, lose some, that's life, kid." I replied, my eyes casted towards my boat once more before it turned back towards them. "Well, I've got a few things to take care of, but I'll see you both in a bit."

"Sounds good." Cantrelle replied with a nod of his head. "We'll be there in a couple of hours."

As I strolled along the sandy beach, I spotted Diana and her coworkers setting up a large pot on the wooden deck near the marina. They were in full organizing mode, getting ready for the shrimp boil she was so eager to get back to. It was crazy how things could be so different in this place than back home, but so similar at the same time.

As I approached my boat, the distant sound of a lively band setting up in the nearby parking lot greeted me. The music was only a taste of what was to surely come later in the day when everyone gathered together.

It was the perfect day for a shrimp boil. Between the cool breeze coming off the ocean to the sleekness of the water and the warm rays of the sun, I don't know if anything could be better.

After a quick shower on deck, and a change of clean clothes I found myself relaxing within the AC to cool off from the intense heat radiating outside. A cold Corona in hand, I sank onto the plush sofa and let my mind wander to memories of Maria. Her smile and laughter echoed in my mind, reminding me how much I missed her. Despite our recent breakup, she was always on my mind.

We were just too different, but that didn't change the love I had for her.

Lost in bittersweet thoughts, I drifted off to sleep without even realizing it, my heart heavy with longing for what could have been.

It was a couple of hours later that I was awoken by the sound of people laughing and music coming from the background. I blinked a few times to fully drag myself from my early siesta and looked at my watch to see it was almost midday. I hauled myself from the sofa, grabbed another cold beer from the refrigerator and headed off my boat toward the Tiki.

My stomach growling with the anticipation of food.

I immediately spotted Jeff and Cantrelle, who were both sitting around a table with half a dozen other men and women, a few I recognized from the party the previous night and others I didn't. Jeff spotted me almost immediately. A smile lit up a seat as he called out to me while he gestured towards an empty chair.

"Have a seat, Gringo."

"His pet name for me," I explained with an overacted roll of the eyes as everyone looked up at me and laughed.

The table in front of us was covered with several layers of newspaper and covering much of the table was a pile of freshly boiled shrimp with pieces of corn-on-the-cob scattered everywhere. Which I was thankful for, considering how hungry I was when I woke up from my nap.

Midway through my third mouthful, I glanced across the deck and saw Diana waiting with a full tray of beers for a table across the other side bar. Her eyes connected with mine once she made her delivery, nodding only once as if reading my mind.

"Look who finally decided to show up," she teased with a smile as placed the beer down to my side.

"Thanks," I told her as I picked up the beer and washed down some of the shrimp. "Sorry, I overslept a bit after our run on the water. But it looks like I made it just in time."

"Oh, more than enough time for the shrimp," she answered as someone called out to her from the other side of the Tiki. "Gotta run, we have lots of thirsty people. I'll be back with another short-ly."

As she strutted off, I reached toward the center of the table and grabbed another pile of shrimp. Only to have Jeff lean toward me at the same moment.

"We are going to Merida this afternoon, that is if you are ready for that ride?"

As much as I was interested in the money and to see what he had in mind, I was actually feeling a little exhausted. Maybe it was the wave riding earlier, the mid-morning snooze or too much shrimp, either way, I just couldn't get my enthusiasm up for it.

At least not right now.

I leaned back in my chair taking a moment to think it over before I looked at Jeff with a heavy sigh. "We're going to have to postpone that, man, I'm feeling totally beat after the party last night and then being out on the water this morning."

Jeff chuckled as a smile fell across his lips. "Really? Did my sister keep you up past your bedtime, ol' man?"

The thought of what Maria and I got up to the night before was only a teasing moment within my memories. As much as I would have liked to do more with her, I didn't get the chance. I nodded my head slightly as I lifted my beer to my lips. Jeff quickly dove into his cellphone to make a call that once again left me alone with my thoughts.

What is it about my connection with Maria that has me so worked up?

The rest of the table returned to chatting and eating as I watched Jeff stand and walk off with the promise of being right back. What was he up to? He suddenly seemed under a lot of pressure and that wasn't like him, not at all. He was always the happy-go-lucky type of man, but he seemed to be bothered. Unable to relax and have fun.

I was lost in my thoughts when Diana tapped me on the shoulder. "How's the food?"

"It's fantastic, my compliments to the chef."

She laughed. "When are you going to take me for that ride on your boat you mentioned?"

"It looks like I am free this afternoon. What time are you finished?"

Despite knowing that getting involved with this woman could lead to trouble, I couldn't resist her charming company. Her face lit up when I asked if she wanted a ride, and she quickly confirmed that she did before excusing herself to gather her things.

Meanwhile, Jeff returned and sat beside me, absentmindedly shoveling shrimp into his mouth. I asked him about Diana, and he casually replied that she was just a cool chick. But his tense demeanor and nonchalant tone revealed otherwise.

"It seemed like she had something going on with Cantrelle," I replied, a grin crossed his face as he shook his head.

"I don't keep track of things like that my friend, but I can assure you if she was... she wouldn't entertain you like that. Diana is a good woman, you should enjoy her company."

Easy for him to say. The last thing I wanted to do was anger someone as intimidating as Cantrelle. Even if Jeff says it wouldn't be a problem.

As we chatted, two girls at the table caught my attention. Tracy and Heather were from a 60-foot catamaran called the Dynasty, and we exchanged small talk until Diana returned to my side with her perfectly curved body bouncing with excitement.

"Are you ready to go?" she asked, her mischievous gaze shining down at me caused me to chuckle as I nodded my head.

"Sure. Why not?"

It's not like I can get into too much trouble, right?

CHAPTER SEVEN

THE SALTY WIND RUFFLED our hair as we stepped aboard the San Blas, ducking into the cozy cabin. Diana's eyes went wide with wonder as she took in the newly varnished wood interior; her fingers traced the smooth surface with admiration. I couldn't help but feel a surge of pride at her reaction, knowing all the hard work I had put into this vessel.

"It's beautiful," she purred, taking in every inch of the cabin.

"I've been fixing her up for the past two years," I said with a hint of satisfaction in my voice.

Diana continued to explore, stopping to look at pictures pinned on a sideboard - one of me beaming alongside my best friend Ramon. Unable to resist showing off my handiwork, I boasted about my upgrades.

"I installed these myself," I said with a hint of pride in my voice. "The inside is almost done, yet, there are some minor mechanical problems left to fix."

"Mechanical problems?" Diana raised her eyebrow. "Doesn't that mean we cannot have a ride?"

I smirked. "Absolutely not. It only pertains to the generator parts. The engine is all perfectly fine. Ready to take her out?"

"Hell, yes," Diana beamed.

"Make yourself comfortable while I finish up," I said, fetching her a bottle of water out of the cooler and a cold beer for myself.

She sat on the cooler, with me tending to the engine at the back of the boat, watching attentively.

"These motors are spotless," she said.

"It's my pride and joy," I said, smiling. "It's not brand new like Jeff's boat, but it does pack some punch."

"I can tell," Diana snickered.

I just smiled, knowing where this was going. I told her as I finished my pre-sail checks how I came across this beauty.

"I actually bought it at a DEA auction in Miami," I said. "It used to be a notorious drug smuggling boat. It's equipped with twin turbos on each engine, capable of producing over four thousand horsepower."

"Is that a lot?" Diana asked.

"You could say that," I chuckled. "Most boats this size usually do 12-25 knots miles per hour. This baby can hit sixty, but it guzzles fuel like crazy."

With a graceful shimmy, she peeled off her damp T-shirt, revealing a black bikini top and matching swim shorts that hugged her curves in all the right places. A sheen of sweat on her tanned skin, she sat on the transom watching me, the sun highlighting golden strands in her hair. I did my best to keep my eyes from roaming down her cleavage; it was no use-I was caught by her smile.

Getting ready for the voyage, I couldn't help but think how comfortable she seemed going about the boat, preparing equipment with ease. I cranked up the engines, the roar of which gave me goosebumps as it usually did. Diana flinched at the noise, so I hastened to shut hatches to soften the racket. As I headed for the bow to cast off the lines, I saw large footprints up there, and I felt a twinge of alarm. Had anyone been lurking around earlier? The thought of setting up surveillance cameras crossed my mind.

Finally ready to set sail, I went to the cabin and put the engines in gear. We slowly drifted away from the marina and once we cleared any potential obstacles, I pushed the throttle up to 2800 rpm. The engines hummed smoothly as we reached our perfect cruising speed of 26 knots, though I made sure not to push them too hard considering my current financial situation.

With a course set to the west toward Progreso, I put us on autopilot and sat down beside Diana on the bench. We chatted and enjoyed the spectacular view of the endless blue ocean stretching out before us, keeping an eye on the radar just in case. Suddenly, Diana's concerned voice snapped me out of my contentment.

"Um.who's driving the boat?" she asked hesitantly.

"Don't worry, it's on autopilot. We're going to this secluded cove I know and then to a great beachfront restaurant for dinner," I said, trying not to show my amusement.

"Dinner?" she echoed with surprise.

"You said you didn't have any plans today, didn't you?"

"Yes, but I didn't bring any clothes suitable for a fancy dinner," she said a little apprehensively.

"Don't worry about it. It's a casual beachside place, trust me—no one is going to be in a suit and tie out there," I said with a chuckle, the contentment warming my skin like the sun outside as she settled in closer against me.

The boat cut through the waters, the melodic hum of the engine mingling with the soft lapping of waves against the hull. Diana and I sat side by side, taking in the breathtaking view of lush mangroves and pristine sandy beaches. The salty ocean air filled our lungs as we cruised along the coast.

For a few moments, we sat in comfortable silence until I finally broke it, asking her when she planned on returning to the States. She turned to look out at the expanse of water, her features with a hint of uncertainty. "I've just been taking it easy," she replied slowly. "I love this lifestyle down here, but eventually I'll have to start considering my future."

"I totally understand," I nodded sympathetically. "I also had always wished to live on a boat. It took much effort in making this dream a reality.

Diana said she had been on vacation in Florida immediately after graduating from Texas A&M University, and I was so excited to hear that she was an Aggie. The two of us lost in discussion about our Alma-mater.

"My dad is with the Border Patrol," she said. "I get a lot of offers from state and federal law enforcement, but growing up with it makes me question life, really. I mean, I don't know if that is the route I want to take."

A tinge of sadness flickered across her expression, and I tried to lighten the atmosphere by teasingly asking her to forget everything she had seen Jeff and me do if she ever became a lawyer.

"It wasn't just you two," Diana playfully shot back. "I'm not innocent either."

Now that was something I definitely believed.

Further out, as we chugged up the coast, reminiscing on past adventures, the humorous side of some of them made us burst into a crazy laugh. In about an hour, I pointed out to her the opening of my secret cove-hidden entrance in a tiny cut of the mangroves, which opened onto a small deserted beach.

"We should go for a swim," Diana said excitedly, and without waiting to hear my thoughts on it, dove into the crystal clear waters.

As much as I missed Maria, Diana was sure able to take my mind off things. Allowing me the opportunity to relax like I want to. Something which I truthfully needed since everything else going on in my life.

"Come on!" She called out, the moment she breached the surface of the water. "It's amazing." I laughed a little and replied "Give me just a minute to drop the anchor."

I walked up to the bow and that's when I saw footprints up there too. I reached down and checked the hatch; it was still secure so I grabbed the anchor and threw it into the water. I watched as it fell to the bottom in the crystal clear water and let out a plume of sand when it hit the bottom.

I stripped off my shirt and plunged into the water, the initial rush of joy overpowered my being. However, going further down, this serene feeling vanished when I saw the pollution scattered across the seabed. It was a very blunt reminder of how careless humans can be, even in such a beautiful place.

I swam back up to see Diana, my adventurous friend, on her back in the water looking very disappointed at my lack of excitement. "Is something wrong?"

"There's trash on the bottom. Some fishermen didn't care what they were doing out here."

She hesitated a minute, swimming toward me, before she let out a soft sigh. "Well, I guess we should clean it up."

As much as I wanted to spend time with her out here... I couldn't bring myself to leave the trash behind. "You don't have to help. It won't take long to do it."

"Don't be silly," she scoffed with a smile. "Of course I'll help you. Do you have scuba gear?"

"Yeah... I do, on the boat."

"Good, let's get it." And with that, she swam towards the boat, leaving me to reflect on her readiness to help before quickly following her. I hadn't expected her to want to help. Most women I know wouldn't have wanted to. But Diana was different. Clearly.

Suited up, we dove back down and worked together to collect all of the trash. Five bags later, satisfaction of restoring the ocean floor filled me, but I couldn't shake off the feeling of anger towards those who had left it in such a state. The once peaceful dive turned into a conflicting mixture of appreciation and frustration.

How could someone be so careless with something so beautiful?

"I think that should do it," I called out to her from the boat as I finished lugging the last bag onto the deck. "Thanks for helping."

"You don't have to thank me," she smiled, still drifting in the water in her gear. "Since we already have the gear out and we still have some air, why don't we go exploring?"

Exploration. I hadn't been thinking about scuba diving today, let alone picking up garbage from the ocean floor, but given how nice it was outside, there was no need to waste any more of the day. We might as well enjoy ourselves while we still have the sun.

I jumped off the boat and descended into the bottom of the water. Brilliant blues and greens wrapped around Diana and me as we explored the magic of the underwater world around us. Her gorgeous body moved through the water with magical ease as she would casually turn to me every now and again to ensure I was still following her.

I wasn't sure what she had planned for me, but with every smirk on her lips and slight brush of her body against mine, I had an idea.

We drifted through the shimmering water, smooth as silk, heading for the cove's entrance. Our bodies sliced through the waves like it was second nature. When we got to the opening, I pointed to a hole in the reef below, glowing with neon colors. Water poured into it, forming a dazzling circle in the middle of the reef's bright hues. It was about ten feet wide and fifteen feet deep, with a sandy bottom.

I signaled for Diana to come along as I sank to the sandy floor, feeling the pressure shift around me. Her eyes sparkled with excitement as she joined me down there. We took a moment to soak it all in before I guided us toward a tiny cave on one side of the reef.

The entrance was just three feet high but led into an awe-inspiring cavern, twelve feet wide. Ahead, about fifty feet away, a mystical blue glow came from above.

I used hand signals to ask if Diana wanted to keep exploring, and she eagerly gave me a thumbs up. As we swam through the narrow passage one after the other, I kept a close eye on her—just in case. The ocean is stunning, but you never know what might be lurking.

A few minutes later, we emerged from the cave into a breathtaking underground chamber that felt like a grand living room. On one side was a ladder leading up to an opening where we could glimpse bits of sky and swaying treetops. A smooth rock ledge jutted out from another wall, shaped by the ocean's gentle currents over time. And at the back of the cavern sat an old wooden trunk, looking mysterious and full of adventure.

She took off her mask and respirator and swam over to me, her eyes taking in everything around us.

"Oh my God, look at this place. It's amazing," she exclaimed. "How did you find this place?"

I didn't reply, simply watched her take it all in while we floated there. I had been much the same the first time I saw it. I enjoyed watching her reaction and then she noticed the chest.

"Come on, is that what I think it is?" she asked as she pointed at it.

I couldn't resist playing along and in mock excitement added, "I have no idea... I've never seen that before."

I raised myself up on the ledge and leaned back to give Diana my hand and help her up beside me. Once we had removed our gear, I continued to act excited as if we'd found the treasure of Long John Silver himself.

"This can't be for real, surely?" she questioned again.

It took everything I had not to laugh as I knelt down to open it.

"Maybe we ought to be careful, in case it is booby trapped or has snakes in it, like that Bond movie from the seventies."

"Just open it," she implored me, her hand clasped over her face like it was the *Price Is Right*. "What's in there... I can't look?" she asked as I lifted the lid.

I grabbed a couple bottles of water from inside. "It's water, you want one?"

"Oh my God! I can't believe you actually did that or that I actually fell for it," she said as she pushed me backwards and laughed.

"Sorry, couldn't resist," I confessed.

You could tell her adrenaline was slowing down, and she continued to show a lot of excitement as she gazed around the cave.

"How did you even find this place?" she asked.

"Much like the cove, pretty much by accident. I was diving for lobster the second or third time I visited, and dove down and found the passage. I was as surprised as you when I first came up through the water," I explained.

"Was that chest even here the first time?" she questioned.

"Errr, no. I made it from some old shrimp boards and brought it down via that hole," I answered as I pointed up the ladder.

"Let me guess, you made that as well?"

"You are correct," I confirmed with a nod. "I spent a few months out here when I didn't have enough money to pay for the slip space. I'd tie up at the day dock in Progreso a couple of times a week, but you have to pay dock fees if you're there after 6 PM. So, at 6, I would leave and come anchor here. I kept a few cases of water and some MREs in that chest just in case."

"Where does the ladder come out?" she questioned.

"In the woods, right beside the lagoon," I replied.

She asked whether we could go back that way, but when I explained we'd have to carry our gear through the woods with bare feet, she quickly changed her mind. Not that I blamed her, I didn't really want to do that either. I stood up and closed the trunk before placing the crushed water bottles in a vest pocket.

"Are you ready to head back?"

"Yeah, let's go. You can definitely bring me back here another time," she suggested with a sly smile. "If you want to."

Her teasing demeanor was enough to make me chuckle as I shook my head, and gestured for her to follow me. She could be trouble, and as much as I tried to stay away from trouble I enjoyed the idea of what kind of trouble she could bring.

We put on our gear again and slipped back into the water. Our bodies gliding through the ocean back the way we came as we made our way back through the hole, the brightness of the water enough to take your breath away. I could see the hull of my boat above and eagerly made my way back up to the surface with Diana behind me.

The moment we were back on board, we removed our gear and placed the equipment back where it came from. Diving is beautiful, but it's exhausting at the same time. Turning toward her, I watched as she wrung the water from her hair.

"I'll be right back. I'm going to grab us some towels and water from the cabin."

She nodded as I disappeared into the cabin, only to reappear moments later. Handing her a towel and a bottle, she began running the towel across her body as we both stared off across the ocean at the late afternoon sun.

"You live some life, Tomas," she declared.

"It's not a life of rainbows and without worry, but I try to enjoy it as much as possible."

I don't think she realized, but she was passing the water bottle from one hand to another, and it looked like she was thinking deeply about something. As if troubled. With quick thinking I changed the topic, hoping to improve her mood.

"If you want to rinse off, there's a shower in there to the right, and more towels on the shelf," I suggested, my voice a little rougher than I intended.

She turned to me with a smile, her eyes bright and sparkling as she nodded. "That sounds perfect. Thanks."

I watched her as she finished her water, standing with an effortless grace that seemed to come naturally to her. My gaze tracked every movement—the way her hair fell over her shoulder, the subtle curve of her waist—until she turned back to me with a frown. Embarrassment prickled along my skin, and I quickly looked away, caught in the act.

"Are you coming?" she asked, her tone light but with just enough of an edge to make my stomach flip.

Coming? Hell yes, I am.

I didn't need to be asked twice. I jumped off the bench like a running back called into the final play of the big game. As I approached, her eyes flicked over me, a slow smile tugging at the corners of her mouth that only added fuel to the fire burning inside me.

My heart was racing as I finally closed the distance between us, unable to restrain myself any longer. My arm instinctively went around her waist, drawing her gently yet firmly against me. The warmth of her body sent a thrilling jolt through mine, igniting a fire that had been smoldering for far too long. And then our lips met in a passionate, unyielding kiss, a clash of longing and urgency that left us both gasping for air.

I had met my fair share of women before, but Diana was something else entirely. She lit my senses in ways I had never experienced. My hands glided over every curve and dip of her body, tracing the contours and etching them into memory like a man yearning for touch. She leaned back just enough to shoot me a smirk, her eyes ablaze with intensity.

"Let's see if you can keep up," she teased, her voice low and sultry.

Before I could say a word, she stepped under the shower and turned the water on. The cold spray caught us both off guard, but neither of us moved to change the temperature. The shock of the cold only intensified the heat that simmered between us as we stood there, drenched in each other's presence.

Water cascaded down her hair, slicking it flat against her back, and for a moment, I found myself riveted, unable to look away. She was simply radiant, with her skin shimmering beneath the soft light, every move she made purposeful and confident.

"Enjoying the view?" she asked, raising an eyebrow.

"More than you know," I said, getting in the shower with her. The icy water hit me like a slap, but I didn't flinch. I was too busy staring at her—how she looked at me with such longing and intensity, like I was the only thing she wanted and needed at that moment.

She reached for me, her hands gliding over my chest and sending shivers of delight racing down my spine. I pressed her back against the cool tile wall, my lips seeking hers again. This time, the kiss was slow and with purpose, but no less filled with passion. Her fingernails grazed against my shoulders, drawing from me a deep growl that rumbled in this small space.

"You're not bad at this," she whispered against my lips, a playful glimmer dancing in her eyes.

"Not bad?" I repeated, pulling back just enough to lock gazes with her. "I think I can do better than that." I cocked up a confident smirk and started tracing kisses to the gentle column of her neck as her breath hitched the fire beneath the collar more and more. My fingers grew taut around her middle, drawing her up and tight in the air as her legs cinched around my waist eagerly. The chilling water kept pouring down all over us, but on that note, it tasted pretty close to steam, so fiercely did we burn.

Her fingers tangled in my hair, pulling just hard enough to make me look up at her. Our eyes met and for a moment everything else fell away. There was no sound but the rush of water, no sensation but the feel of her pressed so intimately against me, no thought but how badly I craved her.

She leaned in a little, her lips brushing against my ear as she whispered in a seductive whisper, "Prove it."

Challenge accepted.

With renewed determination, I surged forward and claimed her lips once more as if our lives depended on it. In that instant, the world seemed to shrink to include only the two of us, caught in our own little passionate bubble where time seemed to lose all meaning and every touch and movement vibrated deep. Each second was an eternity, yet it passed by so fast—leaving both of us breathless and clinging to each other with a wild longing.

When we finally pulled apart, gasping for breath, her laughter filled the small space. It was light and carefree, the sound of someone completely in the moment. I couldn't help but smile, even as my heart thundered in my chest.

"Not bad at all," she said, her voice soft but teasing.

"I told you I'd do better than that," I replied, brushing a strand of wet hair from her face. My thumb lingered on her cheek, and for a moment, I let myself get lost in the warmth of her gaze.

Whatever this was, it couldn't be more than a fling. But for now, I was content to let the water wash over us, holding her close and reveling in the connection we'd just forged.

I woke a few hours later on my bed with Diana's head on my chest. I looked at my watch realizing it was getting late. Two hours had already gone by and my stomach growled with hunger. I softly woke Diana and told her I was going to start the boat as it was time to leave the cove. I rolled over, put on a clean pair of shorts and walked to the cabin to get the engines running.

I hit the keys and the engines roared to life, The sound echoing off the mangroves made me smile. "I guess it's a boat guy thing" but to me it's like when your favorite song comes over the radio. After they had warmed up for a few minutes, I pulled the anchor and idled us around the cover and back out to the open water. Once we were clear, I slowly pushed the throttle's forward to around 26 knots. Diana appeared wearing one of my T-shirts.

"Don't suppose you have any coffee?" she asked as she rubbed her eyes to wake up.

"Ask and you shall receive," I announced. "On the shelf above the sink... and use the bottled water in the fridge."

She came back with two cups, and handed one to me, then sat next to me on the small bench seat big enough for two. We both sat quietly and looked at the horizon as we sipped our caffeine injection. The sun was getting lower in the sky, and the water glistened with an orange glow as it set off the starboard bow.

The engines emitted a low hum, but I closed the door behind us and it was considerably quiet after that. Even Diana noticed and I told her how I'd added a lot of extra insulation to keep the noise down.

"I can see you really love this boat of yours," she stated.

"It's been a life-long dream and lots of sacrifice to get her to where I want her, so it's truly a labor of love."

"I admire your life, but I would have thought someone who has clearly spent his life at sea wouldn't want to retire there?" she questioned.

The irony of it all had always made me smile.

"I spent my entire career working on rusty steel boats doing whatever my employers required me to do to get the job done. Now, I am on a beautiful boat that belongs to me doing what I want to do. It's actually very different," I explained.

"How long to Progreso, Captain?" she queried.

"About 45 minutes. We could do it quicker, but she drinks fuel like an alcoholic on a bender when I do that," I answered.

She leaned against me in the chair and I put my arm around her. "I'm not in any hurry."

Diana lifted her feet up on the console and it made me think about the footprints I found earlier. Had they been small, I might have thought it was kids mucking around, but these were at least size ten. The fact they were also on the bow troubled me greatly.

Why there?

Were they trying to break in?

Did they manage to without causing damage?

I churned around many thoughts, and Diana quickly noticed.

"Are you thinking about something or is something troubling you?" she queried looking up at me.

"You must forgive me. Sometimes, when the boat is cruising along like this, I drift off into my own little world. I guess it is something I do without realizing, given I have grown accustomed to being out here alone at sea," I answered.

"Is being a Captain the only job you've ever had, aside from maybe some part-time stuff when you were younger?"

"No. I had my own business for a while, doing outboard marine repair and a few other occupations along the way, but the Mistress of the Sea always called me back. It may be a bit of a cliché, but the truth is, for guys like me, there really isn't anything else. I couldn't hack a standard 9-to-5 job, with office politics, gossiping, the rush hour traffic. Hell, no, that is definitely not me," I answered.

"For what it's worth, I can see why you love it so much," she said.

About ten minutes later, I saw the entrance buoys to Progreso marina and pointed them out to Diana.

"Almost there," I announced.

Diana asked to use the shower again and disappeared back into the cabin. I smiled when I remembered how Jeff had referred to her as a cool chick and he wasn't wrong. I wondered if there was anything going on between them, or maybe had been, and what about her and Cantrelle? She obviously liked him, that much was easy to tell.

The truth of all was that I liked Diana and Maria, but I only had one true love. She ran a restaurant in Tabasco, Mexico, was Filipino on her father's side and Honduran on her mother's, and she was the most beautiful woman I ever met. She was around 5'4", 100 lbs, with long black hair and mesmerizing hazel brown eyes... oh, and that perfect smile.

From the moment we met, I could tell she came from a high class, high moral family, but I never fully figured her out. What I did know was that she was around a lot of powerful people and always knew what was going on with the cartels, military, and politicians. I couldn't know for sure, but I reckoned she was connected to something with an acronym: CIA, FBI, MI6, there's a long list.

The restaurant was in a small town close to one of the busiest offshore ports in Mexico. That's how we met, and I dated her for a while; if I was honest with myself... I love her to this day. She was the only woman I ever asked to marry me, but she turned me down and told me maybe in another life. What did that even mean? She tore my heart out and placed me in "the friend zone." We kept in touch but we haven't spoken recently, something I would rectify in the coming week or two.

As we approached the buoy, I switched off the autopilot and made our turn. I was looking at the pier to guide me when Diana came out of the cabin. She was in another one of my T-shirts.

"Hope you don't mind that I grabbed a fresh one?" she asked with a grin.

"Of course not."

She sat next to me for the next ten minutes while I guided the boat up to the pier. As we pulled alongside, Diana went to the back deck to help tie things up there, and I couldn't help but be impressed as most "guests" don't bother. Once the boat was secured, we both went to the back deck.

"Now for the fun stuff!" I announced as I lifted a hatch to reveal a compartment where my minibike was stored.

CHAPTER EIGHT

THE MINIBIKE MIGHT HAVE been small, but the seat was big enough for two and Diana stood there and looked down with a smile.

"Oh, this is going to be interesting," she exclaimed nervously.

"You're gonna love it," I promised.

I used the winch and swung it out of the compartment effortlessly and lowered it over onto the pier, all the while Diana watched on from the bench.

"It looks like a well-oiled machine," she cheered.

"I assure you, there was lots of head scratching, planning, replanning and swearing before I came up with that little idea."

"That engine looks so big on such a small bike," she commented, her eyes wide.

"Yeah, well, that's because it's from a full-size motorcycle. A 440 Kawasaki to be exact. And the flame job on the gas tank... that was done by a friend of mine In Panama City." We did our best to make it look like a tiny Harley.

She chuckled, not the least bit surprised as she nodded her head. "How fast does it go?"

A smirk crossed my lips as I shrugged my shoulders. "I'm sure it will do well over 100, but I haven't had the balls to go past 80."

After I locked up the *San Blas* and made sure everything was secure, especially after the footprint episode. Once I checked the oil, I turned on the electric start and it thundered to life. We both climbed on, I hit the accelerator and off we went.

It was a bike that often caused people to turn and look because it sounded like a full-sized motorbike, and as usual, everyone we zipped past, including the fishermen on the rails, whipped their heads around as we passed.

From the end of the pier, we went down Beach Drive. It was a highway with palm trees down the middle and bushes on the sides, but the minibike was suitable as it had a shiny chrome head light, tail light, & blinkers.

I could see that each person we came across looked and pointed, thanks to the custom paint job and the fact I built it with every-thing from a big bike I'd purchased. I'd have loved to turn it into a little chopper, but it wouldn't fit in the small compartment.

Several miles down the road, the unmistakable neon lights of the restaurant *Cilantros* came into view. I pulled into the oyster-shell parked lot and parked the bike near the steps going up to the deck. Diana took a long, slow sniff of the air.

"I had forgotten how hungry I really was, but now I can smell that food, oooo..." she groaned.

"This place belongs to a friend of mine. It's called Cilantro's. He has a few including one in Savannah, Georgia. You are going to love the food here. No question," I said.

The deck was like many you see with tables and chairs set up with individual umbrellas. Among them, there were palm trees that provided additional shade during the day.

The waiter showed us to a table by the rail so we could look out over the beach. A soft breeze came in from the sea and in the background I saw some kids playing football under lights. I ordered some drinks, and we both decided to go for the fried Snapper.

"Diana, I want to ask you something?"

"It wasn't me, I absolutely didn't do it," she chuckled.

I paused to ponder if I wanted to ask the question into reality.

"I want to ask you about Jeff. He seemed pretty tense earlier and yesterday you told me there were "rumors" that he might be in a "bit of a spot" as you put it. Jeff's one of my best friends, if he's in trouble, I want to help if I can."

"Fair enough." She sighed. "It all started with Don Miguel and that sleazy brother of his, Victor. Everyone knows that they are connected to the cartels in Veracruz and they have a reputation for being ruthless thugs! Jeffryn is a trusting soul. You of all people know that, and even he doesn't like them at all. However, he couldn't avoid getting involved with them, at least peripherally. Did you see him shouting on the phone earlier at the shrimp boil?"

"Couldn't really miss it," I nodded.

"Whenever Don Miguel and his brother are around, Jeffryn is always super-stressed. He gets irritated badly by them, but he still does business with them. He sometimes lets them stay at the marina house in the apartment next to me, and it makes me really uncomfortable every time."

I just nodded, taking a sip of my scotch. This was the sort of news I dreaded.

"In the evenings I like to sit out on the deck and a couple of weeks back I heard them talking about some kind of deal or something like that. It was something to do with Jeffryn, that's for sure, and I don't think they trust him either. Luckily, I managed to sneak back in before they realized I was there."

"Any chance you heard what kind of deal they were talking about?"

She looked up, her eyes inquisitive. "I think I heard something about his sister, but they talked mostly in Spanish, and mine isn't that good."

"I talked to Maria last night, and she didn't say anything about Jeff being in trouble, but she did ask me to stick around for a few weeks."

"We're all worried about him," she admitted before she took a mouthful of drink. "I wouldn't be here if it wasn't for him. He gave me a job at the bar and let me stay at the apartment for free."

I weighed a few things on my mind, some of which now seemed more likely based on what she'd said.

"When Jeff worked for me in Campeche, I thought he came from money, but having seen the marina, his mansion and all the toys, I had no idea it was from that sort of wealthy background. When he worked for me, he made a couple of hundred bucks a day, and today he tipped that much at the boil."

The waiter then appeared with our food, and the smell was something approaching perfect. We both squeezed some lime over our fish and dug in. The food didn't last long and after dinner we ordered more drinks—a Margarita and Scotch—and kept chatting.

"If you're comfortable on the back of the bike, do you fancy a little cruise down Beach Drive before we head back?" I asked, as we finished up our drinks.

"Sure, I would love to see more of this city."

After paying our bill, we made our way around the little island bar in the middle of the deck and back out to the bike. I eased us out onto the street and we cruised at 35 mph down the strip. On one side were the bars and restaurants all lit up, the different types and colors of the chairs and tables from each place adding to the vibrancy. It was early evening, and the sidewalks were full of people having a good time.

At the end of the strip, I turned to Diana and said, "I think we'd better head back. It's already going to be pretty late by the time we get back to Cozumel."

She confirmed her agreement with a nod and a smile. I turned around and we made our way back. It must have been a good twenty minutes when we arrived at the boat. I got the winch out and hoisted the minibike back on board.

"Need any help?" asked Diana.

"No, thanks for asking. I just need to be careful to remember not to lean the hot exhaust next to any fiberglass. I leaned it against me once..." and I pushed out my forearm to show a huge burn scar on the inside.

"Ouch, that's one way to remember," she winced.

I repeated my standard oil and water checks, maybe they were even more important now until I found out who'd been on my boat, and then walked inside and started her up. As before, Diana and I took lines at either end of the boat, and once we'd drifted away from the dock, engaged the throttles, backed up, and spun us around, I saw a small boar coming straight at us from the far side of the marina.

There was white water breaking over the front of their boat, which showed how fast they were going, and while I wasn't sure if they were coming for us specifically, it made me uncomfortable.

I pretended not to notice, and eased us toward open water. I glanced back as I reached the jetties and could see they had changed angle. It was now obvious they were coming after us, about a quarter of a mile back but gaining fast. I may have been past paranoid, but it looked like the three men in the boat were all looking at me in the cabin.

"Tomas, I am sure it's nothing, but is that boat chasing us?" asked Diana, concerned.

"Not to alarm you, but that would appear to be the case. Don't worry, we aren't going to deal with any of their bullshit today," I reassured.

As soon as I could realistically do so, I pushed the throttle forward to 3800 rpm. The turbos kicked in. In a matter of minutes, we were in open water, and once I cleared the marina basin, I pushed her to the max and she let out a huge roar.

We accelerated so quickly that Diana stepped back and grabbed the door frame for assistance. The boat quickly climbed to 60 knots and as I looked back again, I could see my wake crashing over their bow a few times. The water washed over their windshield and soaked all three.

They quickly realized they were no match for the *San Blas*, and came to a stop. I saw them turn and head back to the marina. Once

I knew we'd lost them, I eased back on the throttle to cruising speed and engaged the autopilot.

After grabbing a couple of beers, I walked to the back and sat with Diana on the transom bench.

"Okay, what was that all about?" she asked as I handed a bottle to her.

"I have no idea," I stated honestly, "maybe they were going to try and shake us down for dock rent, passage fee or some such shit."

"This boat is amazing. You'd never think something this big could go that fast."

"Like I told you, she used to be a drug smuggling boat, so it's designed to go like a bat out of hell. The only problem is the fuel she drinks at that speed. C'mon, let's go inside," I suggested.

I stood up, and she followed me. Once we were both inside, I shut the door and sat at the helm. Diana placed herself next to me and rested her head against my shoulder. We didn't say anything as we both looked out toward the horizon, me regularly checking the radar.

I was thinking about the state of my finances and the events that just happened. I was actually running out of money quickly and needed to take on some work soon. If Jeff really did have something going on, I knew I genuinely needed to consider it; if I didn't, I wasn't sure if I'd even been able to pay the entry fee for the next tournament. And yet, I couldn't ignore the "coincidence" of three men that chased me the very day Jeff was supposed to tell me about his plans.

We arrived back at our marina a couple of hours later. The Tiki was in full-blown party mode. There was the sound of Reggae music mixed with people having a good time drifting across the water.

Diana had fallen asleep in my lap so I woke her up. I told her I'd tie the boat while she came back to the land of the living, but she insisted on helping. We had just finished securing everything when I heard a voice from behind.

"I wondered if you two were going to come back tonight," said a familiar female voice.

We both looked up to see Maria walking toward the boat. *Oh shit.* I was a bit perturbed for her to see me with Diana, but I still couldn't help but smile.

"And I thought you weren't due back for a couple of days," I replied in a fake accusing tone.

"I never actually left. At the last minute I had some unexpected business come up," Maria told us, an unmistakable, somewhat stern expression on her face when she looked at Diana.

I stepped between them, making myself busy "rechecking" the moorings.

"Everything Okay?" I checked.

She nodded, but didn't say anything.

"I think you know Diana?" I asked.

"I do. Diana, how are you?"

"I'm doing well. Tomas was kind enough to take me out for a ride on his boat," said Diana with a smile.

"Oh, he does love his boat," replied Maria.

There was clearly tension in the air, so I broke it and suggested I would have a quick shower and then we could go for a drink at the Tiki.

"To be honest, I'm exhausted. I think I will go home, have a shower, and crash out," said Diana, who looked as if she felt quite awkward.

I offered her a ride, but she reminded me she was staying at the marina house. Diana thanked me for the adventure, gave me a big hug, and headed off down the dock. I couldn't see Maria's face as she had her back to me as Diana walked off, but I am not sure I really needed to.

"Sooo, where did you guys go today?" She asked, the jealous inflection audible for all to hear, especially me.

"Nowhere special. We just cruised down to Progreso and had dinner at *Cilantros*," I admitted.

She punched me in the arm, and not playfully either.

"God, you took her to your lagoon, didn't you?"

I smirked, not so innocently, and then shuffled about as I picked up the bags of trash we collected and secured them to the rail.

"Honestly, you need a new form of foreplay," said Maria as she rolled her eyes.

I laughed and shook my head. The fact that she was jealous was amusing.

"Don't laugh you dick, just go take your shower and hurry up," she told me.

I walked into the cabin, showered and changed as quickly as I could seeing as Maria was waiting.

"Ready for that drink?" I asked, once I was done.

"Not really, I just wanted to wash her off you," she admitted before pushing me back into the cabin.

Thank god I have good stamina, because these women are going to keep me going for a while.

Chapter Nine

I AWOKE TO THE gentle slapping sound of the water rhythmically hitting the hull of the boat. I turned over, peered at Maria, and paused. She looked adorable, all curled up next to me. I eased myself out of the bed, so as not to disturb sleeping beauty, and put some coffee on.

As I did almost every morning, I walked out on deck, gave the lines a check and then stared at the view in front of me, if only to get an idea of what the weather had in store. There was nothing like the breeze and the fresh salty smell of the sea to give the senses and mind a wake-up call. It was better than a jolt of coffee, but that was always welcome as well. Aside from a few squalls on the horizon, the outlook appeared as good as the previous day.

With coffee in hand, I sat on the transom bench and gazed around the marina. The sun had just come up over the horizon and felt warm on my skin. That was nice, far less so than what my eyes looked at.

The dive gear was still piled to the side and the trash bags were still hooked onto the rail. I also spotted that the windshield was covered in dried salt due to our swift exit the previous night.

"Yeah, I got some chores to do."

I also knew I needed to catch up with Jeff at some point during the day. I was sure he'd want to take that trip to Merida and that would give me the chance to ask him about some work. Whether I wanted to get involved was another matter.

Having finished my coffee, I got myself motivated to get on with the chores that obviously needed doing. I dropped the trash bags and scuba gear on the deck, quietly so as not to wake Maria, then grabbed the dock hose and started rinsing everything down.

"He would build brick walls as a form of therapy."

The quote from Winston Churchill popped into my head.

"I guess I feel the same way about rinsing stuff with the water hose."

I moved about the boat, rinsed everything down and watched the salt and dirt just run off the bow, not thinking about anything else of consequence when I saw the footprints again.

Out of curiosity, I placed my foot next to one of them and thought, *"I was right."*

They had to be either a size ten or eleven, and that wasn't any flip-flop tread. My best guess was that it looked like combat boot tread, and that was something to be worried about. Nobody in the marina wore that sort of thing regularly.

I took a photo on my cell phone and washed them away. Once I'd hosed down the boat and put the scuba gear away, I walked over to the Tiki to drop the trash bags in the dumpster that was out back.

As I emptied the contents of the bags, the sound of car doors closing reached me. I scanned around the parking lot and across the far side I saw Don Miguel and Victor leaving the marina house. They climbed into a car and drove in my direction, pulling up alongside me. Victor was in the driver's seat with Don Miguel in the back.

He rolled down the window and greeted me, "Senior Tomas, Buenos Días!"

"Buenos Días, Don Miguel," I replied as I emptied the last sack.

"Are you coming to Merida today?" he inquired.

I didn't want to divulge too much so I shrugged my shoulders. "I haven't spoken to Jeff today, but I think that's the likely plan."

"Good, okay Tomas," he said, offering his hand toward me.

I leaned over and reluctantly shook his hand, careful to not make eye contact.

"I hope to see you there," he said in a somewhat indifferent tone.

I gave a nod of the head as they drove away. I barely knew the guy and yet I felt like I needed to wash my hands. As I walked back to the boat, I wondered whether Jeff had been speaking to Don Miguel at the shrimp boil when he got so upset. We all knew Jeff had dealings with them, but he was usually the one who called the shots—I wasn't sure that was the case this time.

It was still quiet in the marina, a few people out for their morning runs and some had started the same daily routine of morning chores. I checked in on Maria when I got back and she was still asleep. I poured myself another cup of coffee and continued the daily maintenance chores. Just as I was finishing up, my cell phone rang, the caller ID confirmed it was Jeff.

"Buenos Días, my friend," I answered.

"And Buenos Días to you, Tomas. What are you up to this morning?"

"Just finishing the usual morning chores, and also waiting for you. Are we going to Merida today?" I asked.

"Ah, actually, no. I made other plans for today. I will be down there in about an hour. By the way, is Maria with you?" he asked.

"As it happens, yes. She is asleep on the boat," I confirmed.

"Do me a favor, tell her that Michelle called and needs to speak to her?"

He sounded a bit more cheerful than he had the last couple of days; maybe he had something fun planned for us?

"Will do. See you in a bit."

I really didn't want to wake her, but if Jeff asked me to pass on a message, it could be important. I crawled slowly on the bed next to her and gently rocked her shoulder.

"Sweetie, Jeffryn just called. He asked me to tell you that Michelle needs you to call her."

"Urgh, not now," she mumbled. Maria never was very good in the morning. "Let's just lay here a little longer. The world can wait a bit."

Just laying next to her made the world feel right, so I curled up close to Maria and wrapped my arms around her. I drooped off to sleep once more, and set an alarm for thirty minutes. In what felt like no time, it went off.

"Babe, Jeff is going to be here soon. I will get you a coffee and towel so you can have a quick shower," I said as I slid off the bed.

"Two sugars, please," came a muffled voice buried in a pillow.

I looked out the window while I waited for a fresh pot to boil and saw Jeff pulling up behind the Tiki.

"Wow, he wasn't messing around," I muttered to myself, curious what he had planned.

I could see he was in shorts and a long-sleeve T-shirt; "*Standard fishing apparel,*" I said to myself.

I took the coffee to Maria who was sitting in bed and talking on the phone.

"Jeff's here," I whispered as I pointed in the direction of the Tiki.

She nodded to acknowledge me and continued on the phone. I walked out to the deck to wait for Jeff. Shortly after, he came out of the Tiki and walked down the dock towards my boat. He physically looked happier than I'd seen him in days, his expression matching the tone of his voice earlier.

"If I don't know better, I would say you're ready to go fishing," I exclaimed with a smile.

"Oh yeah, are you ready?" he fired back with a huge grin.

"Hell, yes. Give me a few minutes to get all my shit together."

I went back inside and felt like a kid on Christmas morning. Sure, I fished often, but it had been a long time, way too long, since Jeff and I went fishing together. The only downside was he usually caught most of the fish and liked to rub my face in it.

As I dashed about, Maria appeared from the cabin fully dressed, but her hair was still damp.

"By the looks of it, you and my brother are off fishing?" she asked.

"We are, unless you can think of something better we can do and I'll disappoint Jeffryn," I joked.

"I just spoke to Michelle and I have to go to Miami," she explained, "looks like I will be away for a few days after all."

She grabbed her things and walked out onto the deck as I picked up the last of my stuff.

"Knowing Jeffryn, there'll probably be hookers involved," she said in a disapproving voice.

"It's not that type of fishing," I teased back. "Have a safe trip and let me know when you're back."

Jeff had appeared in the doorway just as Maria walked out. He made himself comfortable on the couch as he watched me, not quite as cheerful-looking as he had been a few minutes earlier.

"Jeff, does it bother you seeing me with Maria again?"

"Come on, man, get your stuff together and let's go," he urged with something of a scowl on his face as he stood back up and walked out.

I didn't think he really cared too much. He never really showed it before.

Maybe just seeing us together in the morning was a bit too much.

I grabbed my stuff, locked everything up—and checked it twice just to be certain after recent events—before I headed off toward the fuel dock where Jeff had his boat docked. Jeff was looking things over a final time as I approached. A look of concern still on his face.

"Jeff, is Cantrelle coming with us?"

"Nah, man, he has to work... anyway, this trip is just for you and me," he replied keenly.

Just like old times.

As I got on board, Jose was pulling off the fuel hose and shouted, "We are ready to go, Jefe."

"Okay, let's go," replied Jeff as he started the motors on the *Maria* and started casting off the lines. Headed straight out onto open waters.

Chapter Ten

I couldn't help but be blown away by Jeff's boat as I stood on the afterdeck and looked around me. Of course, it helped to have money, but this beauty was something else; she was clearly brand new and came with every accessory, toy, and gizmo you could imagine.

"Man, she looks well-equipped, Jeff. Does this thing dock with the International Space Station and form part of NASA as well?" I joked.

"Ha, you haven't seen anything yet... come check this out!" he boasted as he stepped inside the cabin.

I paused as I knew I was about to experience a rather large dose of jealousy, the one you get right in your stomach. I walked around and joined him inside, and what I saw was stunning.

Although the *Maria* was only ten-feet longer than my boat, his looked much bigger. Some of it was a visual thing, but there were also obvious differences, such as the cabin was a bit longer but had less deck space aft.

"Christ, Jeff, this is gorgeous!" I said in amazement.

Everything was either electric or computerized, and that even included the throttles. It had recessed L.E.D. lighting in the overhead and light strips on the bottom of the walls that glowed red. It pretty much had everything top of the market, even down to the marble table tops.

I joked about NASA, but this boat was far closer to the mark than I thought. It made my boat look positively plain by comparison. The smile and nodding by Jeff showed he knew exactly how impressive his baby was.

"This is a world away from your old 22 Mako that we used to go fishing in," I said.

He smiled even more, and I saw that brought a happy memory to mind for him as well.

"Grab yourself a beer from the fridge and come up to the bridge with me," he told me.

"Oooo, the bridge," I mocked. "It's all illogical, Captain," I added in a serious 'Spock' manner.

"Fucking smartass," sighed Jeff.

The fridge was as well stocked as everything else on Jeff's floating palace. He had beer, coke, pineapple juice, lemonade, water... the works. It was still a little on the early side so I went for some pineapple juice rather than something alcoholic. It wasn't that early though, so I grabbed two bottles of beer as well, just on the off chance because it seemed more like a special occasion.

When I stepped outside the cabin, I noticed a narrow stairwell that curved around the back-up to the bridge. It made a nice overhang off the back of the cabin to cover a full bar that even came with a sink under it. The builders clearly took advantage of all the space and it still left enough room for six people to fish.

Unsurprisingly, the fly bridge was decked out like the rest of the boat. It had a full console that stretched across with a long, sofa-style bench wrapped around the cock-pit, which had the same electronics he had inside. Jose was up front and sat at the wheel as we steered through the jetties and out into open water.

We sat there and stared out at sea, just enjoying the ride. The small squalls I spotted earlier looked like they were about to make land, but everything else was clear as far as the eye could see. The 65 Hatteras coasted along and when I looked forward at the GPS, it showed we were cruising nicely at 28 knots. What I couldn't work out was where we were going.

"Where are we heading, Jeff?"

"I'm surprised you haven't worked it out. We are going to our old spot off the north reef and troll over the coral heads," he answered.

"Do we need to get anything ready, or does the boat do that for you as well?" I ribbed.

"No, we don't, and no, it wasn't the boat," he laughed. "Jose took care of getting everything sorted. We're all ready to fish."

It left me feeling a bit out of place. That sort of thing was usually down to me, given I am usually on my own, or at best, fishing with hired deck hands. I just felt like I should do something.

"Just sit back and enjoy the experience gringo"

We were extremely close, but that didn't mean we had to talk all the time. We cruised for another 45 minutes, and I don't think we said much at all. The two of us were just content to enjoy the scenery and fresh sea air. As soon as we reached the reef, Jeff stood up and grinned at me.

"Come on, Gringo, let's see if you can still catch a fish!"

And so it started. I jumped up straight behind him and we went to the rack of fishing poles. I leaned in to grab one.

"Not that one, Tomas. That one is all mine."

"Do you have nitrous on it or something?" I replied sarcastically.

Jeff grabbed his pole and showed me his lure. "Check it out" he said, showing it to me. " I had lost my last lure one time so I used this Rum bottle cap and a slip lead as the head then put the feathers on it; I think the rough edges of the cap makes more white water. I always catch more fish with it!"

I smiled big and replied "if it works so well, why didn't you put one on mine?"

He turned and headed for the stern "Competition Gringo" he said mockingly.

It only took us a few minutes to collect everything up, thanks to Jose, and by that time we were over the coral heads. Jose slowed to around four knots and gave us the nod—and we both released our lines. I spun mine out to about the fourth wake behind us and Jeff did practically the same. The coral heads stretched out for about two miles, so we could just cruise back and forth.

We'd gone little more than a mile when Jeff's line loaded up. His reel started "singing" as the fish took off stripping the line. Jose threw the boat in reverse to help Jeff keep the line, and began to crank mine in fast to give him room. All of a sudden I got a hit too. We both had fish, strong fish, on at the same time.

The fight continued, but it seemed obvious that Jeff had the bigger catch, so I was about to cut mine loose. "Im cutting loose Jeff"

"No way, you stay on it, Tomas," ordered Jeff.

Whatever was on my line was strong and pulled hard, and I had the rod handle braced against my hip, but it felt like it was digging a hole in me. It kept stripping the line and pulling toward Jeff's catch. We were in danger of losing both if our lines tangled, so before he could object a second time, I whipped out the knife and cut my line. It made an almighty twang, like a guitar string snapping through an amp, and the rod snapped back toward my face.

I dropped it on the deck and rushed over to help Jeff with his Moby Dick. The beast was running hard and Jose was not using enough power to keep up with it; he was young after all and had probably not done this too often.

"Tomas, go on the wheel," yelled Jeff.

I ran straight up the small steps where Jose was ready and jumped out of the way without missing a beat. I grabbed the wheel and spun it hard over, then pushed both throttles full astern. I kept looking back to help me steer where I needed to so Jeff's line could remain straight behind us.

He kept cranking every chance he had to gain line, and we saw a black shape in the water.

"She's a hoss," I shouted, but Jeff didn't respond as he was intensely focused on his prize.

Soon it broke water and we could all clearly see that Jeff was locked in battle with a big ass Tuna.

"It's a tuna, baby, a big ass tuna," I whooped.

Some fifteen minutes passed in a flash and Jeff had it within fifty yards of the boat. Each time he gave and then regained line, and the fight ebbed and flowed. Tackle boxes, bait and gear floated around the deck that was now full of water from all the vicious maneuvering I had done to help land the monster on the other end.

Eventually, it began to exhaust itself and we had it about 40 feet off the stern where Jose was standing with the gaff hook. The tuna made a big circle toward the side of the boat, and Jose leaned over with it and hit the bullseye right in the back of the dorsal fin. The fish kicked hard and Jose's feet slipped out from under him and he went over the side.

"SHIT," we both screamed at the same time.

I leaned over and grabbed one of the buoyancy cushions and threw it to Jose before I whacked the throttles once again. It was one of the most exhilarating fishing trips I'd been on in a long time. My adrenaline thundered through my body and my heart pounded like a herd of buffalo. We streamed in reverse at the fish and Jeff relentlessly cranked the reel. Everytime a wave splashed over his head he would shake it off and kept on cranking.

After several more minutes of maneuvering, cranking and fighting, we reached the fish again, and it was clear it'd given up the battle. I sunk another gaff into it as Jeff jumped out of the chair to help me pull it aboard.

"Hell *yes*, now that is fishing," yelled Jeff triumphantly as the fish continued to thrash around on the deck violently. We ended it as humanly as possible and then sat back to admire the prize.

"That is a straight-up beast, Jeff! One for the ages," I declared as he sat catching his breath.

As soon as he caught his breath he looked at me "did you throw one of the cushions at Jose? I only saw it out of the corner of my eye," he asked.

"Oh, shit, Jose!" I said. "He got knocked over several minutes ago. I suppose we'd better go get him before the sharks do."

I ran up to the control and grabbed the binoculars. The bright white cushion was easy to see, and I spotted him a good few hundred meters ahead. I pushed the throttles ahead and carefully came up alongside him as Jeff pulled him out of the water.

"Cap, damn man, you left me," he said semi-shocked.

Jeff and I knew he was in no real danger and both of us couldn't stop laughing.

" I did throw you a float," I chuckled.

"Dude, I can't believe you left him," confessed Jeff, who was sitting on the couch with his hands over his face trying not to laugh. By this point, all three of us were laughing.

"No hard feelings, Jose. We knew you'd be alright," I said.

"No problem, Cap... wow, nice fish," he said as he set eyes on our catch.

We tried to get it in the fish box but this mammoth fish, which had to be at least 250 pounds, wouldn't fit and the tail stuck out almost a foot. It seemed fitting to leave it there just to show off just how big it was.

"I can't see we are ever gonna beat that today," I suggested.

"I think you are right, Tomas," replied Jeff as he grabbed two beers from the fridge. "You are still hardcore, my friend. Damn, I can't believe you left Jose."

"He was fine, and I chucked him something to hang on to." I smiled.

Jose was at the front of the boat as we enjoyed some beers and the sea air. It took us about thirty minutes to get back to the marina. Jeff was intent to have his moment so instructed Jose to tie up under the scales at the fish house. They guys came out and all clapped when they saw the tail sticking out. Jeff, of course, milked the moment for all it was worth.

One of the guys came down and tied a line to the fish's tail while two others hoisted it out of the fish box. It dragged across the dock, then hung high for all to see. We walked over to the dial and it was a bit smaller than I thought, a mere 229 pounds.

"Jeff, that would have won the fishing tournament last week."

"Maybe next time."

Jeff arranged a quick deal with the fish house guys to clean and gut the fish, and then to pack it into one pound bags and deliver to the Tiki.

"So, it's not all for us then?" I joked.

"Hey, Tomas, two hundred dishes at thirty bucks each, plus beers, that's a good day at the office," he explained.

"I might need a calculator for that one," I joked back.

He looked on with a wide grin as they got to work, and I'd have been smiling if such a good day had added that much to my bank account. I picked up the hose to wash the deck when Jeff grabbed my arm and told me Jose would take care of all of that.

He reached into his pocket and handed Jose and one of the dockworkers some cash.

"After fueling the boat, I need you to help Jose," he said to the worker. "We have a 4 PM charter and Captain Cantrelle will be back at about 3."

"Si, Jefe," they both answered.

"Tomas, follow me. I have one more surprise for you today," confessed Jeff. "It's time for us to go ride the bikes," he announced as he put his hand on my shoulder.

"Oh, hell yeah, just let me grab a shower and a change of apparel."

"Cool, I will be waiting at the Tiki."

Jeff headed off toward the Tiki and I continued down the dock to the *San Blas.*

How cool have the last 24 hours been? I contemplated as I walked along.

I'd spent an amazing evening with Diana, spent the night with Maria, gone fishing with Jeff and caught an insane tuna, and now I was about to go for a joyful ride on a couple of bad-ass bikes!

CHAPTER ELEVEN

I continued to the *San Blas* and couldn't help but look over the marina; all the boats had people busy doing chores or getting ready to go out for the afternoon. As I looked down, fish nibbled at the barnacles on the poles that held up the decking. The sun was shining, but it wasn't at its peak.

My watch showed that it was almost noon. I didn't really have to as my stomach felt hungry and that had already signaled it was lunchtime. I dropped my stuff off, had a quick shower and changed into my bike-riding attire—which meant blue jeans, T-shirt and black boots—and made my way to the Tiki where Jeff was waiting. As I arrived, I could see he'd also had a shower and changed clothes.

"You ready?" he asked.

"To be honest, give me a moment to grab something to eat. My stomach thinks my throat has been cut," I answered.

"Sorry, Gringo, they are cleaning the grill. We can grab something on the way. Besides, we are having dinner at Cilantro's later."

"At least grab me a bag of those?" I said as I pointed to the Doritos behind the bar.

Jeff leaned over and grabbed a bag, tossing them over to me.

"Come on, we can grab a burger on the ferry," he suggested.

I followed him to a truck outside, and we climbed in. He drove over the gravel lot and once we reached the main road, he turned east toward his house. I sat back and left the driving to him as I munched on my Doritos. The north end of the island was visible and the gulf, where the water went from turquoise along the coast to deep blue, got much deeper. I assumed Jeff was doing much the same, watching the scenery go by and sifting through his own thoughts.

"He probably sees this view a couple of times a day, but I'd never get bored of it."

After fifteen minutes, we entered through his big black gates and security box, and down his driveway. As we pulled up to the far side of the house, I could see two of his staff cleaning down a pair of Gixxers. "Suzuki GSXR 1000's"

"That one is for you," he pointed as we got out of the black SUV. "Is there a difference?" I replied. He lifted his seat and I saw a small nitrous bottle. I smiled big "Let me guess, mine doesn't have one?" "Competition Gringo." he replied with a smirk. I laughed and shot back "you're gonna need it." His smirk became a little less smirky because he knew I was a much better rider.

You would think it was my first time, and yet the novelty never wore off. I hit the ignition and the two-wheeled stallion between my legs growled into life. I revved it up a couple of times and soaked in the deep throated snarl. I grabbed the helmet hanging on one of the mirrors.

"See you on the street," I yelled with a grin and chugged away toward the gates. I stopped once I reached the main road and Jeff wasn't far behind me.

He pulled up beside me and said. "Do you see that orange sign, Tomas? That one about a quarter of a mile away?" he asked with a grin.

"Just say when." I glared as I revved the bike.

"Okay, three... two..." he said looking at me, "...one!"

The pair of us ripped the throttles back and with a cloud of dust and smoke we were both off. We were neck and neck for much of it, but I heard his R.P.M.s tack out in 3rd gear. I assume the nitrous shot. He beat me by about two bike lengths.

We paused at the next intersection.

"Not bad," I confirmed, a little irritated that I'd lost. "Let's see how you do on a road course."

We rode off side by side, still enthusiastically but not in full race mode, and headed toward the ferry landing. We arrived just as they were boarding, so we parked the bikes next to the guard rail.

"Let's go get that burger," I stated as we took off our helmets. We made our way through the ever-growing number of cars, even though the ferry wasn't even half full by this stage. We got to the concession stand on the far side and ordered a couple burgers with everything on them—a heart attack waiting to happen, as described by an old friend once.

While we sat at the picnic table under the umbrella, I looked over at Jeff and said, "I wanted to wait until we were alone to ask you something."

"What'd ya need to know, Tomas," he replied before taking a huge bite.

"I know you mentioned some business the other evening. Cards on the table, I need to make some money. What did you have in mind?"

As a close friend, it is almost as if he expected me to ask it right about then.

"Funny you should ask. We are going to check on that now."

"Guess I shouldn't be surprised. You know me. Don't suppose you want to share any specifics?" I inquired.

He swallowed a bite of burger then explained. "I have a 210-foot supply boat that we converted to carry fuel..."

"Okay," I put my hand up to stop him saying anything more and looked over my shoulder to see if anyone was within earshot. "I know where this is going... Do you have buyers and sellers?"

"Of course, we have been making this run for over a year but we recently lost our Captain and I need someone I can trust to replace him, someone who, shall we say, knows the system."

That bad feeling returned to the pit of my stomach. I knew it was unlikely to be 100% above board and legal, but that feeling was one I knew very well from dealing with the cartels. I was unhappy to even contemplate getting involved again.

"What *exactly* happened to the old captain?"

Jeff put his burger down and side-eyed me. "Nobody knows for absolute certainty," he answered.

"That is really not the frigging answer I want to hear, Jeff," I fired back.

"It's all fine," he laughed as he took a swig of cola. "Listen, as you know, the money is always transferred electronically before the final fuel transfer goes ahead. We have been doing it the same way for two years with the same people, so everyone was quite relaxed. The last time, they postponed the electronic transfer until after they received the product... but then the transfer was never made. We found the boat abandoned and anchored off La Ceiba Playa. She was out of the water with not a single drop of diesel left in it. Our first thought was that it was the Honduran Cartel involved, but my reliable contacts there say they know nothing about it."

The more I hear, the less I like.

"The job coming up is with the same sellers, but now it has to be all cash. They will not accept any other method of payment. Well, not until trust is rebuilt."

"Nothing like trust among thieves," I chipped in trying to remain optimistic.

"Honestly, I just need you to run it to make sure everything goes as it should," he confided.

Run it. Right...

"Understood," I said, rubbing my chin. "So, how much are we talking here? What sort of money is involved?"

He leaned in closer and whispered, "You will have enough to buy 500,000 gal."

I quickly did the math in my head. *That comes to around 1.3 million dollars. "1.4" he corrected me.*

"That's a serious chunk of cash, Jeff. What's your, or should I potentially say, our cut from it all?" I asked the question that would likely decide my involvement or not, no matter how badly I needed the money.

"Your cut will be eighty thousand US dollars," he confirmed.

That is a lot of money, money I need.

Had it been anyone else, I would probably have walked away from it. In fact, I would not have been there in the first place if I thought it involved the cartels, but this was Jeff and I trusted him.

"Okay," I said after a deep sigh and moment of contemplation, "give me the details."

"Alright then," he said quietly. "We have a collection barge just east of Dos Bocas, off the coast of Frontera; it's anchored some three miles off the coast. You will pick up the boat in Progreso and set sail around noon, so you can arrive around 2100 hours. That should give you around nine hours to load up and get out before day light," he explained.

I heard every word he said, and I was paying attention, I had to, but just a small piece of my mind wondered just what I had got myself into again.

"Once you are loaded, you will set off before daylight and head to a position that I will provide directly to you. The position will be off the coast of Cozumel—I guess an eighteen-hour run. There will be a crew ready to take over from there and also a launch to run you back to Progreso."

"That all sounds good so far, but I will need to select my own crew," I informed him.

"That may cause a problem with the other side," he admitted.

"Jeff, I need the money and I can get this done, but I'm going to need to use my own people. I do not and will not end up in a Mexican prison due to someone I didn't want to work with or know," I stressed.

"Okay... Okay...," he said with his hand up, "who do you have in mind?"

"Let's see, Ramon, Tio, Shirma and Pepe if he is up for it."

"Putting the band back together, huh?" asked Jeff.

"That's all of us, man, except for you of course. I have to ask, how come you ain't doing it yourself?"

Jeff lowered his head a little as he explained, "It's a conflict of interest and for the safety of everyone, they can't know where the money is coming from. FYI, Don Miguel is putting up the money and everything else is in his name. I'm merely supplying the transportation and logistics, nothing more."

The ferry approached the other end of its journey and once the landing was made, we went back to the bikes. We fired them up and made our way off the ramp and once we approached the highway, the two of us went back to racing. It was like a game of cat and mouse, I blew past him in the first turn and after that I was just short of dragging a knee in each turn, accelerating hard coming out before down shifting for the next one. It took me a couple of minutes to realize he wasn't right behind me.

I stopped on the side of the road and waited for him to catch up. I just took my helmet off when he came screaming around the corner. When he skidded to a halt next to me, he lifted his Visor and asked in a shaky voice "why did you stop." I replied with the same smirk he gave me with the fishing and replied "I thought you broke something."

"Tomas, the way you took those corners, you are a crazy son bitch, my friend," he laughed.

"I was about to come back for you."

He bellowed with laughter. "Okay, looks like you win this time!"

We both took off again, and a normal trip to Merida would take nearly two and a half hours. Thanks to our inability to not race each other most of the way, we did it in little over an hour. As we got close, I tucked in behind Jeff as he led us straight to Cilantro's.

It was a few minutes later that we pulled up at Cilantro's and parked next to a black SUV that was not dissimilar to the one Jeff had. It wasn't his, but there was something familiar about it.

"Man, that was serious fun, Jeff. It has been way too long since we did something like that, brother," I said jubilantly as I rested my helmet on the bike.

"If it makes you feel any better, I haven't exactly been out riding much myself. There ain't too many people to ride with in Mexico, not like that anyway," he answered. That's Don Miguel's truck, so he must be here. Let's go in and grab something proper to eat."

My memory obviously works okay. I knew I recognized it.

We went through the open doors and took the steep stairs up to the deck.

"Funny enough, I was here just yesterday with Diana," I told him as we climbed.

"I know, I heard." He smiled.

"What did you hear, and from whom?"

"Don Miguel... he said he tried to catch up with you yesterday at the marina. Someone mentioned you'd been here for dinner, but apparently you tore off like your ass was on fire and your boat was too fast," explained Jeff.

He said that and I felt my temperature go up a bit. "You know what, next time, tell him to make a fucking appointment!" I said sternly.

"Of course, Tomas," chuckled Jeff, who clearly couldn't see why I was upset.

We walked through to an air-conditioned open area with several chairs and tables. At the far end of the biggest one, naturally, was Don Miguel, Victor, and a third man who I didn't recognize. Given what we were doing, I didn't like the surprise.

"Senior Tomas, welcome," shouted Don Miguel as he stood up from the table.

I also didn't appreciate it when he blasted my name so loudly in public. He offered his hand, which I once again took but didn't smile as we did. I'd only heard about Don Miguel, but what little I had seen of the man, I was far from impressed. I genuinely thought he was an overbearing, over-loud, arrogant, obnoxious asshole.

We sat across the table from them and Don Miguel once again loudly announced to all and sundry, "You both already know my brother, Victor, and this gentleman is a close friend of ours, Carlos, who we do business with. Carlos, this is Jeffryn and Tomas."

Carlos looked a bit younger than the two of us, maybe in his low-thirties, had shortish hair, and a rather slender, tall frame. The eyes that peered through the wire rim glass were cold yet nervous, and had the fidgety appearance of someone who didn't want to be there—possibly forced. We greeted each other, then Don Miguel called the waiter over.

"Beers all around please, and would you like anything to eat, Tomas?" he asked.

I'll have a shot of tequila with that beer if it's on offer, and the friend snapper," I answered politely.

"Oh, you like your tequila, fabulous," he shouted, once again making sure all attention was on him.

I thought to myself: If I spend much time with you, I'll need the fucking bottle!

The waiter took the rest of the order and left toward the kitchen.

"So, did Jeffryn discuss our little proposition with you?" Don Miguel asked.

"We've talked about some aspects of it. Just to make sure I understand everything, you have a man on the inside?"

"Straight down to the important stuff, yes, I understand you know the business. Carlos is our guy at Control," he said, pointing to the fifth member of our table.

He looked up, and in a shaky voice that matched his nervous disposition. "I am on vacation right now, but I will be back at work tomorrow."

"Okay, right, and who do you have in Logistics?" I questioned.

Don Miguel put his hand in Carlos' direction and stopped him from saying anything further. "Tomas, you do not need to know this person, just what he is doing."

I shook my head. This didn't look good.

"Listen, I know that Control Marino monitors the movements of all vessels by radar, and it's Logistics that gives the orders for the vessel movements. Without people on both sides of the fence, this simply can't be done."

I couldn't tell if I was getting through to him as he sat there emotionless.

"I need certainty that you have these bases covered. You know full well if I'm caught, they'll throw my gringo ass over the side and take your money!"

"Okay, Okay, Tomas. We have a person in Logistics as well. They will ensure your passage, and I'll even arrange for you to meet them after lunch," confirmed Don Miguel.

The conversation became more generalized and away from business. Don Miguel seemed to speak at everyone rather than to anyone, and seemed more interested in just hearing himself speak.

The waiter arrived with our beers and food. I dug in as the others continued to talk and let my mind drift a little, thinking about how much I had enjoyed the previous night at Cilantro's with Diana—a whole lot more than the present company.

I also genuinely thought about walking away from the job. I had my doubts about it from the start, and nothing I had seen or heard improved anything. What kept me inside was the large payday and that I knew it could be done if I could get my own crew on board.

Jeff sat to my left, and he leaned over and whispered, "You are getting that look, Tomas. Don't worry, we have been doing this for two years with the same people. It's all good," he promised.

I merely looked up from my plate and eventually nodded.

A cell phone near Don Miguel rang and he answered it fairly quickly. Once again, the conversation was in Spanish so I caught about fifty percent. All I picked up was that he ended by confirming he was on his way.

"Jeffryn, when you are finished with your meals, bring Tomas to the boat," he ordered before the trio walked away from the table. Jeff merely nodded with his mouth full of food. I just kept eating like I had no idea what had just been said.

Once they were gone, I turned to Jeff with unmistakable concern and asked, "Are you sure about these guys, Jeff? Like really sure?! Man, I gotta tell you, Don Miguel reminds me of that shifty fucker we dealt with in Tampico."

"Relax, Tomas. I assure you, I have everything covered and I am even going to send Cantrelle with you, just to be sure," he said confidently.

"Okay, but if I see one part of this job I don't like, I'm bailing out."

I took a last bite of my fish and finished up my beer. I then got up and headed to the bikes while Jeff paid the bill; typical Don Miguel I suspected. By the time he came out, I was sitting on the bike with a cigarette on the go.

"I thought you quit those filthy things, Tomas," said Jeff in disappointment.

"I did but today I felt like I needed one," I replied as I took one last drag and tossed the butt away.

Chapter Twelve

We climbed aboard the bikes and I followed Jeff down the Marina Road to the far side of the slip. The deck hands were already deploying a gangway as we pulled up next to the vessel.

Shirma, a Mexican friend I knew, walked toward us smiling and asked, "Capi, are you going to be the Captain for this run?"

"We will see, Shrima," I told him as I looked over at the two other deck hands. "Do you know those guys?"

"Si, Capi, of course I do. They are my cousins."

"Nice, we will talk in a bit. We have to go speak to Don Miguel," I explained as the two of us boarded the ship.

"For sure, Capi, it's gonna be great to work for you again." He saluted.

Shirma was young, but he had experience well beyond his years and knew more than most who'd been around twenty-plus years. He was a street smart kid who could act extremely naive, and successfully, when it suited him or he needed to. The most important thing was that I knew I could trust him.

He returned to stowing gear aboard the boat with his cousins, and I followed Jeff up the stairs to the bridge. Ever since we boarded, I had been looking over the Vessel. She seemed to be well maintained, even a fresh coat of paint had been recently added. Sure, there were a few rust streaks scattered around, but she was in good shape for a supply boat.

When we reached the top and stepped on the bridge, we found four people waiting for us... yet another surprise that was unappreciated nor wanted. Standing before us was Don Miguel, Victor, and Carlos, and I assumed, and indeed hoped, that the fourth guy was the man from Logistics.

"Tomas, I'd like you to me Don Hugo, our man in Logistics that we spoke about earlier," introduced Don Miguel, the first to speak as usual.

"It's good to meet you, Captain," he said confidently as he stretched out his hand. "How can I help you and Don Miguel?"

I shook his hand.

"Pleasure to meet you as well. I just wanted to meet everyone and ensure you have things sorted on your end," I replied as I voiced my concerns.

"Totally understandable. I can confidently tell you that we will have a program for you to receive cargo from a platform close to the collection barge. Once the transfer is complete, we will destroy all the paperwork and it will be as if the voyage never happened."

It was the sort of thing I wanted, and needed, to hear and I nodded my approval.

"That sounds good. Now, Carlos, will you have direct contact with Don Hugo? That way, once the transfer is complete, you can monitor any movements until we exit the field to La Ceiba," I confirmed.

"That's correct, Captain," he agreed.

I paused and looked around the room. It was probably too late to back out at this stage anyway, but I was happy enough to go ahead.

"Okay, from what I can see, it looks like we have a solid plan. Unless anyone has any other concerns or issues, I am happy to go ahead—let's do this," I confirmed.

They all nodded and started talking between themselves. There was a noticeable drop in apprehension and I guessed they were relieved to have sorted their Captain. There were parts of the plan that had nothing to do with me, so I stayed quiet while they talked about the aspects that didn't concern me, I just made mental notes so I knew what else was happening.

"Tomas, you got any more questions," inquired Jeff once they had all agreed on everything.

"Nope, I'm all good. It sounds pretty solid from where I am standing," I replied. "I will get the GPS reading from you tomorrow night before we depart. We will have a copy of the program, a cell phone and numbers for Don Hugo and Carlos, and I will have my crew here in 24 hours,"

"Whoa, you wait there, mister. You will use my crew and that is all there is to it. I am not trusting anyone, anyone at all, without my people," shouted Don Miguel as he waved his hands, gesturing wildly.

I'd already had just about enough of Don Miguel, and I slowly clenched my fist. There was a rush of blood to my face and I felt the overwhelming urge to punch him right in *his* fat fucking face. Knowing me well, Jeff saw what was about to happen and stepped into calm the situation before things got out of hand.

"I am sure we can work this out. Don Miguel, I wanted to bring this up with you, but Tomas beat me to it," he stated

"Let me get this straight," I spoke up immediately, "you are asking me to trust all of you and yet you obviously don't want to trust me. Sorry, this is non-negotiable. I know my crew can get this done and I won't be a part of it without them."

I took a gamble that they really needed me more than I needed the money, and that was badly.

"You know what, find someone else," I said, shaking my head.

I threw my hands up in the air and looked to move toward the stairs.

As would be expected, Don Miguel went into a huge rage as he ranted and swore. I thought it best to leave them to talk about it so I headed down the stairs to take a breather. As I walked away, I could hear a seriously animated discussion, or more like an argument, as both Jeff and Don Miguel went back and forth.

I found myself on the aft deck watching Shirma splicing lines.

"What time we leavin', Capi?" he asked.

"Not sure I'm running this one yet. Let's wait and see."

A few minutes later, Jeff appeared and opened with a statement of the obvious.

"I see you still have the extraordinary knack of pissing people off."

"I do try," I replied with a dose of sarcasm that was greeted with a smirk from both Shirma and Jeff.

"Right, Don Miguel has agreed to your condition, but you have to promise me you are sure about Ramon. You know what he is like. Can you keep him out of trouble that long?" he asked earnestly.

"Of course I can, and most importantly, I trust him!"

"Let's get this thing in motion," declared Jeff as tossed me his cell phone. "Ramon's number is in there, give him a call."

I took it and walked up the gangway so no one could hear the conversation. I found Ramon's number and dialed it. After a couple of rings, he picked up.

"Ramon, this is Tomas," I said keenly.

"Tomas, my friend. What's happening, man? Why are you ringing me on Jeffryn's cell?" he asked.

"Just borrowing it as he had your number on hand. Listen, I have an important run to do in the next 24 to 48 hours. It's for 80k US... would you be interested?"

"Fuck yeah, for sure. Just let me know when and where you need me," confirmed Ramon.

I felt a moment of relief and smiled. It was vital to me to have Ramon involved.

"There is usually a flight departing Mazatlan at 1800 and it lands in Cancun at 2030 tonight. Any chance you can be on it?" I suggested.

"Sure can. Can't wait to see you again," he answered.

"The feeling is mutual. I will have Jeff book your flight and send you everything by text," I explained.

"I'll be there."

"Ramon, one other thing. Does your father still have dealings with the customs dock in Dos Bocas?"

"He does, whadya need?"

"They rent dock space for repairs and I really need to get permission to sail there for the day after tomorrow. Let's just say if the authorities start asking questions, we will need a reason to be in the area."

"No problemo, I will have it sorted by tonight," he agreed.

"Good man, see you soon," I said gratefully and hung up.

As I walked back to the boat, I could see everyone still on the bridge. I continued going over it all in my head because I didn't trust any of the guys in there apart from Jeff.

My friend, I ain't too sure about your judgment right now. You're dealing with some pretty shady characters.

I did my best to dismiss it. Trying to remain positive.

It's okay, you have your ever trustworthy ace in the hole—Ramon—and that should be enough to keep us all out of jail if everything goes south.

Ramon had a lot of high-powered friends, both in the government and several authorities, and that was without his father's contacts. His lifestyle had necessitated the association of people who could help get you out of sticky situations. Ramon loved to party, more even than me, and he owned an escort agency, among numerous other enterprises.

In all the years we had been friends, I had never known him get himself in a situation he could get out of with a quick call. I was sure he had plenty of cash stashed away, another valuable asset to staying out of trouble, and that was probably why he was always willing to make more.

By the time I got back on the boat, Jeff was speaking to Shirma.

"It's good to have you part of the team for this run," I interjected, "but afraid your cousins will not be going on this trip. Tell them I will give 'em five hundred US dollars to take a couple of days off."

"Si, Capi. Who else is taking the trip?" he queried.

"Captain Ramon, Tio, Maggie, you, and Izquierdo if he's available. I looked at Jeff and said "maybe Cantrelle."

"I know Cantrelle, he's a good man. Happy to be involved if both you and he are, Capi," he said.

"I'll pay you at the end of the day," I confirmed and turned to Jeff, handing back his phone as I did. "If we're finished here for now, I need to get back and take care of a few things. I also need you to book the 1800 flight for Ramon from Mazatlan to Cancun. He will sort out the others."

"Consider it done. Let's wrap a couple of quick things here and we can head back." Jeff was happy, Shirma was happy, his cousins were happy with the non-work bonus, we all seemed happy. Frankly, I didn't care if Don Miguel or Victor were happy.

I went and sat on the bike while waiting for Jeff, thinking over the plan in my head, MY plan, not their plan. I also started thinking about the contingency plan I had started with Ramon. It was important not to miss anything, not a thing, as that could result in prison or death. We'd always had a contingency plan over the years and it saved our asses countless times.

With him providing the contracts through his father and getting the permission to sail, I decided I would cut Ramon in for around half the money. He wouldn't expect that much, but it was worth it for the insurance. The permission to sail was a document issued by the Mexican government that would show we would be sailing to the Customs Dock for repairs and not doing something potentially or actually illegal.

The only other danger point was getting caught literally in the act or the authorities finding a suitcase of money. If they found that much cash, we'd be arrested for conspiracy and they'd turn the money in... or more likely kill us and keep the money.

We'd better watch the radar like a hawk nonetheless, and be ready to disconnect if any vessels come in the area.

By that point, Jeff had joined me on the bikes and we were ready to head back to Cancun. As we rode along, the sun began to set behind us and the temperature had lowered slightly. We didn't head off like a pair of wild banshees, but we still managed around 100 mph most of the time.

I preferred to ride that way, it didn't allow time for contemplation, thinking too hard or any other considerations but the road. I always found it a great reliever of stress and anxiety. You don't have time to worry about anything else.

We pulled up to the ferry an hour later but had to wait for it to come back from the other side.

"Can I borrow the Land Rover to get Ramon from the airport?" I asked Jeff while we waited.

"I think Diana has it right now to pick up some things for the restaurant, but hey, you can use the Porsche if you like," he answered with raised eyebrows and a smile.

"Nice." I grinned.

"I gotta ask, man, Jeff said with a sigh. "Why did you decide to take Ramon on this trip and push so hard to have him involved?"

"Simple, for insurance. Ramon's father has some big-time connections and if we run into any unexpected problems, he is arranging for us to have papers stating we are there for repairs."

His frown turned into a smile as he nodded his head.

"Smart thinking, I should have guessed it would be something like that, but there won't be any problems."

"You know I always have a contingency... always."

The ferry eventually arrived, and we were back at Jeff's place about thirty minutes after the crossing. His security men put the bikes away and got the Porsche out for me.

Jeff took the keys from his security and handed them to me. "T hat was a blast," he admitted, "let's not wait so long to do it again."

"It was. I'm off to get Ramon, can I grab a little cash advance?"

"Sure," he answered as he passed me some notes from a good-sized money clip. "Tell Ramon to take it easy, you know what he's like."

"When have you ever known him to take it easy," I replied as I got in the Porsche.

As I slid behind the wheel of the Porsche, everything felt smooth and well put together. Jeff had a few sports cars, but this was the one I'd chosen in the past when given an option. I started up the long drive and at the top of the bluff, turned onto the main, and hit the accelerator. And sped down to the marina, the exhilaration of the pull-away was immense. I slowed down as I reached the parking lot and put it just behind the Tiki.

Got a few hours before I have to pick up Ramon. I can go check on the boat, shower and change, then head off.

I took a moment to run the plan over in my mind to be sure I hadn't missed anything while I still had time to do something about it, and felt confident we'd covered every base. I lifted myself out of the Porsche and made my way around the building, noticing a Range Rover backed up near the Tiki deck with its back hatch open. Diana came out with two men as I walked over. They looked like staff and she saw me just as she said goodbye to them.

"Tomas," she yelled, slightly surprised at seeing me. "Oooo, I see you have Jeffryn's Porsche, now you know you're going to have to take me out for a drink later," she purred with that strong Southern accent.

"'Fraid we'll have to take a rain check. Jeff's had me out with him on the bikes all afternoon and I need to freshen up before I pick up a friend from Cancun International in a few hours," I said with regret.

"Ok, you get a pass this time. Bring your friend by later and I'll buy you guys a beer," she suggested.

"Will do," I confirmed as I gave her a big hug.

As I walked along the pier toward the *San Blas*, the sun was still just above the horizon.

Probably got another hour before sunset.

"Hola, Capi," shouted Jose from the far side as he dropped another bait trap into the water.

"Hey Jose, do you know where Cantrelle is?"

"He's on the boat," he pointed, "over there at the fuel dock. We have a charter tonight, and he's getting everything ready."

"Okay, can you tell him to come and see me if he's free in the next couple of hours?"

"Si, Capi, can do," yelled Jose as he grabbed his bucket of bait fish and walked off.

I continued down to my boat and went to do a few checks before I had a shower. Having seen the bilges were all good, I moved up to the bow where I once again found footprints. They were more prominent than last time and clearer to see—they were definitely size ten or eleven, and certainly some sort of military type tread.

I checked the latch on the forward hatch and nothing was broken or appeared tampered with. I unlocked the cabin and carefully peered in. Once I was sure it was empty, I walked down to my V-birth.

I looked straight down on my bed and saw a piece of toothpick laying on the top. I discreetly tucked it into a crack in the hatch, so if anyone opened it, the toothpick would fall out—and sure enough, there it was.

Luckily, I also had a latch on the inside so the hatch could only be opened about a quarter of an inch. I needed to check around to see if anything had been disturbed, but I thought there was little chance anyone got it fully opened. There was one thing I could be sure about, and I decided it was time to install some surveillance equipment to find out what was going on and by whom.

Once I'd looked around at everything, repeating the drill from the previous time, I made myself a cup of coffee and walked out to the deck. It bothered me that someone had tried to get into my boat again, but I tried to remain calm as it appeared they didn't get in. What I wanted to know was who did it! The sun cast a cooling shadow across everything and it was always a pleasant spot. I scanned around the harbor to see if I noticed anything amiss.

The marina was generally quiet and there were a few people milling around and the odd fisherman. There was more activity around Jeff's boat and I could see Cantrelle as he moved stuff around the back deck.

I didn't want to hang around with the surveillance camera, especially as I was going to be away in a few hours. I tipped the final dregs of coffee into the water and went to the cabin. In one of the desk drawers there was a little wireless remote camera. I'd originally intended to put it up to film tournaments so I could watch things back, but never got around to it.

It didn't take long to add new batteries and sync it up to my laptop. When it was ready, I casually strolled around the boat and when everyone appeared busy, I slipped over the side into the water. I swam under the dock and clamped the camera under the planks where it couldn't be seen. I adjusted the angle quickly and had a direct line of sight to the *San Blas* so I could film whoever tried to board. Having checked everything was secure, I started to swim back to my boat.

I heard footsteps as I approached, so I took off my dive watch and held it in my hand.

"Hey, Cap, little late for a swim, isn't it?" Cantrelle asked with his usual big smile.

"Dropped my fucking watch," I lied.

He boarded the boat as I swam around to the rear deck and climbed out.

"Would ya fancy a beer?" I offered.

"Sure, we got a four-hour charter but they haven't shown up yet."

I grabbed a towel to dry myself off and Cantrelle followed me inside.

"Help yourself." I gestured to the refrigerator. "I'm just going to quickly rinse off."

I wasn't worried about leaving Cantrelle by himself, but I still didn't want anyone, not even him or Jeff, to know about the camera I had installed. A few minutes later, I came out, grabbed a beer, and joined him on the couch.

"Jose mentioned you wanted to see me, Cap," he asked after taking a huge swig.

"I did, and you can call me Tomas."

"Sure, Okay, Cap," joked Cantrelle.

"I wanted to talk to you about this run I am making for Jeff tomorrow night. He told me you'd be riding along. I am sure you know but I just wanted to be sure you knew what is involved and the consequences if we're caught," I said sternly.

It was the first time that I ever saw his smile almost entirely disappear.

"No worries, Cap. Jeffryn told me everything I needed to know and I understand the consequences. Let's do it," he answered keenly, if not happily.

"That's good to know. The crew are all of my people from past jobs. I can assure you I have worked with them before and they're all trustworthy and professional. Just so you know, should the worst happen, I have a contingency plan we will discuss once we are underway"

"Are you expecting any sort of trouble?"

I thought about how best to answer, and followed, "It's best to be prepared for anything in this business. I'm just not leaving anything to doubt."

"That works for me, Cap, I'm with ya," he said as he stood up.

"We can discuss the rest on the drive tomorrow," I confirmed as we shook hands and I showed him to the door. "Enjoy your charter."

There was no time to check the camera so I did it straight away. I went over to my laptop and looked at the angle. It was hard to see anyone on the pier, but if they came onto the *San Blas,* I would. Happy that I'd done something to help remove the clouds of doubt and paranoia I'd experienced with the footprints, I got changed and put some better clothes on. I was certain Ramon would want to go out for a beer or something as we hadn't seen each other in ages. The thought made me smile "He's a maniac in the party sense; I went to lunch with him once and we wound up on a G5 full of hookers flying to Belize for lunch."

Ramos was in his mid-thirties, a little shorter than me but built like a tank—he wasn't fat, just jammed a lot of muscle in a short frame. He had a deep, husky voice with a heavy Spanish accent and sounded like a Latin George Clooney. His enormous smile was framed nicely by his mustache and goatee. He knew how to handle himself in a fight and was like a pitbull that just kept coming.

I remembered when we had a disagreement one night, and I can testify that his punches feel like pillowcases filled with bricks. Another comparison some gave was a Latin Joe Pesci from around the *Casino* time. He has always been unquestionably loyal to his friends and trustworthy, and he loved a party. His problem was that he never mastered the skill of stopping once he starts. We had been through good times and plenty of bad times, and while we have been crew with a pecking order, we were more than that, we were family.

Each man had his own unique talents in our team and Ramon had always been my second-in-command, the one I confided in most aside from Jeff. He was an expert sailor and boat handler, and most importantly, he had the contact list. He knows everyone in the business and they all respected him.

There were still a couple of hours before I had to collect Ramon, so I went to the Tiki for something to eat. It was already quite full up when I arrived, and Diana wandered over and hugged me.

"Come sit at the bar, Tomas. I hope you and your friend come back here later with you looking so delicious," she hinted.

"I suspect he has a different atmosphere in mind," I replied.

"The Bartender Jorge will be over to sort you out," she said as she kissed me on the cheek and headed over to a table where they were holding up empty glasses.

I didn't need to look at the menu, I knew what I wanted.

"Hey, Jorge, a Corona and the grilled tuna, please," I ordered.

"Sure," he replied as he collected the menu and headed to the kitchen.

It didn't take long for me to consume that delightful meal and beer, and once I finished, I stood, threw a tip on the table and headed for the parking lot. Walking past Diana, I waved but she had her hands full with two rowdy tables. Joy filled me as I climbed back in the Porsche and drove off for the ferry. I was a sensible driver most of the way... most of it anyway.

My timing was perfect, and I was able to drive straight onto the ferry. Evening had taken hold by now and there was a cool breeze coming off the gulf. I leaned against the railing and watched the lights on the far shore as they passed by. I couldn't help but ponder the job again and wanted to go over it all again, just on the off chance I'd missed something obvious.

That led me to think about Ramon, the guys and the last time we worked together in Dos Bocas, and that, in turn, made me think of China. I hadn't spoken to her in a couple of months, but that didn't mean I hadn't thought about her.

"She'll always be the one that got away." I sighed heavily.

A call was long overdue, so given she could also maybe give me some new insights on the port at Dos Bocas, I decided to give her a call. I scrolled down my contact list and dialed her number. It rang a few times before she picked it up.

"Bueno."

"Hola, Bonita," I responded joyfully.

"Hey, Tomas, I've been waiting to hear from you. Where are you?" she asked.

"I'm in Cancun, just finished up a tournament here."

"Oooo, hey, are you coming to Dos Bocas? Should I expect a surprise visit?" she teased.

"Sorry, no, not now anyway. I am just about to pick up Ramon at the airport.

"Uh oh, no, Tomas, that doesn't usually mean good things. What are you up to?"

"Don't panic, it's all good. I picked up some part-time work through Jeff. We leave tomorrow or the next day for a run in your direction. I hate for this to be the first thing I ask, but is there anything I should know about?"

Her heavy pause was extremely noticeable.

"Your timing is not good. There is a lot going on these days. For starters, they are in the middle of a power struggle for the port area. Just this week, they kidnapped the owner of a local bar called Soberannis and killed him even after they got the ransom."

"I'm less concerned about that and more interested in anything going on with the Navy or Pemex. Got any insight?"

China's tone got even more serious as she continued, "I heard that the Navy was ordered to apply pressure to the Port Captain regarding kickbacks, and the business you are talking about is under pressure as well."

"Go on, how do you know what business I am talking about?" I laughed back.

"I know enough. I know you and Ramon are back together and that Jeffryn is involved as well."

I contemplated my next question. "I have some business with a guy named Don Miguel and his brother. Do you know these two?"

"Shit, Tomas, really?! These two are major players and usually bad news. There is no proof, but I suspect those two ordered the hit on the sheriff here a couple months ago. This is not wise, Tomas," she urged.

"I had a feeling about those two, that's why I brought Ramon in and insisted on my usual crew. I gotta go in a minute, but I will speak to you before we set off," I told her.

"Okay, but keep your phone close. I am going to do some checking," she suggested.

"Thanks, sweetheart. I will come see you when this is all done. I promise."

"Just be careful," she implored before she hung up.

Leaving me wondering if I'd made the wrong choice in what I'm doing.

Chapter Thirteen

I looked up once the call had ended and saw the ferry was making its usual approach to the landing. I climbed back in the Porsche, and the gate swung open several minutes later. The drive across town was quiet, with a quick stop for cold water as I had some time to kill, and arrived at the airport thirty minutes early.

I parked in the short term car park and made my way to the arrival gates. There was still time to spare, so I went to the bar for a beer. Finishing the last mouthful, I saw people starting to come through. Amongst the group was Ramon, who was in the process of looking around for me when I came up behind and tapped him on the shoulder. He spun around and a huge smile appeared on his face.

"Tomas, good to see you, my friend," he exclaimed as he gave me a bear hug.

"You too, Ramon. It's been too long," I confessed.

He was only carrying a small duffel bag so I checked, "You have any checked bags?"

"Of course."

We made our way to the carousels where the bags began to come down the chute.

"It's sooo good to see you, Tomas," he jovially said.

"That's on me, Ramon, I am genuinely sorry. Since I retired and bought the boat, I don't exactly have a lot of money for travelling."

"Then, it's good I am here so we can both make some money, eh?" he laughed.

"Roger that! You wait for your shit, and I will go bring the car out front," I suggested.

I eased the car out of the car park and pulled up around the front of the building just as Ramon appeared with his duffel bag and a suitcase that looked bigger than a footlocker. I laughed as soon as I saw it.

As I climbed out of the Porsche I shouted jokingly "Did you bring the fucking kitchen sink as well?" He laughed and shot back "I didnt know you were picking me up in a fucking Gocart!"

I laughed as I walked around to the front and opened the trunk, and about fifteen people around us joined in the laughter when it became quite apparent that his case wasn't going to fit into the less than spacious Porsche.

"Sorry, buddy, looks like you'll have to hold it on your lap. We will swing by the boat and drop it off there before we go out for food and drink," I proposed.

Luckily it was a convertible so it made it easier. It was quite a sight as he flopped into the seat and then hauled this huge case across his lap.

"I did tell you this was a two to three day job, didn't I?"

"Yeah, yeah, keep the jokes coming. Just so you know, I am aware, but I have another job after this in Carmen, so it's not all for your benefit," he fired back.

Once we were on the ferry, I walked around and helped lift the case off his lap so he could actually get out. There wasn't much to do while we crossed the water, so we leaned on the railings. It seemed a good time to discuss the job as there were not many people on that crossing.

"Let's talk about the job for a minute. You have the permits taken care of?"

"All sorted, we'll have them by 9am tomorrow," confirmed Ramon.

"Perfect. So, you have any questions?"

"Not so much about the job. Are we going to see Jeffryn tonight? It would be good to catch up with him as well?"

"I doubt it. Jeff seems to have a lot going on, although he came across a little less stressed today when we were out on the bikes," I mentioned.

"Is he making the run with us as well?"

The expression of relief on his face when I shook my head was palpable.

"Okay, that look I don't like. What's up, Ramon? Is there something I need to know?" I pushed.

"Hmmm, look, I have a reliable source who says that the cartels are putting pressure on him to use the construction company's ship to move product into Miami... and the word is that Jeff has declined the, shall we say, offer more than once,"

I ran my hands over my face and looked out over the water. "Fuck, that is not good," I muttered.

"Yep, fuck indeed," he reiterated. "I'm talking about the Veracruz Cartel and you know as well as I that these guys do not play nice."

I took a deep breath and looked him straight in the eyes. "Alright, total honesty here. I need the money from this job but not at any cost. Do you think we should do it, or are your Spidey senses telling you to bail?"

I wasn't sure I wanted the answer as he leaned in and lowered his voice further.

"I doubt you will be surprised to hear that I checked into this Don Miguel and his brother. They have nothing at all to do with the Sinaloa Cartel, but they are major players in Veracruz. The word going around is that Miguel fucker is financing this thing out of personal funds to make up for a previous deal that went bad."

"I heard—something to do with a wire transfer," I added.

"You know I am all in on this with you," he continued with a very serious expression, "but I think we need to be prepared that this things could go either way—good or bad—but if it is the latter, we need to make sure everything is set so it comes out in our favor..

I totally agreed and expressed that with a firm nod. I sat there and digested his information and opinion while he stood quietly next to me and waited for my reply; he wanted to see what I had in mind.

"How about this? Tio has family in Frontera and they own fishing boats... correct me if I am wrong?"

"You're getting that look, Tomas," he added after an affirmative nod.

I smiled. "I am pretty sure we can pull this off, and if they actually do try to fuck us over, we will get an even bigger payday. By the way, did I mention this was a cash job! We'll have close to 1.6 million dollars."

"I think I know where you're going with this. Let's give Tio a call tonight, so we can bring him in as soon as possible," urged Ramon.

"Works for me, but let's not say anything to the rest of the crew until we are underway," I suggested.

He gave me a smile, letting me know he was in total agreement. The ferry had returned to the far side, and it was time to pack Ramon and his case back in the car. The rest of the conversation was more about catching up than the job. As I turned into the Marina, people were pulling boats out at the launch and the Tiki parking lot was almost full.

"Holy shit, this is all Jeff's," said Ramon in some amazement.

"I had the same reaction. Jeff has done well for himself, but trust me, he doesn't appear anywhere near as happy as he used to be."

We parked the car behind the Tiki and the band was playing and the loud chatter of people were having a good time. I helped Ramon take his luggage down to the boat and as we walked past, I saw Cantrelle sitting at the bar. As we strolled down the dock, I pointed the *San Blas* out to Ramon.

"There she is, that's my baby," I said proudly.

"That's a nice boat, Tomas!"

Once on board, he put his cases in the cabin and walked to the front.

"She's a beauty," he uttered.

"She still needs some work, but she's all paid for and all mine. Here, let me show you the best part."

I lifted the hatches and showed him the pristine engines with the twin turbos. Ramon grew a huge smile. He was so impressed he suggested he could line me up with some new opportunities to make more money, but I politely declined and instead steered the conversation on to what she could do.

It made me feel good that someone appreciated the San *Blas* as much as me. "Hold on a minute, I wanna show you something." I walked in the cabin and grabbed a flashlight from my desk drawer. I knelt on the deck while he followed suit as I put the light on the reduction gears under the deck aft of the engines. "Holy Shit!" he exclaimed. "They are huge; what's the reduction?" "Two to one" I replied. "This thing must do about 50 knots?" I smiled big and boasted. "A little better than 60."

He continued looking around and saw my internet dome on top of the bridge."Let me guess, you have internet too?" he asked.

"Hey, gotta have comms. with the outside," I boasted.

I handed him a beer as he looked around then we sat down and chatted for a bit.

"Before we give him a call, have you spoken to Tio lately?" I checked.

"Si, Tomas. He actually doesn't live in Frontera anymore. His wife has family in Progreso so they moved there about a year ago," he informed me.

"Have they had any more kids?"

Ramon laughed and added, "Funny enough, they just had their last 'another boy' about six months ago."

I laughed along with him because Tio was a family man and he had a BIG family.

"Doesn't that make seven kids... all boys? I know we used to call him Golden Rod because every time he has sex, it seems to work, but man, seven!"

Tio, whose real name was Jorge, was nearly fifty and didn't care that he showed his age—it was almost a badge of honor. He was some 5'7" tall with curly black hair, an ever-growing pot belly and a few crooked, chipped or broken teeth. He was always friendly and certainly enjoyed his weed; the sort of man who'd literally get up for the restroom in the night and smoke a joint before he went back to bed. Though he may have loved the green stuff, he was very much against things like cocaine. We were all aware he was very street smart and knew his way around the rough parts of town, and the crew were always very protective of him.

With a large family to support, he would work months at a time, but when he was home, he always made it count. It was heart-warming to see such a dedicated father and his strong relationship with the boys. They had a good enough life, but Tio always had to work extra to make sure it happened, and thus he was always up for side jobs when they came up. Not only was he our first mate, but with his love of weed and food, he was also a fabulous cook. I was looking forward to speaking to him again.

"I need to clean up before we go out," said Ramon as he finished his beer.

"The shower is through that door, meet me at the Tiki when you're done," I told him.

"Roger that!"

Just a few minutes later, I walked up onto the deck of the Tiki and pulled up a chair next to Cantrelle.

"Hey, Cap, I hear you and Senior Jeff caught a big one this morning," he declared as he glanced over.

"Hell, yeah, this thing was a beast. It took all Jeff had to reel the sucker in," I added.

"I also hear you tried to drown my deckhand as well." He smiled before he took a large mouthful of his drink.

"Why's everyone mentioning that?" I laughed and shook my head. "I threw him a float."

"You are seriously hardcore, my friend." He chuckled as he slapped me on the back in a jovial but firm way.

"Hey, it was a monster that had to be caught. Besides, Jose didn't seem too upset once he saw it... and I did apologize."

"I think you might have a new fan club, Cap. He has been running around and telling all his little buddies about what happened and what an awesome Captain he thinks you are." Cantrelle smirked.

"I liked him as soon as I met him, even if he is a cocky little shit," I joked.

"The way you have to be in this business, is it not?" he rhetorically asked.

The two of us continued to chat about this and that for a bit, obviously not discussing the job in such a busy place. Every so often I looked around and saw Diana rushing from table to table with trays of food and drink. We'd been sitting there about twenty minutes when Ramon strolled in. I raised my hand to gesture for him to come over. He looked like a mafia boss in dark trousers, an open black shirt, and his hair all slicked back. It was somewhat fitting as he'd played that role once or twice over the years as part of our endeavors.

I got up and gave him my chair while I grabbed another. " Cantrelle, I want you to meet one of my best friends, Ramon."

Cantrelle stood and shook his hand. He towered two feet over Ramon, who smiled as he shook his massive hand. You could see Ramon sizing him up. Not that I should be surprised.

"Cantrelle is going to make the run with us," I explained.

"A little extra muscle, won't hurt," he joked, to which I agreed. "I need a beer," he said as he looked around for a waitress.

I stared down the far end of the Tiki and as Diana turned toward us. I raised my hand and got her attention. "Two minutes," she mouthed silently as she walked away from the table she was serving. A few minutes later, she appeared at my side.

"So, this is your friend, Tomas," she stated as she looked at Ramon.

I introduced them to each, Ramon not wasting an opportunity for a hug with a pretty woman.

"What can I get ya?" she asked.

"Unless the world has changed and flipped on its axis, we'll have three tequilas and three Coronas," Ramon ordered.

"Cap, before I forget, Maria called a while ago and she said she'd been trying to get hold of you but couldn't," Cantrelle informed me.

"Shit, I heard my cell ring a while ago, but I couldn't pick up the call."

"Same ol' Tomas, never answers his damn phone," smirked Ramon.

"Look, I hate these fucking things, and I don't feel the urge to have it surgically attached to me," I ranted. "Fuck... seven missed called and a text. I didn't hear all of these."

I went straight to the text from Maria, it read:

I swear, you never answer your phone. Give me a call when you get this, straight away, Tomas!

I dialed her number immediately—I didn't even bother to walk to the carpark as usual—but there was no reply. I quickly tried a second time, with the same result.

"Now, who's not answering their phone," I teased with a voice message and then placed the cell back in my pocket. Just as it hit the bottom of my pocket, Diana arrived with our drinks, and 3 shots of tequila.

"Do you mind if I join you guys for a bit? My shift is finished so I can kick back and become a patron instead of the server," she asked.

"Sure, pull up a chair," I told her.

"Hey man, you think we can take Jeff's boat for a little cruise later?" I suggested to Cantrelle with a raised eyebrow.

"I am sure we can do that, Cap. I doubt he'll mind."

The drinks were placed in front of us and Ramon picked up his shot of tequila. We all did the same, downing it in one, before we picked up our beers and took a swig. The band of choice that night was a rock band, and they played numerous American classics, which had the dance floor filled with people who were strutting their drunken stuff.

The Tiki continued to fill, and this band was obviously popular as so many people turned up that the "party" spilled over into the parking lot and surrounding decks.

"Hey, Ramon, I know we said we'd go out-out, but look at the Tiki, this is the place to be tonight?" I implored as I didn't feel up to other parts of the local nightlife.

"Sounds good, Tomas, but we will need to take a ride in a bit to pick up some party supplies," he answered with a wink.

"Jes, Ramon, no trouble tonight, Okay?"

"Don't worry, my man, it'll all be good," he assured.

"Fuuuuuck, I wish I had a nickel for every time I heard you say that," I fired back.

"Ya'll going somewhere?" chipped in Diana.

"Not far. Ramon has to go pick something up. We'll be gone and back in less than half an hour, I promise," I told her.

"Alrighty," she announced as she finished her beer and stood up. "I'm going to my apartment to get changed if we're all going out on the boat. By the way, Tracy and Heather have gone to score some pot with Jose, but they will be back soon. Maybe they can join us?"

"Why not," I agreed with a smile at Ramon knowing he would get along well with them.

She kissed me on the cheek and quickly headed out the back door.

"Okay, Ramon, let's go do whatever you gotta do," I said as I downed the rest of my beer.

"You don't need to tell me twice," he agreed and did the same.

The parking lot was so full that I suggested to Ramon to drag a couple trash cans over to hold the spot for us while we were gone.

"Where are we goin'?" I asked as we pulled out of the parking lot.

"Just down to the fishing docks," he answered.

"Shit, well, we're going to have to park at the store and take a taxi the last few miles or so. There is no way I am taking Jeff's Porsche down there," I stated.

The fishing docks in question were the Laguna Pescaleros, an area known for being extremely rough and far from hospitable to anyone who didn't belong there. By the time Ramon had got whatever he was after, the Porsche would have been stolen, stripped, cut up and laid out in spare parts. I assume he knew someone there and we would at least be relatively safe.

I drove down the east end of the island and we stopped at a parade of shops about three miles from the entrance to the docks. It wasn't exactly the sort of security it deserved, but at least here people would likely recognize it as belonging to Jeff and leave it be.

We flagged down a taxi and it drove us to the entrance, but couldn't go any further due to the poor state of the road. These days, only trucks and large SUVs could traverse that pothole ravaged, washed out track. I gave the driver twenty bucks to wait for us and we walked off down the track with jungle-like vegetation on either side. Once we got to the docks themselves, it all opened up with the boats berthed on one side and a row of low-rent shacks on the other.

"Man, I hope you have this all arranged already. I sure as shit ain't going door-to-door looking for your contact," I told him.

"Honestly, don't panic, man, he's right over there," he said as he pointed to a man who was walking off one of the boats.

I sat on a wooden bench and watched Ramon in action.

That man will never change, I thought.

I couldn't have told anyone an exact reason why, but Ramon and I had always been best friends, pretty much from the first time we met on a job. I trusted him with my life and almost everyone loved Ramon, especially the ladies.

I saw him make the old hand-shake exchange where he placed a roll of notes in the hand of the man as he passed Ramon something in return, which I was unable to see clearly. All had gone to plan, and he was just walking up the dock toward me when I saw two Federales walk out one of the shacks and straight toward Ramon.

"Ah, fuck," I muttered as I quickly moved from the bench and hid inside a little icehouse where I couldn't be seen.

An America found in the fishing docks would promote a number of unformatted questions and a lot of suspicion. I stayed hidden but could see what was happening. From my vantage point, I couldn't hear what was being said but it looked like Ramon was doing everything he could to get out of it. If I knew Ramon, and I did, it was almost certain he had something illegal on him.

Everything changed in a second. The one behind grabbed his arms and put them in a lock while his colleague helped him bundle Ramon in the back of a truck parked nearby. They pushed him face down and appeared to bind his wrist with cable ties. One man got in the front, the other with Ramon in the back. The truck then proceeded to drive past me and up the hill to the exit.

I hurried up the hill behind them in an effort to get to the taxi and tail them. I had to stay out of sight on the long straights so made use of the trees to obscure me from their mirrors. As I reached the taxi and saw the truck park up on the far side of the road and a bit of a skirmish in the back, I called Jeff straight away.

"Hey Jeff..." I stuttered.

"What's up?" he replied with concern.

"Yeah, errrrr, Ramon just got himself arrested," I confessed.

"Already?! He's only been here a couple of hours," replied Jeff in a jovial way. "Was it transit cops, locals, or Federalists?"

"Federalist, down at the fishing docks."

"Yeah, no problem." He chuckled. I don't even want to know what you're doing down there, but I can guess. Leave it with me."

Chapter Fourteen

When the taxi driver arrived at that Porsche, I quickly paid him and made my way toward the car trying to wrap my head around what to do. This wasn't how I had imagined things going, at least not yet. Jeff was good at working his magic, not that I knew what that entailed. All I could do was wait. Either for a phone call telling me I was fucked, or good news that didn't typically happen often.

I was just about to call him back when the Federal truck came to a skidding halt in front of the car. My eyes went wide as I contemplated that they were coming for me, but the door was thrust open and suddenly, Ramon was pushed out rolling down the shoulder of the road as they slammed the door and sped off.

What the fuck?

When Ramon stood up, I could see his shirt was torn in three places, a few streaks of blood flowed across his skin, and it looked like both sides of his face were swollen. They had obviously given him a bit of beating in the short time he was in the truck. He walked over, almost nonchalantly dusted himself off, and got in the car.

"Well, that was an unexpected, somewhat unpleasant experience," he joked as he whipped some blood off his face on his shirt sleeve.

All I could do was smirk. "Hey, good times, man," I added sarcastically.

"You're such an asshole," he joked in return.

I almost snorted because I laughed so loud. "Man, you bring all on yourself, my brother. Let's get back to the marina so you can clean yourself up."

As we drove back, there was something gnawing at me.

"You know, I gotta ask," I broke the silence, "what on earth happened to make them jump you like that?"

"I'm not entirely sure myself. They said they knew why I was there and that I needed to get myself the hell out of there. I said, 'Fine, I'm just leaving' and then the younger punk pushed me against the wooden railing and asked me where the fuck I was going. Now, let's leave aside the fact they'd told me to leave, which I attempted, you know how I hate it when people push me!" he explained.

"Yes, all too well, and I have the scars to prove it too. Life is never boring when you're around my brother; I don't know anyone who gets himself into as much shit as you do." I laughed.

"It's a finely tuned skill," he fired back with a proud nod.

We pulled into the Tiki's shell parking lot about fifteen minutes later, and the place was so busy they had begun parking along the side of the road. Luckily and surprisingly, no one had taken the parking spot. We even had to wait for people to move out the way as we crawled across the lot.

"Man, look at how busy this place is. Jeff must be making an absolute killing," suggested Ramon.

"That's what I'm telling you. It's been like this every weekend I have been here, without fail. It's not the sort of place you expect to be so popular and yet somehow Jeff has made it work."

Under the lot lights, I could see Ramon better and he did look worse for wear.

"Go clean yourself up on the boat and I will get everyone together, and you can meet us down on the dock over there where Jeff's boat is tied up," I told him.

"Works for me. See you in a few minutes," he said with a wave as he walked toward my boat around the deck so no-one saw the state of him.

By the time I got back to the Tiki deck, Tracy and Heather were back with Jose from picking up pot. Sometimes ships only dock for a day or two and move on, but we must have made a big enough impression for them to hang out with us. By the amount of laughing going on, I assumed they'd been successful in their hunt for weed. I then realized that I hadn't asked Ramon what exactly he went to pick up.

Cantrelle and Diana had moved to the bar to sit and chat with them.

"Now listen here, Mister, that was longer than thirty minutes," she queried.

"Yeah, let's just say we had a little trouble. Everything is okay, but Ramon ingratiated himself to some of the locals and ended up in a little bit of a situation, but he's alright. He just went down to my boat to clean himself up. No need to worry, this is pretty much par for the course with Ramon and a night out," I explained as I leaned against the bar.

Heather and Tracy said almost in unison. "We heard you've invited us on a little boating trip," giggled Tracy.

"Are you interested?" I replied.

"Sure, but how's this for an idea? If you captain it, we could maybe take our catamaran; it has more room," suggested Tracy.

Cantrelle and I looked at each other. "Even better," I confirmed.

By this point, Jose had moved to another table and was busy chatting up some girls closer to his own age.

"He looks busy," I said to Cantrelle, "let's leave him to it and let him enjoy his evening," I proposed, to which Cantrelle nodded his agreement.

Everyone was just about to finish their drink so I grabbed Diana casually, and turned to Tracy, "We're going down to my boat for a minute to get Ramon. We'll meet you at the catamaran. By the way, I assume you have a grill?" I asked.

"Oh yeah, a big one," she exclaimed with her hands held apart.

"Nice. I have some lobster tails, I will bring them with us," a suggestion that seemed to excite everyone.

Diana and I navigated our way through the various groups of dancing or chatting people and strolled down to the *San Blas*.

"I don't think I have ever had a late dinner on a boat. This is an awesome suggestion, Tomas," she said as she held onto my arm.

"It's as much a necessity as for joy. I have been on the go since this morning, what with Jeff's bike ride, picking up Ramon and his little excursion. I am ready to kick my heels up and have a relaxing evening with good food and fine company."

We soon reached my boat, and I helped her aboard. Ramon was in the Sala and already dressed when we came in.

"Holy shit," Diana said loudly when she saw Ramon's face, "what the hell happened to you? Are you okay?"

"I'm all good. Just a little disagreement with a member of the local government. It looks a lot worse than it is," he assured her.

He may have fooled her, but not me. I knew he was playing it down because I had a full bottle of tequila on the side, and as I glanced over I noticed it was a quarter gone. I didn't say anything, I knew that was Ramon's way of dulling any pain. Instead, I went to the refrigerator and grabbed everyone a beer.

"Here, let me fix that up a little for you," suggested Diana as she reached into her purse and pulled out a makeup bag.

Ramon nodded his agreement and sat on the sofa with his shot of tequila. There was a nasty cut on his cheek, but Ramon, being the man he was, he'd already used some super-glue to seal the wound. The fact he carried it around on him said as much as anything.

There may have also been another aspect to it as well. He'd been a fighter himself and also worked as a cut man for other fighters when he wasn't involved in his own battles. He knew how to take care of himself when it came to all manner of injuries and had regularly fixed his own wounds over the years.

Diana went to work on him for around fifteen minutes and once she was done, she stood back and admired her efforts.

"I've even impressed myself. That looks much better," she stated.

"You're not wrong there, you can hardly see anything but the swelling," I added.

"Oh, man, you gotta teach me how to do that," asked Ramon as he looked at his reflection in a mirror.

"Better still, how about you stop fighting losing battles instead of learning how to make yourself presentable afterward. There's such a thing as walking away," I joked.

"Yeah, yeah, I know," was his only retort.

I went to the kitchen area and grabbed a case of lobster from the freezer under the steps and also picked up some olive oil and garlic. Given it was now open, I also stashed the bottle of tequila in a bag as well.

"Okay, let's roll," I said as I ushered them out of the cabin.

The three of us walked around the slips and over to where the catamaran was moored up. Cantrelle already had the diesel engine running by the time we had climbed aboard.

"Ready when you are, Cap," he declared.

"Let's do it," I added as I set the lobster case and bag down on the deck. Ramon and I then cast off the lines, and once we were free on the water, Cantrelle handed the controls over to Jose.

"Good call, bringing Jose," I told him as we got underway, "someone to drive!"

The six of us grabbed a space on one of the plush sofas in the large cockpit which had a nice blue glow from the multitude of blue floor lights. I started to pour us all a shot of tequila as we idled out of the marina.

CHAPTER FIFTEEN

THE CATAMARAN EASED OUT of the marina and once we reached the jetties, we encountered a slight swell that had rolled in, but it was no problem for the large catamaran which took it nicely.

"Jose," I hollered up to the elevated bridge above us, "how about we cruise inside the outer reef and then get to the south side of the island?"

He leaned back and nodded, then turned off toward the east. We all continued to have some drinks and share some snacks that Tracy brought out on a silver platter. As we enjoyed ourselves, Jose skillfully navigated the cat around the coral heads. They looked a little close on the port side at one point, but Cantrelle assured us that he knew the reef like the back of his hand.

As everyone continued to get to know each other, I went over to the bar to get the lobster ready. As I prepared them, the girls had already stripped down to their bikinis as everyone laughed, joked, and told stories.

Once Jose had maneuvered the cat around the south side of the island, the water became insanely calm, slicked to almost a mirror finish. The moon glistened off the surface and you could even see the reflection of all the lights from Jeff's place high on the bluff above us. I gave Jose some directions, and he eased the cat between the reefs before we anchored in a sandy spot. I made sure the anchor held and told Jose to shut the engine down.

We joined everyone toward the rear of the cat, and Tracy flicked a few switches on a console. Suddenly, the water lit up brightly around the boat. The lights built into the hull must have lit up the water for nearly sixty feet in every direction. Not satisfied with standard white lights, the water was bathed in a blue glow on one side and an exotic purple on the other.

The water looked amazing already, but we were in water shallow enough that the whole reef and coral heads below us lit up. It was one of the island's most colorful and beautiful sights, but the addition of the colors from the lights took everything to a whole new level. Well known fish took on different shades to their appearance in daylight. It was the first time I had seen lights like this so close to a reef and it was breathtaking. I found myself memorized as I stood for a few minutes and stared down into the water.

"I am going to add similar lights on the *San Blas*," I mused to myself.

Diana appeared at my side and grabbed my arm. "Isn't it just amazing," she said, more as a statement than a question.

"It truly is, and it's given me some ideas for my boat," I replied. "Hey, everyone, why don't we go for a swim while Jose keeps an eye on the lobster?"

I didn't wait for a reply. I threw off my shirt and deck shoes, then stood on the side and dove in. Diana was already down to her bikini, so she wasted no time and launched herself into the water straight after me. Heather came over to the side and looked at us treading water.

"Can you touch the bottom?" she asked hesitantly.

"No, not here, but there is a sandy spot upfront that is less deep. Grab a few beers and you can ease in over the left side of the bow," I suggested.

Diana and I swam to the front of the cat and stood there as the others slipped into the water. The lights were so bright you could actually see the bottom and the sandy puffs of powder whenever someone moved their feet. We stood there, beer in hands, and looked out over the brightly lit coral heads as we enjoyed the moment with some Reggae music that flowed out of the ship's speakers.

I looked over at Diana, and from the corner of my eye, I spotted Tracy swim over to Ramon and she wrapped her legs around his waist. I had pondered at what point the girls would decide who got who. Just a minute or two later, Heather swam over to Cantrelle. That nicely left me with Diana.

I looked up and caught sight of Jose, who was sitting there texting on his cell phone. I didn't feel bad he wasn't joining as I knew Cantrelle would pay him nicely for the extra work. He also looked quite content and was always surrounded by groups of girls whenever I saw him.

Diana put her arms as well as her legs around me as we enjoyed our beers and chatted. We had almost broken off into three spaced out couples around the front of the boat.

"I've had a wonderful time the last few days, Tomas," she told me. "How come someone like you isn't hooked up with someone?"

"I've had plenty of girlfriends, a few pretty serious, but for one reason or another, sometimes the jobs I have done, they didn't work out. I'm not so sure I am cut out for long-term commitments," I answered honestly.

She said something else to me, but I had suddenly switched off and my mind had flowed to thinking about China, if only for a few seconds.

"You okay?" she asked as I snapped back to the present moment.

"Sorry, a thought just popped into my head. It's nothing. Is anyone getting hungry?" I asked as I quickly changed the subject.

A chorus of quick "yes" came rapid fire. I playfully pulled Diana over to the bow and helped her back on deck before I lifted myself out of the water. After we'd dried off in the cockpit, I got to work with the lobster tails.

I placed them on a tray and seasoned them with the items I brought along with a few others that I found.

"Perfect," I declared.

"Looks like you've done this plenty of times?" inquired Diana.

"I have," I smiled. "An old friend in Honduras taught me a few ways to cook them so they come out spot on every time."

I pulled out the large grill mounted on the back of the boat beside the swim platform and got to work. Once they were all cooking nicely, I joined Diana on one of the sofas. She had already opened two fresh beers and handed me one as I sat down.

There were sounds of whispers and loud female laughs from the front of the boat, and it was obvious everyone was having a good time. I laid my head back against Diana's arm.

"You look tired, Tomas."

"It's been a long couple of days. I have barely stopped, and I suspect once we eat, I might actually pass out," I admitted.

"Well, make sure you don't pass out too soon," she winked.

The delicious smell must have attracted the others, and they all appeared at the back of the boat like it was feeding time at the zoo. I dished everything up and everyone sat in their pairs on different sofas and benches. Diana was the first to take a fork full of lobster, dip it in butter, and ease it into her mouth.

"Oh, *wow*, this is delicious," she exclaimed.

The others soon joined in with their praise on the dish that had just been served up. None of us said much after that as we all tucked into our food. Nothing much needed to be said based upon the satisfied faces in front of me.

Just as we finished, I looked over and saw an expression I hadn't seen on Diana's face before.

"Everything okay?" I asked as I wiped the butter from my lips.

I certainly seemed to snap her back from whatever she was thinking about.

"Yes, sorry." She smiled as she put her hand on my leg. "I am having an amazing time, and I was just thinking about the last two days with you. It has been a bit like a fairy tale; is it always like this?"

"Honestly, no," I confessed, "but I try to live my life as simple as possible. I suspect most people would call it a boring life on most days, especially when dealing with chores or maintaining the boat.

"I like boring, that is just fine with me," she added. "Do you mind if I ask how well you know Jeffryn?"

Her face had a semi-serious look, and the question seemed a little out of place, but I was happy to answer.

"I know him very well. We have worked together for many years, and I even dated his sister as you found out the other night. What made you ask?"

"I know you have some kind of business thing going with him, and I know very well that he deals with some bad people. I've really enjoyed spending time with you, and I can't help but worry that something might happen to you and I would hate that," she said with a sorrowful look.

"You don't have to worry about me," I promised as I pulled her close to me. "I am genuinely touched that you care, and I like you too, but you don't have to be concerned about me. My job with Jeff is just a boat delivery, and I have my own crew to watch my back. After all, I have Ramon with me and he is a badass that makes sure I don't get in any trouble."

"He seems like the type who gets into trouble," she added.

"You are correct in some cases, but he is pretty much untouchable. He has a family high in the government."

"Really, who is that?" she continued.

It felt a bit of a bizarre conversation that I didn't want to spoil the evening, especially as it looked like we might be staying the night based on how the others were getting along.

"Let's talk about that another time," I said as I closed off the conversation.

"I am sorry, Tomas, I didn't mean to pry," she came back quickly.

"No problem, no worries, just we have better things to do and talk about."

Maybe it was the creeping sense of age, or maybe just residual fatigue, but the conversation did feel heavy for a second date. Diana had dredged up some deep, existential questions, and while I found her thoughtfulness out of place, I put it down to her trying to find common ground, to dig into things that were really important to me. And still the load of the moment remained, and I had to drive it from my thoughts.

The sea breeze clung to my skin, salty and sticky, so the thought of a shower was irresistibly tempting. "I'm going to rinse off," I announced to the group, yearning for a brief escape.

I chose one of the cabins that bore no apparent signs of someone else's possessions strewn about.

It was neutral enough, unclaimed, without personal possessions. I closed the sliding door behind me and exhaled, relishing the quiet for a moment as I peeled my damp shirt off and flung it over a nearby chair. The cabin carried a faint smell of sunscreen and cedar. For a moment, there was just me and the promise of warm shower water to scrub the day away.

The water sputtered to life as I turned the handle, cold at first but gradually warming up. Just as I was about to step under the stream, the door creaked open behind me. My head whipped around, my pulse quickening. There stood Diana, her dark eyes glinting with mischief.

"What's up?" I asked, my voice tinged with a mix of surprise and curiosity. Wordlessly, she reached behind her neck and pulled the ties to release the bikini top. The brightly coloured fabric fell away from skin, the garment dropping without fanfare as her smirk deepened: the unyielding confidence of the lips curving in self-assurance admits no doubt.

"What does it look like?" she retorted, airy and almost teasing, as she slid out of her bikini bottoms. She walked with a confident air of a woman who knew exactly what she wanted and wasn't about to ask for permission.

Before I could say a word, she stepped under the shower, and the water tumbled over her like some miniature waterfall.

Drops clung to her skin, catching the light and outlining every curve with exquisite detail. The cabin door clicked shut behind her, and after that, we heard, in rapid succession, soft noises of other doors closing in unison. It seemed everybody had decided to turn in for the night, so we were left in this little cocoon, alone together.

Diana, leaned in closer. The nearness of her was magnetic; warmth from her body and the misty coolness from the shower made an erotic combination. "Dont think, Just go with it."

Her hand trailed down my chest, and where it passed, it left an iron-like warmth in its wake. My resolution started to slip when she rounded her lips into another flirtatious smile; her smirk was to dare me to try resisting her. She brought her hand up and, with her fingers under my chin, lifted my face so that our gazes could meet. Unmistakable was the profundity of her gaze—a maelstrom swirling beneath the facade of her playfulness.

"I don't bite... unless you want me to," she said, her voice lowering to a sultry whisper.

Her laughter was light and playful, but it did little to mask the tension crackling between us. I wish that I could say that I faltered—that I stopped for even a moment of reflection—but the truth was that the sane thoughts had long since vanished.

My hands found their way around her waist, drawing her closer as the water tumbled over and around us, the world outside growing farther and farther away. Her lips pressed against mine were soft, yet unyielding—just the perfect balance of fervent desire and submission.   The heat between us was more than enough. Steam spiralled around us, mingling with the rhythmic patter of water cascading to the floor. My fingers wove through her damp hair, drawing her nearer as her nails scraped gently down my back, sending shivers through me that had little to do with the cold.

"You're full of surprises," I whispered against her lips, my voice husky with longing.

"You have no idea," she said, her smile returning, mischievous and full of promise.

She turned, pulling me fully under the spray with her. Water drenched us to the skin, plastering her hair to her shoulders, but she seemed oblivious to it all. Her hands worked deliberately, searching, teasing, leaving no inch of me unexplored.

The air around us grew thick and electric, the space between us shrinking until it was as if nothing else existed but us. Time stretched, every moment unfolding with each sensation. The tile against my back, the warmth of her skin next to me, and her breath mingled softly with mine. I couldn't tell where I ended and she began, and for the first time in what felt like an eternity, I didn't want to know.

Whatever this was, it was wild and thrilling—everything I hadn't known I'd been craving. As the water kept falling all around us, washing away the debris of the day, there was one thing that came clear: Diana was a force, a storm I had no hope of standing against.

CHAPTER SIXTEEN

I AWOKE THE NEXT morning to find myself alone in bed. I checked my watch and it was just after seven in the morning. There was sunlight already appearing through the porthole, and you could hear the sound of the seagulls squawking above the boat. I realized I could hear voices and people going about doing different things.

I got dressed, used some mouthwash by the small sink and headed up on deck where I found Tracy sitting with Ramon. It seemed we had sailed back to the marina in the early hours while I was still asleep. It wasn't the first time I'd slept through while sailing.

"Good morning. Where is everyone else?" I asked.

"Heather is still sleeping. Cantrelle said he had to go get ready for your trip, and Diana had to get the Tiki ready. She did also say you should come and have breakfast when you are up. There's coffee if you're in need," Tracy pointed..

"I'm sorry I called time a bit early last night," I admitted as I poured a cup of coffee, "it was one hell of a long day."

"It's okay, man, we had a wonderful time," she confirmed as I sat next to both of them.

Ramon was rather quiet. He was sitting there with his shades on and his head rested back against the sofa, and he had said nothing since I appeared.

"Hey, brother, are you alive there?" I asked in mock concern.

The only reaction he gave was a visibly painful groan and a thumbs up. I was trying to work out if he had a stunning hangover, if Tracy had worn him out, or if his beating had been worse than I thought yesterday.

"Man, you do look like crap," I admitted.

His arm repeated the same action, only this time he gave me the middle finger rather than a thumbs up.

"Finish up your coffee, my friend. We have a lot to do today. Tracy, do you two fancy joining us for breakfast?"

"That's lovely of you to ask, but we'll have to pass. Heather and I are going to Cancun today to do some shopping," answered Tracy.

"Thanks for the hospitality. Next time we can take my boat," I suggested.

"We'd love to," Tracy agreed as she gave me a hug.

"C'mon, Ramon, it's time to show some life." I said as I slapped him on the leg.

He grumbled something and hauled himself off the sofa, then gave Tracy a hug before he followed me off the cat.

As the two of us walked across the marina, we saw Cantrelle already down on the dock talking to Jose.

"Man, go get cleaned up. I got to talk to Cantelle quickly," I told Ramon.

I handed him the boat keys, and he continued onward to the *San Blas*. Jose was loading bags of ice into the ice machine.

"Morning, Jose. Morning, Cantrelle, how was your date last night," I asked.

"It was a fine night, Cap. Jose brought us back to the marina about 6 am this morning and then woke me so we could get a few things sorted before our trip today," he answered brightly.

"Sorry for bailing early last night, I was whacked. I am planning to head to Progreso later this morning. Is that all good with you?" I checked.

"All good here, Cap. Jeff gave me the truck and I have most of the supplies all loaded up, so that works for me" he replied.

"Perfect, I'll get my stuff together and have some breakfast. Pick us up at about eleven by the Tiki."

"Will do," said Cantrelle.

I continued across the marina to my boat and heard the shower running as I entered the cabin. I fixed myself a fresh cup of coffee and wandered out on the deck to phone Jeff.

"Tomas, good morning. Did you get Ramon back yesterday?" he answered.

"Yeah, thanks for the assist. They roughed him up a little, but I've seen him in worse shape before," I told him.

"Try to keep him out of trouble, at least until after the job," he stressed. "By the way, Gringo, I think your ass is in some hot water. Maria went down to the Tiki looking for you last night, and she stayed until closing waiting for you to show up."

"What?! Shit! I thought she was still in Miami."

He let out a loud laugh. "I think she is all love-struck again, my friend. She came back yesterday evening. I can't see her car so she may be on her way down to see you," Jeff informed me.

"I'll give her a quick call. Speaking of the job, I have arranged for Cantrelle to pick us up at eleven and we should be in Progreso by two," I told him.

"Great. Don Miguel's people are dropping off the package for the exchange at three. What time will you guys get going," Jeff queried.

"As soon as we have everything we need, Don Miguel's package should do it," I confirmed.

"Fine, give me your ETA when you depart and I will handle the rest. Let me know if you need anything else?" he checked.

"Will do," I said as I hung up.

I called Maria as soon as I got off the phone with Jeff, but it went straight to voicemail. I hung up and walked back inside just as Ramon walked up to the Salon. He still had his sunglasses on but has fully cleaned himself up.

"At least you look better," I exclaimed.

"I may look better but I feel like shit," he fired back.

I poured him a cup of coffee and headed to my cabin once I'd handed it to him. As I stepped into it, I noticed the piece of toothpick was once again on my bed.

Now I gotcha mother fucker!.

Instead of taking a shower, I changed into shorts to retrieve the camera. Ramon was on the phone when I reappeared in the Salon. I told him I'd be right back and quietly went to the transom and lowered myself into the water.

I swam out and retrieved the camera from its mount and swam back to the boat. Ramon was still on the phone and seemed to barely notice I was wet. I dropped the camera quickly in a drawer and took a quick shower. As much as I trusted Ramon, I wanted to see the footage when I was on my own. Ramon had finished his call by the time I dressed and returned.

"Good news, my friend, I have sorted the permits for the API dock and the declaration of security has already been filed with the Port Captain," he announced with enthusiasm.

"Nice work, brother. Let's grab something to eat at the Tiki and get this show on the road."

Diana was already on shift when we walked down the dock and into the Tiki.

"Don't you ever take a day off?" I joked.

"I'll have you know, I get Thursday, and a half day on Friday and Sunday. Other than that, yes, maybe I live here."

"I can think of worse ways to make a living," I mussed as I stared out over the marina, the moving boats causing the sun's reflection to glint and glisten in rhythm.

We ordered some breakfast—a couple of omelettes and orange juice—and Diana headed off into the kitchen. I hadn't noticed that Ramon had taken off his glasses as I chose our food. As my head turned, I let out a riotous laugh.

"You look like a fucking raccoon man!," I told him.

"What do you mean?" he asked while he looked for a mirror.

I took out my phone and took a picture of his face as he looked at me. I then handed it to him.

"Shit, look at my eyes... man, and I think they screwed up my nose."

"I guess that happened when they kicked the shit out of you," I sniggered.

"Yeah, thanks for the help by the way."

"You know, someone had to stay out of the way and call for help," I amusingly reminded him.

"That snotty-nosed Federali deserved it," he defended as Diana walked up to our table and put the plates in front of us.

"You guys still heading out to Progreso today?" she asked.

"Yep, I should be back in a couple of days if everything goes as planned," I confirmed.

"Before I forget, Tomas, Jorge told me Maria was in here all evening last night waiting for you."

I couldn't tell if there was concern in her voice or if it was jealousy.

"I did try to call her but she didn't answer. Thanks for letting me know. Maybe we can get together for lunch when I get back," I suggested as a way to move the subject along.

"Sure," she smiled, "You know where I'll be."

The tone in her voice was odd, not jealousy, not friendly, just off. She just seemed less chatty, a bit off character. Ramon hadn't noticed and tucked straight into his food. I guessed it was just me, so I did the same.

As we ate, he looked over at Diana as she cleaned the bar.

"So, you're getting serious with this one?" Ramon questioned.

"Don't go there, man, not this morning," I replied semi-serious.

"You do seem to have this habit of falling in..." he started.

"What is that supposed to mean?" I snapped back.

He could see I was irritated, so he refused to let up.

"I'm just saying, China got you all messed up, then Maria did the same and now there's this cute thing, even if she does seem to suit you the best," he continued.

"Oh, bite me. I met her a few days ago at Jeff's party, and we have been to *Cilantro's* once," I defended.

"And... the lagoon?"

"What the hell, does everyone know about the lagoon?"

He just smiled. I whipped my hands and stood up.

"Fuck you, bro. Eat your food and meet me on the boat."

He just laughed and resumed eating as I marched off.

Chapter
Seventeen

I observed a small family playing in the water and some of the old guys at their usual fishing spot as I walked back to the *San Blas*. I contemplated whether Ramon was right after all.

I knew I loved, and still loved, China, and it screwed me up big-time when we broke up. I still thought that Maria didn't bother me as much, simply because she would always go off to college and that would be the end of it. As for Diana, he was right again; she did seem to fit my personality and adored my lifestyle.

I'd done my best the last few years to avoid any serious commitments. I was someone who always gave my all in relationships, often putting their needs and wants above my own, but now was my time. Metaphorically, I tried to snap myself out of it—I needed to focus on the job and there was one other matter that needed attention.

I stepped down into the Sala on my boat. The room was cool and a fresh blast of air-conditioning hit me.

"Time to see who's been fucking with my boat!" I muttered as I grabbed the camera from the drawer.

I had just plugged it into my laptop and was fast-forwarding through the static footage and saw nothing for the first half. I looked at my watch and saw it was almost eleven, so I had to put the camera and laptop away again and get ready for the job.

After a quick shower, I put on some black cargo pants, a plain black T-shirt and my holstered SIG Sauer 45 Caliber pistol. I clipped the holster to my belt near the small of my back and pulled the loose T-shirt over the top. I knew full well if I was caught with a gun in Mexico that I would go to prison, but that was a more agreeable option than being dead.

I gathered the rest of my stuff—dive knife, jet fins, masks, snorkels, underwater light, compass, two small dive tanks about the size of a two-liter bottle called pony bottles which had built in respirators and allowed you to go down to about fifty-feet and stay submerged for about thirty minutes. I also threw in some extra weights and belts, just to be safe.

Once I had everything packed, I walked up to the Salon and started locking up. As a last minute thought, I decided to hide the camera in a much harder place to find.

Better to be safe than sorry, just in case someone does get in, I thought as I tucked it under a hard to spot sideboard.

Ramon appeared at the door just as I was ready to leave.

"Damn, man, you look like you are ready for a mission," he joked.

"Very funny," I replied as I threw him the keys. "Grab your stuff and meet me at the Tiki as quickly as you can. We're getting picked up soon," I told him.

"Yeah, yeah, no rest for the wicked, I get you," he muttered as he eased past me to get to the spare cabin.

I noticed that a number of people stared and looked at me as I walked back up the pier. It was nothing to be worried about, that I could see anyway, and I just nodded as I passed by. I understood they weren't used to seeing a guy dressed all in back with a black sea bag. Cantrelle was already sitting at the bar talking to Diana and waiting for us when I arrived.

"Aren't you a little hot in all that?" she asked me.

"Yeah, how about a cold one," I quipped back.

"You ready, Cap?" he checked.

"As can be. Just waiting on Ramon to grab his crap and drag his ass up here," I confirmed.

Diana still seemed less talkative and to me appeared to be banging and crashing more than usual. The problem was that I didn't know her well enough to be sure, but I would have bet that she had something on her mind. At that moment, Ramon appeared in the doorway.

"Ready when you are," he stated as I downed the last of my beer.

"Diana, we'll see you in a couple of days," I said in the hope of seeing some positive sign.

She came round the bar and gave me a big hug, the reaction I hoped for.

"You be careful," she demanded.

"Always."

We grabbed our bags and walked out to the truck outside. Once we'd stowed all the gear, Ramon sat in the front with Cantrelle and I took up a spot in the back. I stretched out in the back and tried to call Maria one last time, but yet again, there was no answer and it cut to voicemail.

I rested my head back and stared out the windows as we drove along. At points, I must have drifted off as it didn't seem like two hours had passed when Cantrelle snapped me out of my doze and called out for directions.

"Hey, Cap, which way do you need me to go?"

"Go up to Cilantro's over there, and take a right into the marina parking lot. That is where the boat is docked," I answered.

"Roger that," he came back as he accelerated away from the junction.

As we pulled in and parked, I saw Shirma and Izquierdo directing a fuel truck to back away from the boat.

Shirma was in his early thirties, six-foot tall and a couple of hundred pounds with curly black hair. He may have had a bit of a potbelly, but he had cat-like feminine eyes with long lashes. As a man, he was humble with a friendly nature, but like Tio, he was also street smart, which made up for his lack of schooling.

His close friend Izquierdo, who he was raised with, was also six-foot tall with black hair, but he styled his with a really short crew cut rather than the tasseled mass of Shirma. He was a quiet, shy man who rarely spoke unless spoken to and relied on Shirma to do most of the talking. He'd always been a great worker and always the first out the door when it came to assignments.

I could also see Tio up on the deck smoking away; I let out a mild laugh as I knew he never smoked cigarettes.

That's my band of outlaws and rogues, I mussed.

"Cantrelle, back up to the gangway and the guys can unload the gear."

As he re-parked the truck, Ramon walked over to Shirma and Izquierdo, and they all shared a hug.

"It's good to see you both. Are you ready for this?" he asked.

"You bet," they both replied.

They quickly set to work removing the bags from the back, and I walked over to Cantrelle.

"That's Shirma and Izquierdo. The three of them have a lot of catching up to do, so I will introduce you later. There is actually someone else I want you to meet."

He nodded and followed me inside the boat and upstairs to the bridge. I'm sure he noticed the big smile that appeared on my face when I saw Tio.

"Tio, it's great to see you, my friend," I hollered as I gave him a big hug.

"Capi, you too. So happy to be working with you again," he answered.

"Tio, this is Cantrelle, a friend who works for Jeff and I thought he'd be a good addition."

"Nice to meet you. Could've used him at Ancla," he added with a large smile.

"You're dead right there," I laughed to Cantrelle's bemusement. "Let me explain, Tio and I were at a bar in Tampico one night, called the Ancla, and we almost got our asses kicked because this idiot was drunkenly putting moves on a married lady."

"Yeah, but she was hot," confessed Tio as he laughed loudly.

"So, how have you been, Tio," I checked.

"Good, man, ready to make me some money," he declared.

"We are going to do that for sure, and it may be a bigger payday than we thought," I told him.

"Really?!" as his eyes lit up.

"Let's get everyone together later and we can discuss that. Cantrelle, Ramon, and I will stow our gear and then we can grab lunch."

"Works for me. I have the position for the fuel barge and just received all the charts. I can plot our run and have it ready when you're done," suggested Tio.

"Roger that. Cantrelle, let me show you to your room," I gestured.

The two of us walked down the stairs to the next deck, which had four rooms. Each was impressively equipped with a bathroom and larger-than-usual beds for a work boat. Shirma and Izquierdo appeared with our bags.

"Shirma, put mine in there," I pointed, and Captain Cantrelle is staying in the room opposite mine on the starboard side.

The two of them dropped our bags just inside the rooms.

"I'm going to take a walk around the boat, do some checks. You go ahead and make yourself comfortable," I told him.

"Roger that," he replied as he went into his room.

I descended one set of stairs to the galley and mess level, then down another set to the engine room. It was well maintained and also had a fresh coat of paint with sixteen-cylinder engines about the same size as one on a locomotive. I reckoned it could hit around twelve-knots.

Not enough to outrun anything, but a comfortable speed.

I made my way through the engine room back to the steering compartment and then found what I was looking for—a ladder with an escape hatch to the main deck. There were a few shipping containers on the main deck, and I decided we could stagger them around the hatch and it would provide a temporary way to hide if we were boarded... or at least hide the money.

Shirma and Izquierdo were loading supplies when I approached them on the main deck.

"Shirma, do we have a crane here?"

"Si, Capi, it is over there. We can have it here in an hour or so," he replied.

"Great, both of you follow me."

I led them over the containers and explained my plan, where I wanted the containers and how it could help us move from inside to outside unseen, and that they had to ensure the hatch wasn't covered. They got to work to make it happen as I walked back toward the cabin.

I always communicated things to Shirma when I spoke to both of them, even though he was the younger of the two. Izquierdo had tons of experience and had worked with me a number of times, but I didn't think he'd said more than a dozen words to me in all that time. At least I never had to worry about him having loose lips.

As I made my way to the cabin, I noticed a bench swing hanging from an overhead in the shade. I had a few moments so I pulled out my cell phone as slouched into it; there were three missed calls from China that must have come in when I was dozing in the truck. I hit dial, and she picked up straight away.

"Tomas, where are you?" she said with urgency.

"I'm on the boat in Progreso; we just arrived about thirty minutes ago," I told her.

"Listen to me, you need to cancel this run and get away from there and everything to do with it right now!"

"Okay, calm down, back up a bit. I assume you have some new information?"

"Yes, and it's serious. From what I have found out, it looks like this whole thing is a set-up. As I told you, Don Miguel is in serious trouble over a deal that went bad where he lost almost a million dollars of the Cartel's money."

"Okay, we already knew that," I cut in.

"I have a reliable source that's told me Don Miguel was supposed to pay for the diesel from his own money to make it good with the cartel, but it looks certain the plan is for some 'unconnected' guys from Don Miguel's group to meet you, steal his money back, and kill you so it looks like you and your crew robbed them. Just walk away!" she urged.

"Listen, I have the entire team here and we're about to pause for something to eat. We will talk it over and will get back to you in the next hour or so," I explained.

"Tomas, please walk away from this," she begged.

"Relax, China, I'll call you back," I said and hung up.

What China wasn't aware of was the fact that we had hoped this was how things might play out. We knew there was a good likelihood that we would have a chance to double-cross the double-crossers and make a large amount of money in the process. If the deal was legitimate, we could never have considered it because the entire cartel would be after us. Since this was an "off the books" job for Don Miguel, they would blame him when it went bad and just kill him!

Now I knew this was going to happen, I sat there on the swing and started to put the alternative plan through its paces. I was in mid-thought when Ramon came out the back door.

"Hey, Tomas, just thinking once the guys have moved those containers, we could get everyone together, go over the plan and have something to eat?"

"Let's go to the bridge and see how Tio is coming along," I suggested.

From the bridge, we saw Cantrelle and Tio outside on the bridge wing talking. As I poked my head out the door, I noticed Tio had another joint in his hand.

"You partake in the smoke as well, Cantrelle?" I asked him with a smile.

"Not me, can't do that stuff. If I smoke that, we won't have enough food for everyone," he joked.

"I know what you're saying, it gives me massive munchies as well. Hey, Tio, put that thing out and come inside.

"Si, Capi," he agreed as he stubbed it out in the handrail and put the remainder in his pocket.

They followed us in and I joined Ramon at the chart table where he was looking at the suggested course from Tio.

"How's it look, Capi?" he checked.

I saw that he had plotted us a course that kept the boat three miles off the coast all the way to Frontera.

"Looks good. There's a few things we need to discuss before we get started. Let's get everyone together while Ramon and I get some food, and then we will go over all of it?" I suggested.

The guys left the room and closed the door. I turned to Ramon and explained to him what China had told me during the phone call. I got the exact response I wanted.

"Fuck, *yeah*," he roared as he rubbed his hands together. "Let's go make some real money," he added with delight.

"You and I are going to split the original cut. The extra we will split eighty percent between us, with the remaining twenty diced up between the crew," I proposed.

We both grinned and shook hands.

"Ramon, we are the only ones that know the exact count of the money, so let's keep it that way."

He nodded enthusiastic agreement. We walked down to the main deck and saw the guys were already loitering by the truck. We all climbed in and I drove us across the marina and pulled into the parking lot behind *Cilantro's*. As we walked in, I saw it was busier than usual with a large amount of people.

We looked around and every table was taken. A waiter came over and informed us it would be a thirty-minute wait to be seated. I nodded, then walked outside to make a call on my cell phone—I called my friend and owner of Cilantro's.

"Tomas, what's up, my friend?" he answered after a couple of rings.

"Hey, Carlos. I hate to ask, but we are here at the restaurant and it is pretty busy. We are on a bit of a tight schedule so I was wondering if you could pull some strings to arrange an extra table?"

"Sure, Tomas. I am in Houston right now, but leave it with me," he replied. "How long are you going to be in Merida?"

"Not for long, I'm afraid. We have got a run this evening, but I will catch up with you soon. Thanks so much for your help," I added.

"I will get you taken care of and stay in touch," he finished before he hung up.

The guys all smiled.

"Pulling the VIP card, nice," smirked Ramon.

The waiter returned a few minutes later and told us the table would be ready shortly. He also took a drinks order for six Corona's. Across the deck, I saw two of his colleagues hastily arranging a new table. I felt a little embarrassed when they interrupted a couple's meal to move their table to make space, but we didn't have time to wait; it's good to have friends in the right places.

Once the table was ready, we walked over and took our seats. It didn't escape my attention that people waiting on the bench outside looked at us as they tried to work out who we were to get such treatment. I nodded our appreciation, and they all went back to their meal as we sat down.

The waiter came and took our order, then replaced all the bottles of Corona. We started with a little catch-up chat and then moved onto the business at hand.

"Ramon, everything seems on schedule but we are still short an engineer," I began. "Has anyone heard from Alberto?"

Magdaleno, or Maggie as he was often called, was our usual Chief Engineer. He was in his early forties, a short man at just under five-foot and almost as wide. His black hair was usually cut in a Barney Rubble type parting on one side, to which I often referred to him as the Latino Barney Rubble. He was a quiet, humble and friendly guy, but supremely confident when it came to engines.

"Si, Capi, he boarded a bus at 6 am this morning and will be here at 8 pm," confirmed Tio.

"A bus?!" I exclaimed. "We could have arranged a flight. No matter. Tio you take the truck and be there when he arrives. We will set off as soon as he's on board."

"Roger that, Capi," confirmed Tio.

I looked around and moved my chair closer to the table, and then gestured to the others to do the same.

"Okay, listen up, things have changed somewhat in the last hour or so and I need to know if everyone still wants to take part. It's going to be extremely complicated and dangerous, but you will get triple the current payoff."

They looked at each other and smiled.

"A close contact of mine who is very well-informed regarding movements of the cartels and Mexican Navy has given me some new intel. The man financing our operation is in a bad spot with the cartels over a previous deal that went bad. Now they intend to double cross us, take the cash, the diesel, and kill everyone involved.

The smiles all dropped.

"Now I have your attention and you understand the risk, my plan is to out fuck the fuckers," I announced as the smiles returned. "I want you to think it over while you eat and let me know if you're in once we get back to the boat. I will then discuss the specifics of the plan."

Ramon and Tio smiled and raised their glass to confirm they were in, and the rest of the crew did the same. I was never in much doubt but they deserved to know. As we went back to eating and chatting, Tio leaned in and quietly told me he needed to talk privately with a concerned expression.

Shit, this will be hard without Tio.

I loved Tio like a brother, but he had a lot of children and intended to respect his decision if he wanted out—we would have to make do without him.

Everyone seemed in good spirits and they dug into the food as soon as it arrived. There was a moment when it felt almost like a family reunion and that made me feel more responsible. I thought about every part of the plan as I toyed with my food and wondered if I was leading us into serious trouble. Ramon noticed how I just picked at my food.

"You Okay?" he asked.

"Yeah, I'm all good. I need to go and make a couple of calls, and afterward, you and I need to have a private meeting."

"Gotcha," he answered.

"Tio, bring the guys back to the boat once you've all finished and then go wait for Maggie."

"Roger that, Capi," he confirmed as I finished my meal, left some money and headed for the door.

I had shit to do, and it wasn't going to get done with me sitting here.

CHAPTER EIGHTEEN

THE SUN WAS SETTING and slowly dimming as it dipped below the horizon, but there was still an hour of daylight so I walked along the beach to the marina. It was slightly cooler than usual with a nice breeze that blew in off the Gulf. I walked over to the rocks piled against the sea wall and sat down.

I took my cell out of my pocket and gave Maria a call, but it once again cut to voicemail after a single ring. I then whipped through my contacts again to call Diana.

"Tomas, did you make it to Progreso?" she checked upon answering.

"Yep, we arrived a couple of hours ago and just had a late lunch in *Cilantro's.*" I confirmed.

"When are you leaving on your trip?" she continued.

"We're leaving tonight," I answered before coming to a slightly uncomfortable question given my closeness with the two of them.

"I hate to ask, but have you heard anything from Maria since last night?"

"No, but you're not the only one looking for her. Jeff came by about an hour ago and asked the same thing," she answered.

"I may not have a phone signal once we set off, but I will have internet. Can you send me a text if you hear anything?"

"Sure, and take care," she said.

I thanked her and hung up. The next item on the list was to speak to China again so I dialed her back.

"Bueno, Tomas," she answered.

"Hey, China, do you have any further information for me?

"I do. I spoke with some people and it seems Don Miguel is definitely planning to use some muscle to double-cross you. There are rumors he has borrowed the money for this job and my guess is he intends to steal the money, not pay it back and blame it all on you and your crew. He has a lot of firepower and has planned to ensure none of you live. Don't do this job, Tomas, it's not worth it," she pleaded again.

"I am going to chat to Ramon and chew a few things over. I promise I will call you back in the next hour."

This could still work, but it means someone might have to metaphorically go down with the ship.

As I returned to the restaurant, the other guys were just about to get in the SUV to go back to the marina. Ramon had moved from a table to the bar, so I grabbed a stool next to him.

"Any news?" he asked in a hushed tone.

"Yeah, and I'm not sure we can actually pull this one off," I answered quietly.

"What's the problem?" he continued with concern.

"This Don Miguel character is a big fish. My contact tells me that he has a lot of firepower, and I suspect if we double-cross him before he can do it to us, we will be running and hiding for the rest of our lives. I hadn't accounted for him having such reach," I explained.

"You wanna scrap the whole thing and head back?"

"I reckon we can still do it," I continued after a swig of the spare beer Ramon had ordered. "My contact has Mexican Navy connections and could set it up so we were 'busted' but to do that, someone would have to stay onboard to make the connection."

"Man, if we have the money already, why don't we just set the damn boat on autopilot and jump on Tio's cousin's boat" he suggested.

"We could, but then they will know who took the money, and Don Miguel and the cartel will be constantly after us. The plan I am reformulating is for you and me to drop the guys off once we get close to the location. Once we get there, you can drive while I tie up—it will give the appearance of a full crew on board. Once we tie up, you will go to the engine room and wait for me. I will hook up the hose and when I go down to line up the valves, we will escape through the hatch hidden by the containers... hopefully unseen.

"Hopefully unseen?" he questioned with a raised eyebrow.

"I get your worries, my friend. I have a couple of pony bottles with me with about thirty minutes of air. The area has really strong tidal currents according to the charts. We will tie up the boat so the back will be on the down-current side. The current will assist us to get far enough away before we run out of air.

"I'm with you so far. If they can't see us, how will Tio and the guys?"

"Ah, there are always a lot of fishing vessels in the area. If we stay a few hundred yards down current, no-one will suspect anything. Once we surface, I can signal Tio with the light, facing away from our ship, to pick us up.

He took a drink and looked at me while I waited for his reaction.

"Shit, I'm in," he responded in less than a minute.

"Hold up, you haven't heard the scary part yet!"

"You mean it gets scarier than double-crossing cartels and a big honcho?" he asked.

"I intend to start a fire fight with the Mexican Navy," I added.

"Not a good idea," he roared and looked at me like I was suicidal.

"Hear me out. If they have firepower, they have a lot of guns. We will be receiving the diesel when the Navy boat arrives. I will take out a pistol and fire shots toward Don Miguel's men, then quickly send a volley at the Navy boat as it arrives. They won't know who is shooting and will absolutely fire back. Once that happens, I will duck into the hatch, meet up with you and we'll escape into the water.

"That's a brilliant change of plan. Even if Don Miguel isn't killed, he will be too busy hiding from the cartels for losing their money a second time to come after us," added Ramon as he nodded.

"Bingo. The Cartel will assume the Navy confiscated the money as the seized amount is never the same as the reported amount, if it is even reported," I finished.

"I have no idea how you think this shit up, but that all works as far as I can see," Ramon finished.

"Have yourself another beer, then meet me on the boardwalk. I have a call to make," I told him as I stood up and left. I decided to walk along the beach again as it was far less crowded than the boardwalk. The breeze had eased to nothing, and I looked out at the steadily growing illuminations streaming across the glass like surface for more than a hundred yards.

It better not be this calm when we make the connection, otherwise it will be too easy for them to spot us in the water. We need at least two to three foot seas to help conceal our getaway.

I knew I needed to check the weather report when we got back to the ship. It was a vital check that could decide our ultimate course of action. I reached the same mass of rocks and sat myself down to make the call I promised to China. As before, she answered immediately.

"Hey, China. I spoke to Ramon and we have a new plan, but we are going to need your help to pull it off," I started.

"I'm listening," she confirmed.

"I need you to set some things up with your Navy contacts. Let them know in the next day or two there will be an illegal diesel sale off the coast of Frontera."

"I guessed you'd be crazy enough to go through with this," she sighed.

"I don't have an exact time yet, but will give you at least twelve hours' notice before it goes down," I continued. "Tell him it will happen about three miles off the coast of Frontera. It will be night so if they display lights for a fishing vessel, they should be able to get close before everyone else realizes it's a Navy ship," I proposed.

"Anything else, while you are at it?" she asked.

"Actually, find out from him how much money we need to leave on the vessel for him to skim off the top but still show enough for a legitimate bust?"

"Tomas, I'm aware that you and your merry band of pirates know what you are doing, but you do know there is a chance my contact could screw us over and kill you guys for the money too?" she warned.

"Don't panic, gorgeous, none of the team will be there when it goes down."

"And just how will you manage that?"

"That's all I can say right now. Listen, I gotta go, but I will be in touch soon," I assured her.

"Okay, watch yourself," she added before she ended the call.

I called Jeff, but it went straight to voicemail. I left him a message but the moment I hung up, my cell rang.

"Hey, Jeff," I answered.

"I've been trying to track Maria down all day. Have you spoken to her?" he asked in a panic.

"No, I heard she came down to the marina last night but no one has heard from her since," I told him as I became more concerned myself.

"I found her car at the airport and I am taking the 10 pm flight to Miami to follow up where she went. I am sure she is fine but it's unlike her to do this."

"Text me as soon as you know anything," I asked firmly. "I just called to let you know I'm going to check the weather reports and wait for Magdaleno to check the engines, then I will give you a call to let you know what time to arrange the meeting with Don Miguel."

"Okay, let me know," he finished as we ended the call. A heavy breath escaped me as I tried to process everything I was about to do. If this went wrong, we were all fucked.

I continued to be concerned about Maria, but I didn't know her routines anymore. The fact that Jeff was so worried very much escalated my fear. She had always been the sort of woman who could take care of herself, but big brother Jeff had always kept close tabs on her to make sure.

I strolled up the boardwalk and sat on an empty bench as I waited for Ramon. There was no sign of him after thirty minutes so I started to walk around to *Cilantro's* to see what the delay was. I just caught sight of him walking around the corner of the bar with a girl on his arm. He kissed her and they both laughed, then she walked off in a different direction.

"Good ol' Don Juan... he can't even keep it in his pants for a day." I chuckled. "So how long have you known her?" I asked with a smirk.

"Oh, about twenty minutes." He grinned.

"I'm not even gonna ask. Still, that must be your second-longest relationship," I joked.

"And a massive fuck you," he shot back.

We walked back around to the boat and the guys were sitting on buckets behind the cabin, playing on their phones as usual. They looked up as we arrived and Shirma stood up.

"We all squared away, Capi. Do you need anything else?" he asked.

"No, thanks for asking, Shirma. Just let me know when Tio gets back with Maggie."

"Si, Capi, will do."

Ramon headed to his room to check on his kit while I walked up the outside stairwell to the bridge. Cantrelle was in the middle of a nap on the couch, so I quietly went to the computer to pull up the weather report.

The report initially came back much as I'd earlier feared—slick calm overnight—but the wind and seas were supposed to increase the following day. It was obvious we needed to delay our departure by a day. I knew that wouldn't be a problem once Magdaleno arrived as he could temporarily disable something that would "force" us to push our departure back.

That would cause Don Miguel to throw a huge fit because he would have to alter his plans to kill us.

It must be such a high-stress logistical nightmare for him, I thought sarcastically, *especially as he knows if it goes wrong again, they'll melt his head in a vat of acid—poor guy*!

I printed out the report and was just about to go downstairs when Cantrelle sat up on the couch.

"What's up, Cap," he asked as he rubbed his eyes.

I perched on the seat next to him and explained the plan to him in exact detail, right down to the delayed departure.

"I understand everything, Cap, and I have no concerns you haven't thought of," he replied. "Just so you know, if you need me to stay on board, I have a lot of diving experience as well."

"Really, how much?"

"I'm a retired Navy SEAL, for one."

I sat back in my chair with a huge grin. "Now that makes a lot of sense."

"How's that?" he questioned.

"I couldn't help but notice that you brought a pretty big seabag on board for what's supposed to be a two-day trip," I added. "Do you have supplies?"

We both knew I meant more than an extra bottle of water and protein bar.

"Never go anywhere without it, come check it out." He gestured as he got up.

I followed him down to his room and closed the door behind us. He lifted the bag from the floor, placed it on the bed and began to pull an exceptional array of gear from it, which included a compact AR-15 assault rifle, two SIG Sauer pistols similar to mine, a couple of tactical knives, boots, watch, wetsuit, jet fins and a small re-breather. The latter was similar to my pony bottles, but whereas that allowed me twenty minutes, the re-breather scrubbed the air and allowed it to be run back through which gave nearly 2 hours of air.

"Oh, that impressive," I said as I picked up the AR-15 and ejected the magazine to see it contained military grade ammunition.

I reloaded, checked the safety, and handed it back to him.

"Okay, let's change it up and you stay onboard with me, just in case something goes wrong and we need the additional firepower," I suggested.

"You got it, Cap," he confirmed as he started to pack everything up.

"Seeing as we are not leaving tonight, why don't you go and kick back with the crew in town and have a good time?"

"Thanks for the offer, Cap, but I think I will stay with the boat. I am going to go for a swim later and burn off some of the beers and food from today," he told me.

"That's fine, you go do your thing. I am going to meet up with the guys and then I'm probably going to get some rest," I said.

"You got it," he finished.

I went back on the deck to call Jeff back—he didn't sound any better than he had before when he answered.

"Hey, Tomas, what'd ya need, I'm just about to jump on a plane," he asked in a hurried and stressed manner.

"I'll be as quick as I can. When you get a chance, tell Don Miguel's people that they can drop off the money and that it looks like an on time departure," I lied because I wanted to keep what was going to happen to as small a circle as possible.

"Right, they should be there within the hour," he informed me.

"Thanks, Jeff. Please send me a text as soon as you find Maria," I asked.

"Will do, speak later," and he hung up.

There was another reason I didn't tell Jeff what we were doing. The less he knew, the better and the further he would be away from it all. Besides, he had enough on his mind with Maria.

I paused and looked out across the quayside and saw that Tio was just climbing out of the truck with Magdaleno. I went down the gangway to meet them. Maggie dropped his bag and rapidly walked over to me to give me a big hug.

"Tomas, it is great to see you again, Captain," he said enthusiastically.

"Likewise, Maggie, how have you been?"

"Good, I have a new baby boy, so I'm ready to make some money." He grinned.

"Congrats, brother. I am sorry to jump straight to business, but we will catch up later. I have something I need you to look at immediately," I stressed.

"Just say the word, Cap."

"I need you to go down to the engine room and find an unobvious way to disable the steering or engines themselves. It has to be something that will keep us from departing until noon tomorrow," I explained.

"Ah, Cap, consider it done," he said with a wink as he picked up his bag.

"Maggie," I yelled as he walked across the deck, "meet us on the bridge when you are done and we'll fill you in on the rest."

His acknowledgment consisted of a waved hand.

"Tio, while Magdelano works his magic, let's go and have that talk," I suggested.

The two of us went over to the bridge wing and sat on the lawn chairs that were scattered untidily.

"So what did you want to talk about, Tio," I asked calmly.

He didn't say anything and had a glassy-eyed look that indicated he was upset about something.

"Man, we definitely want you with us on the job, but if you're really concerned about something or don't want to make the trip, it's all good," I promised him. "You don't have to explain anything and nothing changes; if you want out, we'll book you a flight home and catch up in a few weeks."

"No, Capi, that's not it. It's nothing to do with the job itself." He swallowed and looked me in the eye. "I was feeling pretty rough a few weeks back and went to the doctors. They did a load of tests and told me a couple of weeks ago that I had bone cancer!"

Those two words hit like a sledgehammer.

"Bone cancer! Fuck. Is it treatable?"

He shook his head, and tears appeared in his eyes. I slid my chair over to him and put my arm around my friend.

What can you possibly say to news like that?

"Tio, you are family and we will do whatever we can for you."

"Si, I know, Capi," he said as he wiped a tear away. "I don't want the others to know, you understand?" he asked.

"Of course, but don't you want to go home and be with your family? I will make sure you get your cut."

"Everyone is crying and feeling sorry for me. To be honest, I need this trip with the guys again, some normality—that's why I don't want them to know," he explained. "It's my last round, let me enjoy it."

I nodded my agreement and felt tears slowly starting to seep from my eyes. I wiped them away and stood up.

"I love you like a brother, Tio. I totally understand, and this stays just between the two of us. You tell them when you are ready."

"Thank you, Capi," he said as he also stood up, cleared his eyes and took a deep breath.

We both headed to the bridge and as we entered it, something caught Tio's eyes.

"Cap, we might have a man overboard," he said, slightly bemused.

I moved over to him and looked where he pointed. I could see a man swimming across the bay and out toward the jetties.

"Ah, that's Cantrelle. He mentioned he might go for a swim," I confirmed.

"A swim?!" He laughed. "Looks like he is heading out to sea."

"He's an ex-Navy SEAL, so he probably is."

Tio continued to watch in amazement as I checked some of the print-outs.

"You know what, I was planning to go to bed early, but as we're not leaving until tomorrow, how about we go out for a few beers once Don Miguel's goons have dropped off the package?"

"Sounds like a plan, Cap."

A few minutes later, Magdelano appeared on the bridge in the process of wiping grease from his hands.

"All systems go, or rather not," he laughed to himself. "I disabled the steering and we won't be able to get the part I need until tomorrow morning. I'm so annoyed," he mocked with a wink.

"Great work, Maggie. Go get yourself cleared, we're going out for some drinks once the package arrives."

Chapter Nineteen

I WENT TO THE kitchen area and grabbed a beer from the fridge. I might have felt more relaxed now the whole team had arrived, but I was still numb from Tio's news. Now that Magdelano had arrived, the wheels were slowly being put in motion.

Maggie was one of the most important parts of the team. The key to any job that involved a boat was the engine room—no engine, no movement—and Maggie was the engineering doctor and one of the best I'd ever known.

Jeff, Ramon, and Maggie were the first guys I worked with when I was assigned a job in Mexico many years ago. The rest of the crew we acquired along the way, but you had to know someone to get into our merry little band. We didn't accept just anyone, and you had to have that special craft and, most importantly, be trustworthy.

I glanced over at Tio who was sitting on the other side of the bridge talking to his wife on the phone, and thought I would leave him to it. I decided to go and unpack my gear. On my way to my room, I knocked on Ramon's and let him know that Maggie had arrived.

"Speaking of Maggie," I said as he poked his head out, "I checked the weather and decided we are going to push our departure back until noon tomorrow. Before you ask, yes it will no doubt cause a hissy fit from Don Miguel, but I had Magelano temporarily disable the steering and wouldn't you know it, the part won't be here until tomorrow!"

"Where do you come up with it all? Do you need anything else from me?" he asked.

"Nah, but since we're not leaving till tomorrow, Tio and I decided to go for drinks—you up for it?"

"Oh, for sure. What time?"

"I dunno. We're waiting for Don Miguel's hired gorillas to drop the cash," I explained.

"Fine, just give me a twenty-minute heads-up," he said as he closed the door.

As captain, I had the stateroom. It was twice as big as the others and also had an office that was fully equipped with GPS maps so I could track our position without having to walk all the way to the bridge.

In the corner of the desk was a stack of small monitors that allowed me to see what was going on in the crucial parts of the ship. I clicked a few buttons and changed the feed to the one that could be repositioned to show the parking lot and see when Don Miguel's people arrived. I wasn't too worried about it because Shirma and Iqzueirdo would let me know if anyone showed up.

I reached over and hauled my bag off the floor, placed it on the bed and started emptying the contents. I put the pony bottles on the floor, and grabbed my SIG Sauer and its ammunition.

Now, where can I hide you?

I decided to stash it behind one of the ceiling panels above my bed that came out. When I removed it, there was about a foot of space between the false ceiling and the steel bulkhead where the wires and plumbing went from room to room. It was the perfect place.

As I packed away all my scuba gear in the locker, a black SUV pulled up next to the gangway on the monitor. Two men, one with a large hard-shell black suitcase, got out.

"And here comes our money," I exclaimed in my head.

I reached up above my bed and grabbed my pistol, checked it was loaded again, then clipped it to my belt. I was genuinely sure it wouldn't be necessary, but I wanted to have it and not need it, rather than the other way around. I walked down to the galley just as Shirma escorted them in. The goon holding the briefcase purposefully walked up to me.

"Are you Captain Tomas?" he asked, to which I nodded. "I was instructed to allow you to confirm the contents of this case. I am then to report back to Don Miguel with your departure time and estimated arrival at the barge."

He followed me upstairs to my room, but refused to enter when I opened the door.

"I am forbidden to see what is inside the case," he said sternly. "It is for your eyes only."

He passed me a key and unlocked the handcuff around his wrist. I took the key and closed the door, then placed the case on my bunk and opened it. My heart almost leapt out of my chest when I set eyes upon all that money. I could understand why Don Miguel didn't want his guys to even have the temptation of seeing it.

I tipped the contents out onto my bed and quickly had plenty of thoughts about how that money could change my life. The packs of money—each pack contained $10,000 in $100 bills—filed the bunk. I picked up each one and flicked through it to ensure they were all money and not blank pieces of paper as I'd seen done before.

It was impossible for me to know if they were counterfeits or not, but given Don Miguel expected to get his money back and the diesel, it was unlikely he would jeopardize everything but using fake money. He was too arrogant for that. With this much money involved, it would be easy to start a fire fight between the two cartels and the Navy as they would each assume they were being double crossed.

It was no small task and took me a while, but I eventually counted the whole $1.4 million. I piled it back in the suitcase and placed it under my bed. I opened the door and the delivery man stepped forward.

"Tell Don Miguel I accept the package and have confirmed its contents. We will be leaving tomorrow morning and will be there that night at 2100 hours."

He said nothing, just turned and walked away, swiftly followed by his colleague, and left the boat. I closed the door again and pulled out some trash bags from under my sink. I broke it all up and split it between three bags. Payoff money, crew money, and me and Ramon's cut. "The biggest one of course!" I then placed them in the hide-away in the ceiling. On the off-chance something happened, I wanted the payoff bag to look big as a distraction, so I added some books with 100k cash and locked it up before I placed it under my bunk. That will be the only bag going with us.

I returned to the bridge afterward where Tio was waiting for me.

"Has Ramon come up yet?" I checked.

"No, Capi, I have not seen him."

"Okay, well go check on him and Maggie to see if they are coming while I go talk to Shirma."

I found him sitting at a table in the galley with Izquierdo.

"Hey, Shirma, we are going into town for a bit this evening. While we are gone, I need you and Izquierdo to rotate watches until we get back. You know the drill. Do not let anyone on board without calling me first," I told him.

"You got it, Capi," he answered.

I went out on deck and called China one last time before we left. She sounded half asleep when she answered.

"Hey China, sorry, did I wake you?"

"Not really, I just dozed off. What do you need?" she asked wearily.

"I just wanted to let you know that Don Miguel's men have been and gone, and we arranged the meeting for 9 pm tomorrow night. Let's put our little plan into action at, say, 9:15 pm?"

"Okay, Tomas, listen, you be careful!" she pleaded.

"Don't worry at all. Just be sure to tell them it's important they are not too early or too late," I pointed out.

"Will do, call me in the morning," she asked before she finished the call.

Hearing her half-sleep voice dragged memories from my mind of the time when we were together. She could be a contradiction, one moment looking to live in the moment and enjoying life, the next she could be weighed down with something. I often thought it was work related. There were times when she got up in the middle of the night to go outside with her Sat. phone. I always knew if she wanted to talk about it, she would have.

A few minutes later, the guys all came walking out the door. We piled into the SUV and headed out the lot. We were close to everything so we could have walked; I just felt better having the truck there.

"Any place in particular?" I asked Tio who was in the back.

"Wherever suits you, Capi," he answered with a smile.

"Hey, what about Lipsticks; the girl I was with earlier said she worked there."

I shook my head. "Lipsticks sounds like a great place." I laughed.

As we pulled up in front of the club, it was everything you would expect with a name like Lipsticks. The name shone in bright pink neon lights that flashed alternatively with an outline of a woman in a bikini. We all made an enthusiastic entry inside and were greeted with the sight of naked women on poles or scantily clad waitresses serving drinks.

"I know this is where you met the girl from today; C'mon now, admit it," I whispered to Ramon.

"Honestly, Tomas, I didn't know this place existed," he protested.

I smirked and sarcastically followed up, "Yeah, right!"

A waitress came over and showed us to a table. I took the seat with the best view of the entrance and anyone coming in—an old habit I picked up long ago, something I did every time, regardless of what I was doing. The waitress quickly came back with a bucket of ice and some beers. We each grabbed one, cracked it open and raised out bottles.

"To our family and our success tomorrow," I toasted.

The DJ announced a change in dancing girls and all the new arrivals had the sort of exotic dancer names you would expect: Mercedes, Jasmine, Sapphire. As I looked over at the guys who were clearly enjoying the view, it made me think about the old times, all the scrapes we'd gotten into and out of together. We used to do this sort of thing often, but then one by one we either got married or just tired of the scene. Everyone was chatting, enjoying the show and in good spirits, but I quickly noticed Magdaleno had two beers to one for everyone else, and he was also ordering shots of tequila all around.

"Maggie, are you on some sort of mission tonight?" I shouted above the music.

He looked puzzled for just a second, then smiled and nodded. He could handle his liquor so I wasn't too worried about that from the job perspective. I decided to keep an eye on him just to be safe.

The place was busy for a weeknight. I then reminded myself that it was a port town; where there are sailors, there is liquor and women. Just to prove my point, I spotted Tio and Ramon making several trips to the private dance booths. At one point, a girl yelled Ramon's name from behind me. It was one of the dancers who pointed to a beer, a gesture asking him to buy it for her.

"Yeah, never been here before," I muttered with a smirk.

He was such a playboy at times it surprised me that he hadn't contracted something after his wayward actions all these years. Much to my surprise, he shook his head to indicate that he wouldn't pay for it. She tried again and once again he shook his head. After the third time, she started shouting some hostile words in Spanish, and the next moment, the bottle she was holding flew in our direction. We all ducked and it smashed into a mirror behind us. Large shards of reflective glass flew in all directions, and we all jumped out of our seats.

"Gentlemen, time to go... vamanos," laughed Ramon.

In that instance, vamanos meant get the hell out of there, in a very literal sense. We all grabbed our cell phones and anything else, and headed for the door. About halfway there, a bouncer came out to see what all the commotion was about. He jumped out in front of Ramon, who as usual, was the first in line running for the door.

Without missing a beat, Ramon hit him hard in the chest with the palms of his hands, which pushed him backwards onto his back. As he slid across the floor we all trampled over him like cattle as we charged out the door.

We all hurled ourselves into the truck, I whacked it in gear and slammed on the gas. The truck sprayed gravel and oyster shells all over the other vehicles and even the people in the parking lot as we made our escape. The last thing they would have heard was the sound of unstoppable laughter as we all fell about in hysterics.

"Damn, man, we can't take you anywhere without you getting in some shit," I chuckled at Ramon. "Gentlemen, that's it, I think we're heading back to the boat.

It didn't seem to dampen the mood as everyone regaled their view of what had just taken place to great amusement. It was like retelling the best parts of a movie you all just saw. When we arrived back at the boat, I told Ramon to put the truck behind a container not far from the boat as I was confident the local police would already be looking for it.

The rest of us walked to the galley. I took a seat across from Shirma, who was sitting at the table, while the others raided the refrigerator for more beer. Magdelano was the only one who seemed a little drunk, but not too bad when I totaled up how much he'd had. The guys just seemed contently happy to all be together again.

After I explained Ramon's latest escapade, I told him, "You can go to bed now if you want, but I want you and Izquierdo to come on watch at 6 am sharp."

"Si Capi" he confirmed as he got up, stretched and headed toward the cabins. The guys were having a boisterous time in the Galley, so I left them to it for a bit and went to make some final calls. I went to the bridge, checked the weather before I grabbed a bottle of water and went out on deck.

I tried to call Jeff first, but it went straight to voicemail. I assumed he was likely still on the plane or hadn't turned off Airplane Mode, which he often did. I tried Maria again, a part of me deep inside hoping she would answer. She didn't—it went straight to voicemail again.

I let out an audible sigh and looked out across the marina, where the lights reflected from the barely rippling surface. There was a merchant ship moored to the long pier that jetted out into the far end of the bay. It was a customs dock, and that was where all the ships that came from foreign ports had to go before they could dock and offload all their cargo.

I found myself just staring at it as I tried to work out what the hell could have happened to Maria. More importantly, if she was okay? I knew Jeff would have tried all the hospitals, police departments, Maria's associates, friends... morgues. I shuddered to think of the last one. It was not like her to just outright disappear. She always let Jeff know if she planned to be out of touch.

As I tried to figure it out, I heard some people yelling in the distance toward the merchant ship across the bay. It was too far away for me to hear exactly what was going on, but from the amount of shouting it was pretty serious. People were not happy, that much I could tell.

An alarm suddenly went off, and the crew scurried about the deck with flashlights as they shined lights out into the water.

The alarm stopped a few minutes later, but crew members seemed to continue to look into the water as the bridge officers barked orders as they stood outside the cabin on the upper deck. Four crew members then launched a fast rescue boat into the water and drove it around the marina and the bay. They continued to shine lights and investigate the water.

They passed within a hundred yards of our boat and shined their lights right at me. I put my hand up to shield my eyes and they quickly turned around and headed toward their ship.

What the hell is going on over there and what are they looking for?

"What's up, Cap?" asked a soaking wet Cantrelle, who was standing in a puddle of water behind me.

"*Jesus*, Cantrelle, you scared the shit out of me. Where did you come from?"

He just smiled and pointed to the merchant ship.

"Are you responsible for all the mayhem out there?" I inquired with a shake of my head.

"Errm, yeah, that's my doing, Cap. It's just a little exercise to stay sharp." He grinned.

"What did you do?" I asked, not too sure if I wanted to know.

"Here, check this out," he replied.

Cantrelle held up his hand and showed me a tool that he was holding.

"This is a grappling hook and repelling tool that we use in the SEALS. The hook shoots around sixty feet and it has a motor that can pull a three-hundred pound man up to wherever the hook is attached. Of course, it works the same to repel down," he explained.

He passed it over to me. It was quite small and not much bigger than a normal-sized handgun. The wire was extremely thin and the hook looked like it only opened when you used it.

"How loud is it when you fire the hook?" I asked.

"It uses a CO2 cartridge, Cap, and it's silenced. Try it for yourself," he suggested as he pointed at the water.

I aimed downward and pulled the trigger. There was a barely audible "poof" and the hook flew rapidly into the water. Cantrelle pointed to a switch on the side. I flipped it and pulled the trigger, and the entire sixty-foot of wire recoiled in a couple of seconds.

"That is super cool. Okay, where can I get one?" I smirked.

"It ain't on the civilian market, Cap, could you imagine what damage those Somali pirates could do if they got their hands on kit like this?" he answered.

"Good point. Hey, have you been swimming all this time? We saw you heading out earlier."

"Yes. I only swam eight miles, though; I usually do twelve at least," he replied proudly.

"Man, I'd have drowned after one," I added with a laugh.

"Ah, don't do yourself down, Cap. We're all just trying to make use of the skills we are born with. I'm pumped up and ready, so when are we leaving, Cap?"

"We'll depart at 0900, so go ahead and get some rest," I told him.

"Roger that, Cap. I will be up at 0600, see you then."

Cantrelle went inside and I saw him head down to the cabins through the window.

I pulled my phone out for the last time and called Diana. She answered after a single ring.

"Hey, Tomas, I wondered if you'd call tonight."

"Great minds and all that," I joked. "I just wanted to see if you'd heard from Jeff or Maria?"

"No, sorry, hunny. All I know is that Jeff flew to Miami earlier this afternoon, but no one has heard anything since then," she replied sadly.

"Okay, I thought as much, but just wanted to check while I could. I am going to be out of touch for a couple of days, but will text you my email address. I know I sound like a broken record, but please let me know when you hear anything?"

"Of course. Now, be careful out there. Let me know once everything is finished," she told me.

"Will do, goodnight," I added before I ended the call.

As there wasn't anything else I could do, I went back to my cabin. I checked everything was where I left it, then sat at my desk and poured a scotch. I took a few sips as I went through the plan in my head. Being the meticulous planner that I was, I took out a notepad and jotted down every step, and next to it I added any contingency plan we had arranged.

I grabbed a second shot and read over everything again as I slowly drank it. Like any plan, the only blind spot was the unknown. I couldn't help but snort as it brought to mind the "Unknown Knowns" speech from Donald Rumsfeld. As far as the plan went, that meant unknown people, such as Tio's cousins.

I couldn't think of any new ideas or wrinkles, and so I decided to split everyone's share of the money to enable me to pass it out before we met Don Miguel's people. Rule number one was that you never split the take in front of everyone, especially if people were getting different amounts.

As I placed the money in piles, it dawned on me about the Navy Captain.

They could kill everyone and take the money! In fact, why wouldn't they?

How well did China really know the guy, and would he go after her if we tried to screw him out of his cut? I shook off the concern because it really scared me that something could happen to her. I packed up the Captain's money as well, but decided to keep the second-biggest rule in mind—hope for the best, plan for the worst.

I decided to have a shower once I finished my second drink. As I stood with my eyes closed under the steaming hot water, the jetted liquid running across my head and shoulders, I realized how tired I was. My whole body was tense and I felt exhausted. It has been nice to be retired. I may not have had much money but my stress levels had been virtually zero, and that was well worth it.

I put on some sweatpants and a T-shirt after I finished, and laid back on the bed. The lure of the money was huge, but I couldn't help but wish I was on the *San Blas* in my own bed. I love the stress-free life of retirement since I bought my boat. Nothing could beat waking up and drinking coffee on the deck as you looked out over the crystal clear blue waters of the Caribbean. That happy place was enough to relax me and I drifted off to sleep.

I awoke the next morning at 5 am. It took me a moment to place myself due to the unfamiliar surroundings, but once I got my bearings, I got up, dressed, and headed to the bridge. I found Tio fast asleep on the sofa.

"Tio, why don't you go get a proper nap?" I asked as I shook his foot.

He woke up and his bloodshot eyes looked around.

"I need you on watch at 0900, so grab some proper shut-eye. Anything to report before you go?" I checked.

"Si, Capi, Captain Cantrelle went for a run and said he would be back by 6 am. We have a grocery truck that will be here at 0700, and I have all the charts laid out with the course plotted so you can check everything," he informed me as I made a fresh cup of coffee.

"Perfect, thanks, Tio," I replied.

He gave me a nod and shuffled off to his bunk while I poured a cup of coffee and went out to the lawn chairs on the bridge wing. I took a seat in one and propped my feet up on the railing. The bay was still calm despite a slight breeze blowing across. I saw several small fishing boats right outside the jetty and a pilot boat pushed up next to the merchant ship.

They are obviously getting underway after last night's shenanigans.

I also observed from the corner of my eye Shirma, Izquierdo, and Magdaleno laughing and joking around on the back deck. I couldn't make out what they were saying, but Maggie laughed several times quite heartily. That made me smile. It was almost like a proud parent watching the kids play. We might have been similar in age, but they all looked up to me as their leader. I had earned their respect and their trust many times over.

I went inside and grabbed another cup of coffee and then went to check my emails. Just as I stood next to the computer, Cantrelle came up the stairs.

"Morning, Cap, I couldn't sleep so I got up at four and went for a run," he told me.

"Well, it's 0545 now, grab yourself a shower and some breakfast. We have the groceries arriving at seven and we'll depart at 0900."

"Works for me," he affirmed and headed below.

"He's probably just ran twenty plus miles. He's like the fucking Terminator," I joked to myself.

With a second cup in hand, I saw that they guys were back to work. I wandered down to the engine room to check on everything with Magdelano. I passed Ramon's room en-route and poked my head inside to check he was on board—I found him snoring his head off, so closed the door quietly.

I walked into the engine room and saw Magdelano bent over the bow thruster screwing in a new filter.

"Hey, Maggie, what's up, any real problem?" I asked.

"Hi, Capi, nothing serious," he replied as he wiped his hands on a rag. "I found a small restriction on the fuel filters. Just to be safe, I swapped them out."

"Have you been through everything else?" I checked.

"Si, that was the last check. We are ready to go," he replied positively.

"Great, we depart at 0900, so have them warmed up by then."

"Roger, that," he answered as he took off toward the main engine compartment.

Chapter Twenty

THE SIGHT OF A fully laid out breakfast greeted me when I entered the galley. Shirma had obviously been busy and served up Huevos Mexicana, black beans and tortillas. I'd become quite accustomed to Latin food and found American meals quite bland in comparison, even if there were things that Americans did better like pizza, steaks... and seafood gumbo.

I got myself a plate and dug in, but my mind was still on other things, most notably the lack of calls, texts, or emails from Jeff or Maria. Once I'd finished, I went up on deck and called Jeff again. After several rings, he answered.

"Hey Jeff, how's everything there? Have you found Maria?" I asked with urgency.

"No, she is not in Miami. I stopped overnight, and I am heading back to Mexico on an early flight this morning," he told me exasperated.

"Right, we need to postpone this job," I added swiftly. "We will meet you in Cozumel as soon as possible."

"No, Tomas, I really need you to go ahead and make that run, then get your ass back here as quickly as possible," he said firmly.

"What the fuck is going on, Jeff? Is there something you're not telling me?" I added sternly.

"Listen, Tomas, she is being held, but I can assure you she is okay," he came back.

"Held?! What the hell does that mean?"

"Look, I can't say anything right now, but she is okay and you need to know that. Just make the run and get back here as quickly as you can," he explained.

"Fine! Whatever you need," I started as he quickly hung up.

I threw myself back in my chair and felt like I wanted to jump out of my skin. My mind was racing, my heart pounding, and my head was full of numerous thoughts. My blood pressure shot up and if I wasn't stressed before, I certainly was after the call.

Just what have I got myself involved in?

I had finally got myself out of all the illegal dealings and work that I had previously been involved in, and now I'd managed to get myself sucked back in. I leaned forward and grabbed one of Tio's cigarettes from an almost empty cigar box on the table.

I inhaled a few drags, then launched myself out of the chair then grabbed it by the top and repeatedly smashed it on the railings. Various plastic shrapnel flew all over the deck. To finish, I launched the chair with a roar over the side.

I needed to calm myself down because being this emotional often risked oversights or mistakes on the job, and the consequences of that would be just as serious or worse. I dropped down a deck and was just in the process of calming myself down on the railing when Ramon's head popped out from the deck below.

"Everything Okay, Tomas?" he asked with a concerned look.

"No, man, it's far from alright. Jeff has just told me that someone has snatched Maria," I replied as I vented some anger.

"Right, let me get my shit together and we can go deal with this," he added without hesitation.

"No, wait," I shouted.

He looked up at me with concern and surprise. He obviously felt the same way—a member of the family was in trouble and it needed to be sorted.

"I talked to Jeff, he knows who is holding her and why. He was adamant that she was okay and that he needs us to make this run. Honestly, I don't know anything more than that. We need everyone with maximum focus, so don't say anything until we have finished the job. You and I can then head back together," I told him.

"Right, let me get dressed and I'll be right up," he added.

I finished the last drags on the stolen cigarette, then composed myself and headed back inside. I hadn't sat on the sofa for more than a minute or two when the bridge phone rang. It was Cantrelle calling up from the galley.

"The groceries are here, Cap," he informed me.

"Good. Tell Shirma that once you guys get everything stowed away, we are leaving.

He agreed and then I called the pilot to arrange our escort out. We didn't need it physically, but it was Mexican law for any vessel over a hundred tons. He immediately asked for our permission to sail, which had been covered by Ramon's father. I took their number down and faxed it straight over. They called back minutes later to confirm a pilot would board at 0855 for a 0900 departure.

I hung up and made my way downstairs. Ramon was just leaving his room when I passed the cabins.

"Ramon, the pilot will be here at 0855. Get yourself some breakfast and then take us out," I told him.

"Roger that. Do you have a route planned out?" he questioned.

"Yep. Tio laid out the course, but make sure you run slow. I want to arrive at 9 pm and not a minute sooner," I reaffirmed.

He nodded his agreement, and I went to my cabin. I sat at my desk to collect my thoughts, to digest everything that I'd been told. I couldn't do anything so I decided to finish splitting the proceeds. I carefully counted out the remaining share and finished packing them into trash bags with duct tape. Once the crew had been sorted, I took out enough to pay the Navy Captain and put it into a spare briefcase we would leave behind. I put the rest into two piles of 400k each for Ramon and me.

A nice pay day, but we are risking our lives for it.

I pulled out the list I'd made the previous night, assessing it one more time. The "Unknown Knowns" still gnawed at me, a worry I couldn't shake. I closed my eyes and in that moment of silence, I came up with one more part of the plan. I called down to the gallery and asked Shirma to send Ramon up. A few minutes later, he knocked on my door and I let him in.

"I want to discuss a new idea with you. I have split up all the money, $400k each for us," I started to be rewarded with a big Ramon smile, "but there is a concern about something that came to my mind. We do not know Tio's cousins at all, and in the scheme of things, their share is quite small."

"I think I know where you are going," he interjected.

"You and I are going to take a ride, just you and me. We will find a place to stash our cut, then we can come back for it after things have settled down," I suggested.

"Okay," added Ramon with a now deeply serious expression.

"I'm going to make a few dummy packs for the two of us using books. That way, no one will have any questions."

"I think I might know a place not far from here."

"Perfect, let's go," I said as I packed money into a smallish duffle bag and followed Ramon downstairs. On our way out, I told Shirma to get some steaks out and grill them for lunch and that the two of us had to pop out.

We jumped into the truck and Ramon told me to drive to the highway and head east out of town.

"It's a freshwater spring out in the middle of nowhere. One of my more serious girlfriends brought me out here once with her kids to go swimming."

I gave him a quick look as it didn't seem like his sort of thing, but he'd had many different lady friends over the years and I couldn't picture Ramon playing Dad.. We drove for about twenty minutes as Ramon stared out at the trees and passing scenery. He saw what he was looking for. "Take a right here between the trees." I turned right onto a dirt trail.

It was barely wide enough for the truck and the trees scraped the sides as we trundled along. It widened out after about a quarter mile to reveal a large sandy lot around a freshwater spring with a small waterfall about ten to twelve feet high. We were lucky it was early enough that no one was around. I backed the truck up to some trees at the far end of the lot.

"Let's go in here and make our way back toward the rocks," Ramon suggested as I grabbed the bag.

We jumped out and Ramon led the way. Once away from the lot, it turned into dense forest-like terrain. That made me relax as there was little chance anyone would be walking back there. We made our way carefully to ensure that no foliage was broken that could give our path away. Once we reached the top of the rocks, I spotted a large flat rock nestled against one side.

"There," I proposed, "help me move it."

It looked perfect when we rolled it over. We couldn't bring a shovel with us as that would look too obvious all around, so I pulled out my knife, used it to loosen the earth and we dug a hole with our hands. We placed the bag in and covered it over again, making sure not to leave any fresh earth exposed and threw all that we removed into the bushes.

It took us nearly an hour to fully bury the bag and remove all signs of footprints and disturbed ground. Once we were sure we'd been as thorough as possible, we hiked back to the truck. By the time we got back, we were both soaked in sweat. I checked my watch and I told Ramon that we had forty minutes before the pilot arrived.

Once we got to the highway, I held back just in the bushes and opened my window to listen. I wanted to ensure no one saw us pull onto the highway. I couldn't hear any cars, so I eased out onto the highway and flew off back to the marina.

As we pulled into the marina, I looked over and saw the pilot boat was pushed up against the hull.

"The pilot is here. Go straight up and get us underway. I will just go and park the truck. I will come and relieve you at lunch," I told Ramon.

As soon as I came to a stop by the gangway, he jumped out and raced up to the bridge. Once I was aboard, I went to the galley and instructed Shrima to give me a call when it was ready. I grabbed a bottle of water and sat across from Magdelano who was at the table with his laptop.

"Everything is still good to go, Maggie?" I asked.

"Si, Capi, I was just talking to my daughter. She graduates from university next week," he told me with immense pride.

"Pass on my congratulations. Listen, Ramon will be taking the ship out and I'm going to catch a quick nap before taking over. If there are any problems, just call the bridge," I told him. I then walked to my cabin to wash up and recuperate a little.

A couple of hours later, the phone in my cabin rang. It was Shirma letting me know that lunch was ready. I pulled back the small curtain that covered my porthole, and to my relief, it looked like the wind had picked up as forecasted.

The sea was rising about two or three feet, which didn't affect a vessel this size, but it would make all the difference for someone in the water. If we'd been moored up, the boat would have slowly rocked from side to side, but we were headed straight at them doing a slow six knots and the ride was pleasant.

Izquierdo was washing the dishes when I arrived in the galley. The rest of the guys were under a tarp out on deck.

"You already eaten?" I asked him.

"Si, Capi," he confirmed.

"Okay, go steer for a bit so Ramon can come down for food?"

I grabbed a plate of food and a bottle of water, and walked out on deck. The guys were sitting in a sort of circle under the tarp with their plates in their laps. I knew the food had to be good because they were all silent, a very rare occurrence. I suddenly noticed Tio wasn't with everyone. I checked if anyone had checked to see if he was coming for lunch and Shirma confirmed he was coming down. With everything as it should be, I dug into my food.

Tio arrived shortly after, so I waited for him to load up his plate and take a seat before I spoke to the crew and updated them on the situation.

"Alright, listen up guys," I started as they all looked up from their plates. "I want every one of you to get some rest. Shirma and Izquierdo will take a four-hour watch each, then Tio will take over at 1900. He can then make the arrangements to meet up with his cousins at 2030hrs. We should be around five miles from the exchange site by that stage. At that point, everyone will disembark apart from Cantrelle and myself."

Magdelano raised his hand and asked, "If we are going to pick you both up, why don't we all stay onboard and leave together?"

I understood his question.

"Tio's cousins will have two small fishing boats. I want you, Shirma and Izquierdo in the first, with Ramon and Tio in the second. The latter vessel with Ramon and Tio will remain one mile behind the ship and the rest of you will stand by where you disembark at five miles. After lunch, I will give each of you your cut and you will be responsible for your own."

I was pleased everyone nodded at that point.

"Once we all reach the standby location, we will run upriver together into Frontera. I have bus tickets for everyone to Villahermosa, and from there, you will be on your own. Does anyone have any questions?"

My query was met with silence. I stood up and held my bottle of water aloft in salute. "Okay, guys, let's get this done."

Each one of them joined, and then they returned to their meal and chatted between themselves. I shuffled over to Tio and Cantrelle.

"I will meet you both on the bridge at 7 pm," I told them.

They both nodded their agreement without saying anything. With everything sorted, I finished the remaining bits of my meal before I returned to my cabin. I set out some clothes for later and flopped on the bed for a nap.

My alarm woke me up at 6:30 pm and I had a shower, got dressed, all in black again, and went upstairs. I stepped onto the bridge and saw the entire crew sitting on the sofas. They all greeted me in unison and I acknowledged as I walked over to the coffee pot to pour myself a fresh one.

The next job was to check for any updates, so I sat at the computer and checked my emails. There was a tinge of apprehension as I had no idea what might be contained there, especially if it was news from Jeff. All I found was one from China that read—

Tomas, it's a go. PLEASE be careful!

"It's a go, gentlemen," I told the crew.

They all started talking to each other about the plan and what was expected as I walked over to Tio.

"Is everything set with your cousins?" I checked.

"Si, Capi. I got a message that they were already underway to the coordinates we gave them. We should be there right on schedule.

"Great, nice work," I praised as I went and sat in the co-pilot chair.

Around forty five minutes later, I spotted lights from several small fishing vessels up ahead. I picked up the binoculars and scanned for two that were close together, which I found after a minute or two.

"Tio, I think I spotted them about ten points off the starboard bow about a mile."

He flipped the spotlight on and off twice, and moments later, the two boats flashed a smaller light, maybe a flashlight, in the same way back at us.

"That's them. Okay, guys, it's game time," I announced.

I reached down and picked up one of the duffle bags I had carried on the bridge with me and handed them their packets of money and bus tickets. I left the dummy packs in the bag with the payoff money for the Navy guys for Ramon to carry. It was important no one knew the switch we had made, in case someone might be crossing us.

"Bro, if anything goes bad or something happens to me, give my share to China," I leaned in and whispered to Ramon as I gave him the bag. He said nothing and nodded, and made his way downstairs. I looked over at Tio.

"There is another bag over there," I said as I pointed to a second bag I prepared earlier. "Take it with you—it has a change of clothes for me and Cantrelle.

He came over and gave me a big hug after he collected the bag. "Watch your ass, Capi."

I reached over and pulled the throttles back slowly as we made our approach to the two small boats. Once we were fifty yards away, I eased them back into reverse and we came to a stop. Tio's cousins pulled both boats up to the port side gate. I quickly walked over to the window at the back of the bridge to watch them leave the ship. Cantrelle quickly appeared alongside me.

"What do you need me to do?" he asked.

"Nothing yet, just stand by," I replied.

Once the guys had boarded their respective fishing vessel and pulled away to a safe distance, I pushed the throttles full ahead and we continued toward our rendezvous at the barge. The recent calm waters had been replaced with sea running at around three feet.

I eventually saw the lights from the barge up ahead. Checking the radar, it confirmed the barge was little more than four miles away. I calculated needing to arrive at 2045 so I would have fifteen minutes to get the vessel secured to the barge before the Navy vessel showed up.

I turned up the range on the radar and looked for the Navy vessel. Most boats only just show up as a little spot, but you can still tell the difference between a skiff and a ship. I found a contact about twelve miles to our west. I quickly calculated that its speed was a little over fourteen knots.

That has got to be the Navy ship."

Exactly at 0845, I pulled up next to the barge. It was bigger than usual and appeared to have containers forward that were constructed as living quarters. As far as I could see, there were eleven men on the barge. I turned to Cantrelle.

"That's a lot of men to work a fuel line. You got your bag set up?" I asked hastily.

"Yeah, it is in the engine room," he replied.

"Okay, here we go," I announced after a deep breath.

I put the engines back in gear and slowly chugged our way up to the barge. Don Miguel's men were already on the deck, but I couldn't see any clearly visible weapons. That didn't mean there weren't any.

"Cantrelle, I am going to get alongside about ten meters away, then I'll pass it to you at the aft controls. You will have to maneuver us into position. Once I get the stern line on, you just push the bow thruster over to hold us against the barge. Then, run like hell to the engine room—I will meet you there," I told him.

I had just put the engines into reverse to stop alongside the barge when a bright spotlight suddenly lit up the bridge. I instinctively put my hand up to shield my eyes from the light which allowed me to see it was coming from a small Navy skiff with a large machine gun mounted upfront on a tripod. They pointed it directly at me.

"Get the fuck down!" I screamed as I dove to the floor. Without any warning, the windows immediately exploded in a hail of bullets.

Chapter Twenty-One

THE SOUND OF THE machine gun fire was almost deafening, even for someone familiar with being shot at. Shards and large pieces of glass exploded throughout the bridge, some sticking in the walls and ceiling like serrated teeth that had chopped down. The main bridge console and chart table exploded like fireworks on New Year's Eve before some of the electronics caught fire. It looked like something out of a *Star Trek* movie when the Enterprise got ravaged.

Cantrelle and I had both thrown ourselves to the floor as the shower of debris rained down on us. He crawled in my direction over the broken glass and then we both shuffled our way to the stairs on our stomachs. He was so close behind me that he landed on me at the bottom of the stairs.

In unison, we jumped to our feet and sprinted down the next flight of stairs, through the galley, and to the engine room. Once we were inside, I slammed the hatch closed. I turned around and

Cantrelle already had his bag over his shoulder and had loaded a magazine into his rifle. I rushed to the corner and grabbed my bag as well.

"Let's get the hell out of here," I shouted.

We quickly made our way down past the engines and to the hatch that led to the rudder compartment.

"Go!" I yelled as Cantrelle ran through the hatch.

The passage to the rudder room was actually a small crawl space only around three feet high. As soon as Cantrelle was through, I jumped in and secured the hatch behind me. We crawled on our hands and knees through to the rudder room in single file. We could still hear the sound of gun fire, now coming from multiple directions, along with numerous men shouting, but the overwhelming noise was our hard breathing.

"What the actual fuck, Cap!?" asked a stunned Cantrelle.

"I have no idea," I huffed, "just get your mask on. We are getting the fuck out of here."

Bullets continue to rebound and ping off the metal hull of the ship, more often than not sounding like it came from the front. I reached into my bag and pulled out my mask. I hung it around my neck, strapped my pony bottle over my shoulder and placed the respirator in my shirt.

"Follow me, and stay close," I urged Cantrelle.

I grabbed the ladder that led up to the hatch and opened it slightly once I got close enough. The sound of gunfire became much louder and it was obvious it was coming from all around us. I could hear men shouting and yelling in Spanish, and it sounded much closer than I would have liked. I looked below at Cantrelle, who nodded at me, before I raised the hatch and peeked through the crack. It was all clear in our immediate vicinity, but countless bullets were hitting the containers around the hatch. I climbed out on my hands and knees with Cantrelle close behind. We crawled to the aft bulwarks, and I poked my head to quickly observe what faced us. Exactly as planned, the containers were perfectly placed to block anyone's view.

"Lets get the fuck out of here," I told Cantrelle.

I put the regulator in my mouth and slipped over the bulwarks into the water. I tried to make the process as fast but as minimal as possible to avoid a huge splash. Cantrelle entered the water right behind me.

I grabbed my gauge to check on our water depth, the pressure in my tank and the compass on the rear. I sank down to 20 to 25 feet where the water was pitch black, but we didn't use any torches in case the lights in the water gave away our position. The gauges had a light, but I kept them beneath me and out of sight from the surface.

Based on my calculations, with the current in our favor, we needed two hundred kicks to reach two hundred meters. It may have been dark with virtually no visibility, but the water itself was lukewarm. I kept checking my compass and continued to kick eastward. Cantrelle swam alongside with his rifle still in his hands. Once I counted the kick two hundred, I looked over at Cantrelle and gave a thumbs up.

Carefully and slowly, we swam upward to the surface and once we reached it, I saw we were further away than I anticipated—by around three hundred yards. The gunfire now more in the distance cracked away like fireworks and I could see the muzzle flashes from some of Don Miguel's people as they fired back from behind the living quarters on the barge. Their light illuminated like high-speed blinkers.

"What the hell just happened, Cap?" asked Cantrelle again as he treaded water next to me having removed his respirator.

"It would appear that the Navy Captain decided he was going to keep it all."

I reached down into the water and grabbed my dive light off my belt. I carefully shielded it in front of me and started flashing it in an easterly direction where Tio and Ramon's fishing boat was located. They were in the distance when we hit the top of each wave, but lost sight when we dipped down.

Within a few minutes, they chugged slowly alongside the two of us and helped us into the boat. In next to no time, Tio's cousin had spun her around and accelerated in the direction of Frontera.

"Capi, we heard all the commotion from here. What happened over there?" asked Tio urgently.

"It's all about double-crossing, and that is exactly what the Navy Captain tried to do to us!" I explained, catching my breath against the side of the boat. I kept looking behind us at the barge and the rate of gunfire has slowed considerably to a few shots. I assumed they were likely finishing off the wounded. My hands still had the shakes and my heart continued to pound away even though the worst was likely over. About ten minutes later, I heard the voice of Shirma and the others as we had reached the meeting point.

"Is Capi and Cantrelle okay?" yelled Shirma.

"They are all good, we got both of them," replied Cantrelle.

Tio's cousin guided his boat next to theirs and we were about to take a moment when Shirma raised the alarm.

"Capi, look, look," he yelled as he pointed behind us toward the barge.

I didn't need binoculars to see the Navy skiff heading straight for us.

"Shit, there is no way we can outrun them," I said with deep concern as we pounded in the waves heading for frontera. "We are going to have to split up!" I yelled. Cantrelle had already taken position laying down on the deck ready to return fire.

"Capi, give me your gun," demanded Tio".

"Why, Tio? What are you going to do?" I asked in surprise.

"I'm going to lead them away, just give my cut to my wife."

He reached down and tossed his bag to my feet.

"Make sure my wife gets this!" Then hollered to his cousin to get the other boat close. We had to slow to an almost stop to make the exchange..He grabbed my pistol and jumped into the other boat.

The shock on the faces of the others was unquestionable, myself included, but the others didn't know what I did and I understood. He didn't have long and it was logical—one life that hadn't long to burn left for several others. There wasn't time to cry, mourn, debate a different direction or really even to say goodbye. The skiff was going to be quickly on us.

"Everyone, get your asses over here now!" I screamed.

For a moment they all stood and looked at Tio.

"Go, go, go, go," he yelled as he started pushing them into the second boat. He swiftly made his way to the controls and slammed the throttles to full as he sped away from us toward land. At the same time, I rushed over to the lights and yanked out any wires I could see; the lights went out and everything went black. The lack of protests from Tio's cousin left me thinking they already knew about his health situation.

"Go that way," I yelled to him.

He spun the boat around and continued in the direction of Frontera. As he did so, we all watched Tio speeding toward the coast. It was impossible to tell if the Navy skiff had taken the bait, but then I saw two muzzle flashes. It was Tio firing my .45 at the skiff, which immediately returned fire with its powerful machine gun.

"It worked!" I thought sadly, knowing the cost that would be paid.

The skiff continued to fire and veered off in Tio's direction. Everyone on our boat sat and watched in silence as we skipped across the top of the waves, except Tio's cousin, who was steering the boat. Just as we reached the entrance to the river, a large volley of fire and muzzle flashes erupted from the Navy skiff, then everything went quiet. That was the moment the dam broke. Tears welled up in all our eyes, even Tio's cousin, as the events sank in.

"Why did you let him do that, Capi," asked Shirma in desperation.

I wiped away my tears and took a deep breath as it was hard for me to even talk.

"Guys, Tio told me that he was dying of bone cancer. He didn't want you to know yet or to feel sorry for him, and he wanted to just enjoy a final job together. I have his money here, and I will add some of my cut and give it to his family. Right now, we need to make sure we get away to be able to do that. The time to mourn will be later," I told them as strongly as I could manage.

A few moments passed before everyone nodded at me. They all looked out across the water, muttered their own thanks to Tio and got back to work. Tio's cousin turned back to the controls and took us up the river. We soon arrived at a nice looking little house with a small dock.

"This is my place," Tio's cousin confirmed. "There is a shower in the boat house if you and Cantrelle want to freshen up or change. I will go and tell my family what has happened and get the truck ready to take you to the bus station. I nodded as the crew pulled the skiff off the bank.

Cantrelle and I grabbed our stuff and headed over to the boat house. It was set up like a studio apartment with a small kitchen in it. The walls were bare wooden planks with gaps you could see through.

"What's the plan, Cap?" asked Cantrelle as he broke down his rifle.

"Don't worry, I planned for this contingency. The two of us will stay together while I send the guys on the bus. I'll explain the rest later, but for now, we need to get going," I told him.

Once everyone was ready to depart, we climbed into the truck. Around forty-five minutes had passed by the time we pulled into the bus station parking lot. Everything looked as quiet as I'd hoped. I pulled out the money I had packed for Tio's cousin and handed it to him. That seemed to be the moment it all hit him.

"Jorge told me about you and how you've helped him through the years. I am sure that, in his eyes, laying his life down for you and the rest of the crew was a better way to go than slowly dying in a hospital bed.

"It's been an honor and I want you to tell your family how much we loved Tio," I said as we shook hands. "Take care of yourself and your loved ones."

We all piled out the truck and walked over to the seats to wait for the bus. I sat by the window and watched the highway for any sign of trouble. Ramon and Cantrelle came and sat beside me while the others took a seat across from us. All we could do was wait.

Chapter Twenty-Two

THE BUS WE INTENDED to take was already parked in its bay, but there was still over an hour to wait before it left. Cantrelle had his long seabag placed between his feet and the rest of us carried small backpacks.

"I assume your rifle is in there?" I questioned.

"Affirmative," he responded.

Ramon had spent much of our time there staring out of the window. I assumed he was on the lookout for trouble as well.

"Tomas, that went to shit real fast tonight and you can bet they are going to be on the hunt for us," he warned.

"You're not wrong there. You all stay here while I make a call," I told them.

I grabbed my phone, walked outside, and once I was out of earshot of everyone, I called China.

"Tomas, are you okay?" she asked.

"Yeah, I'm okay, but we hit a serious snag on the job. Apart from Tio, we're all okay, but it seems the Navy Captain had some different ideas. They tried to kill us, obviously, after the money for themselves. I'll fill you in on everything later, but I need you to get hold of Chivo and Omega. Give them my number and get them to call me," I asked.

"Oh, Tomas, I am so sorry. I don't know what to say. He has always appeared trustworthy and there has never been any red flags around him," she added sadly.

"Hey, for all you know, someone could have recently got to him. You know how it is with things like this, everyone knows someone who knows someone. It's not your fault. You'll probably find he has some family connection cartel-wise somewhere," I tried to reassure her.

"Well, I'm still going to look into him later, but for now, let's stay on track. I'll get hold of the guys as soon as I can."

She didn't waste any time and hung up. I sat on the curb and waited for the call, and hoped they would contact me quickly. I didn't have to wait long and a couple of minutes the phone rang.

"Hey, Tomas, China just called and said you were in a jam. What'd ya need," asked Chivo, the urgency very evident in his voice.

"Thanks for calling so quickly, man. I need you to get hold of Omega and come pick up me and a friend, but come in separate cars. We don't have much time, so I will fill you in on the rest when you get here," I replied with equal gravity.

"No problem, where are you?"

"Pick me up on the east side of the bridge in Frontera. Call me when you get to the bridge."

No problem, consider it done," he confirmed and hung up.

He hadn't finished the words when the phone flashed up a call from Omega. I told him much the same and to reach out to Chivo who'd explain the rest before he agreed and hung up.

I felt a light sense of relief that I had managed to speak to them both so quickly. I hurried back inside and sat next to Ramon and Cantrelle again.

"Ramon, I've been doing some thinking, we both know they are probably setting up roadblocks and initiating a manhunt for at least one American. I want you to go with the others on the bus to Villahermosa. I have already reached out to Chivo and Omega to take me and Cantrelle to Progreso."

"Is that wise, Tomas?" he said with a concerned look.

"It will take us a while to get there, but I have asked them to come in two cars and one of them will act as lead car and advise of any roadblocks or major problems before we get there. I want you to go straight to Cozumel and help Jeff with Maria. I promise I will be there as quickly as I can," I explained.

"Just watch your ass," he told me as he got up and hugged me.

"Get your stuff and let's get outta here," I told Cantrelle.

He followed me away from the station and down a back road.

"Where we headin', Cap?"

"There's a bridge about two miles west of us. We can get there using back roads to avoid being seen. Once we get there, we can hide out under the bridge until the ride I have arranged arrives,"

I looked at my watch and saw it was just after midnight. We made our way down some residential dirt roads that ran two blocks off the highway. There was a flashing glow from TVs in some windows, but the majority were in darkness. It was so quiet that our footsteps set off some dogs, so we made several trunks down different roads until we reached the river.

We soon reached the bridge and climbed the embankment underneath and waited for the call.

"Do you mind if I ask who's coming to get us?" inquired Cantrelle.

"They are my taxi drivers. Every time I go to a new country, I find a couple of very trustworthy taxi drivers. They always know where to get whatever you need and, most important, they know how to get around unnoticed," I explained.

"Gotcha, makes sense," he agreed.

We both sat there quietly, lost in our own thoughts. I've known Chivo and Omega for many years. Chivo was roughly my age and had three small children. Whenever I went back to the States, I always used to buy shoes, backpacks and school supplies for them. I met Omega through Chivo when I needed someone to get me to Del Carmen. He was a bit younger than me but both were extremely trustworthy. My relationship with them was more of a professional one compared to the crew who were family.

Close to an hour had passed when my phone finally buzzed.

"Tomas, we are both here," confirmed Chivo, "but there's a problem. There is a roadblock already set up at the other end of the bridge. Where exactly are you?"

"We're under the bridge," I told him. "Have Omega ready to take the lead, and my associate and I will get in the car with you."

He told us to stand by and I held my hand up to instruct Cantrelle to wait. Chivo stayed on the line and I heard his breathing increasing. A few minutes later he told us he was clear, and I motioned to Cantrelle to move. We grabbed our bags and scampered to the top of the embankment, and found Chivo's car right next to the bridge. We dove in the back seat and huddled down.

"Let's go, Chivo. Give Omega a call and have him run a couple of miles in front of us. We're going to Progreso and I'll pay you both a thousand dollars U.S. when we get there."

"You got it," he declared as he grabbed his phone, called Omega and passed on what I'd said.

He told us we were clear a few minutes later and we sat up. I quickly reached over and shook his hand in thanks.

"It's good to see ya, how are the kids?" I said.

"They are doing good... growing up too fast. Do you mind me asking why the Feds are after you both?"

"We had a diesel deal go bad and now we need to get back to Progreso," I admitted.

"No problemo, we'll get you both there," he answered positively.

"I know you will, my friend," I confirmed as I patted him on the shoulder.

I scrunched down in the back seat and pulled out my phone to check my messages. There weren't any so I decided to update China with a message which read—

En-route with Chivo. Send a text if you need me.

Her reply came back straight away—

Okay, stay safe!

I put my phone away and allowed my eyes to close for a few minutes. The events must have caught up with me and I slept for almost an hour. By the time I woke, we were in a small town some ten miles from the bridge to Ciudad Del Carmen. I looked over and Cantrelle was still asleep with his head against the window.

Maybe even his engines had worn down. I leaned forward between the seats.

"Chivo, let's slow down a bit and let Omega get a bit further ahead of us," I suggested.

"Si, you got it," he replied.

He eased off the accelerator, and our pace slowed.

"Is there a problem, my friend?" he queried.

"I was just thinking, if they had a roadblock in Frontera, I'm pretty sure they would have one up here in Del Carmen. If that happens, I want you to drop us off while you and Omega go on ahead. "Make your way to Playa Caracol on the east side of Del Carmen and get a room at the Fiesta Hotel. It's right by the beach. Get a room that you can park in front of so we know which room you're in. It may take us a while, but we'll get there on foot." I explained.

"I got it, where do you want me to drop you if needed?" he continued.

"There is a wooded area before you get to the bridge on the south side; that will do." I suggested.

"Si, Tomas. I will stay on the phone with Omega until this is over."

"Perfect."

He got on the phone to Omega and I decided it was time to wake Cantrelle. I gave him a nudge and he sprang to life like he'd simply been looking out the window. I explained the plan to him and he simply smiled.

"Another swim, eh, Cap." He laughed.

It brought a smile to my face, although I didn't share one iota of his enthusiasm to be back in the water. I didn't know whether to chuckle or fume once I realized I would have to swim in my underwear if I wanted dry clothes.

We only had to wait twenty minutes to have my suspicion confirmed when Chivo turned and said, "You were right, Tomas. Omega is going through a roadblock right now."

"*Damn it,*" I thought, even if it was an obvious expectation.

"Once we get past this little town, I will have you drop us off," I instructed.

No one said anything for the next few minutes until I broke the silence.

"Cantrelle, when the car stops, we'll both haul it out on your side and hit the woods."

He grabbed his bag and placed it firmly on his lap, "Just tell me when."

We drove along a far emptier-than-I-would-have-liked road for a couple of miles. I watched ahead as we passed the outskirts of town and started on a long curve in the road. I knew we could have waited until we got a little closer, but I knew once we'd made our way down to the bay, a walk across the beach would be an easy proposition. We had four hours until daylight... and counting.

"Right here, Chivo," I alerted him and he came to an abrupt halt.

Cantrelle and I sprang from the back of the car like a pair of repeat-fire jack-in-the-boxes and sprinted into the woods. There was a quarter moon in the sky but under the jungle canopy, it was pitch black. We both pulled out our mag-lights to illuminate our way. We might not have bothered as the brush was extremely thick in places and it wasn't like we could see much in front anyway. The dense foliage restricted us to slow moving, especially when we had to go around obstacles.

It was a sticky, hot night and our constant effort meant we sweated a lot, but thankfully, there was a lack of mosquitos—likely due to the equal lack of water. Our journey to the beach took nearly an hour. The mangroves grew out into the water, but it wasn't as bad as it could have been. It just meant in places we had to wade through the water, sometimes waist deep.

So much for dry clothes, at *least I won't have to swim in my underwear.*

We didn't say much between the two of us, we just concentrated our energy on the journey. I knew Cantrelle could probably swim around the bay, but there was no way I could. I needed to launch from near the bridge as it was only a few hundred yards. I knew if we made it to the other side before daylight, we could avoid being seen.

After thirty minutes of humping through the vegetation, I spotted the bridge. What I couldn't see were any roadblocks or fed trucks. We stayed close to the jungle for cover and made our way closer to the bridge. Eventually, I saw the roadblock, but they'd set it up about a hundred yards before the bridge. From our previous angle, we were already past them. All we had to do was swim across and then hump it for about three miles to the hotel.

Once we made it to the bridge, the two of us waded out into the water and swam slowly through the pilings underneath. Cantrelle powered ahead easily, but about halfway across, I grabbed onto one of them for a quick rest. There were some small pieces of rusted iron that I was able to grab onto around all the oyster shells. The choppy water made it harder to cling, and I ended up cutting my hands on the shells.

I soon let go and opted to swim backstroke to conserve some energy. By the time we reached the two-thirds mark, I was struggling. My arms and my legs were burning, and I genuinely felt like I wouldn't make it. Cantrelle stayed close, but the swim was nothing more than a short stroll to the bottom of the garden; his breathing barely raised above a rest.

I told him I had to rest, so I pulled off my shirt and wrapped it around my hand to protect it as I grabbed another of the pilings. It took a few minutes, but the burn in my legs began to subside. Cantrelle simply treaded water next to me with his bag.

"How the hell do you swim with that thing?"

"It's waterproof, man. If you trap some air inside, it damn well floats on its own," he came back.

As if a penny dropped in his head, Cantrelle unstrapped it and pushed it over to me.

"Hold on to it, Cap, it'll save you some effort," he suggested.

I grabbed it from him and jammed it under my stomach to use it as a float. It made all the difference and I paddled my way across.

"Shit, I should have used this from the start," I joked.

We were eventually within touching distance of the shore on the far side and I put my foot down to touch the bottom. We both stood up, waded our way out of the water and onto the beach. I looked at my watch and estimated we had about an hour before daylight.

"Don't suppose you got any dry clothes in your bag?" I checked.

"Sorry, this was my last pair too," he answered.

"Thought so."

We both unbuttoned our pants and took off our shirts, wrung them out as best we could and put them back on again.

"We'll walk down the beach until we can get up on the back roads. There's a taxi station on the outskirts of town, some two miles from here," I told him once we were dressed.

"Works for me," he confirmed.

We walked about fifteen minutes behind the low-end houses that lined the beach and came to one that had a low brick wall, about waist height, around the property. We leapt over the wall and quickly made our way around the side of the house to the street.

Daylight was fast approaching and there was a glow in the east; we had about thirty minutes before people started going to work. Everything was quiet and the streetlights were still on as we made our way toward the taxi station. It was on the main highway, so I decided our best approach was to wait in an alley and flag one down.

We waited a few minutes and I saw one heading down the highway in the direction of the station. I waited until he got close, then stepped out on the curb and waved it down. He stopped right in front and the two of us jumped in.

The driver didn't seem overly surprised to see two Americans, but it was a port town with a lot of foreigners, something I hoped would work in our favor. I instructed him to take us to a small restaurant about six blocks from the hotel, just in case he was aware the Feds were on the lookout for two Americans. The drive took about ten minutes, and just as the sun peeked above the horizon, we pulled up in front of the restaurant. There was a young girl sweeping the sidewalk as we loitered and waited for the taxi to drive off. As soon as it left, we smiled at the girl and walked to the hotel.

When we arrived, I spotted Chivo's taxi outside one of the rooms and Omega's parked on the other side of the lot by the street. I walked up and tapped the door lightly, and to my relief Chivo opened straight away. We quickly entered and I grabbed the nearest chair to sit on.

"Where's Omega?" I asked when I noticed his absence.

"He's next door," Chivo answered.

I asked him to go and get Omega and the two of them came back a few minutes later. Omega looked like he had just woken up.

"Omega, I need you to pick up some jeans and T-shirts for Cantrelle and me," I said as I reached in my bag and pulled out a few notes from the packet Tio gave me.

I leaned over the table and we wrote our sizes down on a sheet of hotel paper before I handed it to him with some money.

"I leaned over to Chivo, who was sitting on the edge of the bed and gave him some money as well.

"Can you get us some food and coffee while the two of us clean up?" I asked.

"Si, no problem."

"Make yourself comfortable," I said to Cantrelle as they left, "I will be out in a minute."

I knew it was a nice little hotel with larger-than-normal bathrooms and very comfortable beds because I'd stayed there a few times before. I stripped out of my wet clothes and stepped into the running shower. The hot water instantly calmed the tension in my muscles. I leaned my head against the wall and let the water cascade down on me and did my best to think of nothing other than the hot water. I felt like I could sleep for a week.

Chapter Twenty-Three

I WRAPPED A TOWEL around myself after my relaxing shower and told Cantrelle it was his turn. He took his bag into the bathroom and closed the door. I slumped on the bed and took out my phone. I tried to call Jeff so we could update each other, but it went straight to voicemail. I decided to send him a text—

I'm on my way back and should be in Cozumel by early morning. Call me.

I also called Diana, who picked up straight away despite it being quite early.

"Tomas, are you okay?" she asked, but there was something about her voice that sounded funny.

"Yeah, it's me. Everything is alright at the moment. Are you okay?" I fired back quickly.

"I'm fine, we were just worried about you."

"Who are we?" I quickly asked in confusion as hardly anyone knew about the job.

"Ummm," she said with a momentary pause, "everyone here at the marina. I was expecting you to call last night... when you finished the job."

She sounded really nervous, but I decided not to let on that I suspected anything or that I knew something was wrong.

"Everything is just fine here. It was a long night, and I just overslept. We're in Villa Hermosa and will catch the evening flight tomorrow to Cancun," I told her.

"Do you need to be picked up?" she offered.

"We're all good. I have someone picking us up. I will see you at the marina around ten."

"Okay, will see you then," she finished, and we hung up.

I laid there quietly for a moment. My sixth sense told me something was amiss. That was why I told her we were 160 miles in the opposite direction. I'd learned to trust my instincts because they had saved my ass several times. I reached out to China next via text—

I'm out. Will call you tomorrow.

She texted back shortly after—

Be careful. People are looking everywhere for you. Most have just started looking toward Villa Hermosa for you, but they've set up roadblocks all the way to Del Carmen and Palenque.

Do they know who I am?

No, they are just looking for two American men traveling together.

Thanks, I will call you tomorrow.

I relaxed back on the bed and waited for Chivo and Omega to come back. Despite the new concerns, my biggest worry was Maria.

I hoped she was okay and it sounded like Jeff had things under control when we last spoke. It didn't stop me remembering that the cartels often kill people whether payment is made or not. I hope that Jeff's political connection through his father would be an added incentive for them not to hurt her. Either way, Ramon would be there soon and many of his contacts were on the other side of the law.

If they hurt her, there won't be a place on the planet they can hide.

In case even that wasn't enough, I tried to think of any added insurance I could bring to the situation... and then my mind hit upon Javier. Just the idea made the hairs on my neck stand up and I shivered.

Javier was around 6'2" with curly black hair, good teeth, an olive complexion and a solidly muscular build. He spoke with a British accent and was always serious. I'd never heard him laugh, but he did get a sinister grin in the corners of his mouth when something amused him. He was of Mexican descent but grew up in Europe. He almost always dressed in black and was an expert in martial arts and combat—he was one man you didn't fuck with. At one time, he was in MI6 Special Forces, someone heavily involved in the Balkan wars, and was now a straight-up mercenary.

I didn't have a number for him, but I was sure I could get a message to him via his brother Antonio. He was a boat captain and a friend of Magdelano. That was how I first met Javier. He also retired about the same time as I did, so I knew there would be a good chance he was home. I scrolled through my cell and tapped his number.

"Hey, Tomas, my good friend. How is it going?" he answered.

"Good and bad, long story. I am sorry to cut to business but I need to get hold of Javier," I cut in quickly.

"Everything okay?" he said seriously.

"No idea. Jeff's sister has been kidnapped and while we should be able to handle it, I could really use Javier's back-up if he is in the country. Can you get him a message to meet me in Cozumel tomorrow night?" I asked in some desperation.

"You bet, I will get word to him now."

I expressed my gratitude and we hung up.

There was no doubt in my mind that Javier would help if he was available. We'd been close friends and I still trusted him with my life. His involvement would easily tip things in our favor. I'd seen him do things to people that would scare the shit out of anyone. He was like a machine, similar to Cantrelle in some ways, and had the reflexes of a cat. If you were a threat, you were already dead before you knew it.

I hadn't long finished the call when Chivo came in with a sack of tamales and cups of coffee. I got up and sat at the small table with him.

"How'd it look out there?" I asked.

"Normal, my friend, I couldn't see any sign of any federal trucks or local police," he answered.

"That's a good sign. When we leave, we'll do the same as before and give Omega a five-minute head start," I suggested to his agreement.

Centrelle soon finished his shower, and we were just finishing breakfast when Omega returned with two bags of clothes. He picked up two pairs of jeans and two navy-blue T-shirts.

"Perfect, thanks, now get yourself something to eat while we change," I told him.

Chivo explained the plan to him as he ate, then I told him the route I wanted him to take out of town once we were dressed. When he was finished, he grabbed his keys and went on his way five minutes ahead of us. As soon as my watch beeped, having completed its countdown, we walked out to the taxi and followed behind. I let Cantrelle have the front seat so I could stretch out in the back. I was awake until we crossed the east-bound bridge off the island before I laid out and took a nap.

The journey remained uneventful. I woke up periodically to the sound of Chivo talking to Omega on the phone as he got status reports from up ahead. The journey took us nearly seven hours to get to Merida, and I awoke feeling more refreshed than I had the previous few days. Cantrelle was laid back in the front and looked asleep, but with him it wasn't easy to tell.

I poked my head through and suggested to Chivo, "Tell Omega to take the turn by the plaza and head straight to the marina."

He picked up the phone and relayed my instructions. I looked at my watch as we pulled into the marina lot and it was 1500. I told Chivo to park by the containers at the back of the lot and Omega followed close behind. It was ecstasy to get out and stretch our legs after the drive. I walked over to both of them and gave them a hug before I reached into my bag, pulled out $3k from Tio's packet and gave each of them $1500.

"Thank you, truly, guys. I owe you big time for this. There is an extra five hundred in there for both of you. I really appreciate you coming through for me. Drinks on me next time," I told them.

" Give us a call, anytime," replied Chivo.

We hugged once again, they went back to their cars and left together. Cantrelle and I walked around the container and climbed into the SUV. The keys were in the console where I asked Tio to leave them. I paused, just for a moment as I picked them up, and thought of him. It still didn't feel real.

"Rest in peace, brother," I whispered as I made the sign of the cross. I started the truck and drove it across the lot. It had already become a typical sunny day and it appeared our luck had finally run out. Everyone was out and about early and the traffic was heavy. I was hungry but waited until we had passed the outskirts of town to stop at a roadside taco stand. I ordered us some food and we quickly ate it in the truck before we hit the road again toward Cancun. I reckoned it would take us about two and a half hours.

Let's just hope we don't run into issues along the way.

As we drove along, we passed the road where Ramon and I stashed our money. I trusted Cantrelle and was half-tempted to pick it up so we could avoid having to come back for it. However, I decided against it in case we had to ditch the truck at any point and run.

That made me think of Ramon, and I pulled out my phone and gave him a call. As expected, he answered almost immediately.

"Hey, Cap, where are you at?"

"Cantrelle and I should be in Cancun in around two hours," I advised

"Shit, you guys made good time," he exclaimed.

"Have you talked to Jeff?"

"No, he's just not answering or returning calls. I left three messages."

"I tried a couple of times too and got the same. Listen, find yourself a place in Cancun to hang out for the next couple of hours and we will come pick you up."

"Will do, see you in a bit," he replied as he ended the call.

"Knowing Ramon, he probably has several ex-girlfriends in the area," I chuckled to myself.

"Everything alright?" Cantrelle asked curiously.

"As it can be," I replied. "We're going to pick up Ramon, then I can drop you wherever you need to go."

"Sounds good. I stay at the marina, three doors down from Diana," he confirmed.

"Cool, I can drop you there."

The two of us remained silent for the rest of the trip. As we entered Cancun, I called Ramon.

"We're here. I'm just coming up to the Euro Hotel," I told him.

"Nice, pull in there. I'm in Room 211 on the second floor. I picked it as I guessed it would be one of the first you passed," he stated.

"I'll pick you up in front of the lobby."

"Roger that," he confirmed.

We pulled into the hotel, and I parked out front of the lobby. A few minutes later, Ramon came strolling out the double doors. It looked like he'd literally thrown on his clothes and ran out the door. He jogged over and jumped in the back with a smile. I put the truck in drive and headed toward the ferry dock. Ramon must have sensed I was not in the best of moods and worried as he was unusually quiet.

Once we came to a stop in a parking place on the ferry, I climbed out and called China.

"Where are you?" she asked breathlessly.

"I'm back in Cancun. We just boarded the ferry."

"Oh, thank God. The Navy ship just got back, and I heard reports of a body."

I took a deep breath in. "That must be Tio, unless it is one of Don Miguel's thugs," I stated.

"Tomas, fuck, *Tio*?! What happened?" she asked breathlessly.

"We didn't know, but he was dying from cancer. He chose to go out on his own terms and to save us. I will tell you the rest later. I'm absolutely shattered by it, but there are other things to worry about right now."

The memory of him telling us is still fresh in my brain. I hated that I left him, regardless of the situation. But I had to respect his wishes. It was what he wanted.

"Just call me if you need me. As far as I know, they are still looking in the surrounding area here, so if you're in Cancun, you should be good. I'll update you if I know more. Just don't make waves!" she ordered.

"Yes, ma'am," I responded as we hung up.

Ramon and Cantrelle strolled over to get something to drink from the concession stand, and I rested up in the truck with A/C on full and blowing in my face. I wanted to go over the next stage of the plan and that helped fire up my tired mind. I needed to call Jeff to find out what had happened with Maria, and I knew I'd best make a quick personal call to Diana. It wasn't like I could slip by and onto my boat given she worked about fifty feet from it.

The thought of my boat sent my mind off on a tangent. I contemplated how nice it would be to simply cast the lines off and go anchor my lagoon until everything had blown over. I couldn't do that. If Jeff needed my help, there was no way I would let him down. I had always been, and always would be, loyal to my friends.

Just as the ferry made its landing on the other side, Cantrelle and Ramon climbed back in the truck. They handed me a water bottle that I quickly consumed. As soon as the gate lifted, we drove off. I saw the marina as soon as we reached the top of the hill and a sense of relief washed over me. It had only been a couple of days but felt like ten.

I turned down the marina road and rumbled into the shell lot behind the Tiki. Rather than park in my usual space, I rolled down to the fuel dock to split the distance between the marina house and my boat. We all climbed out and I walked over to Cantrelle and shook his hand.

"Thanks for the help," I told him. "I think we can take it from here."

"Roger, Cap. I'll be around so just shout out if you need any help."

Ramon did the same, and then we headed back to the boat. I swore I heard Cantrelle whistling happily. As we strolled on the boardwalk by the sea wall, Ramon looked over at Tracy's catamaran. I just looked beyond that at the Tiki. There was a decent crowd in, even without a band. As I peered over, Diana came out of the kitchen with two trays of food.

"You go ahead. I'll be there in five," I told Ramon as I threw him the keys.

He caught them and headed to the *San Blas*, as I walked up towards the Tiki. Diana saw me as I walked up to the deck. She gave me a huge grin, and wandered enthusiastically over and gave me a hug.

"I am so glad you're back. I was worried when I didn't hear back from you last night," she admitted happily.

"Yeah, sorry, we got a little busy but everything went to plan."

"Cool. I am here until twelve. Will I see you later tonight?" she asked with a wicked smile.

"Sure. Come down to the boat later. Ramon and I are still trying to track down Jeff. We might need to catch an early flight to Miami, but I'll be here all evening.

She grinned and kissed me on the cheek, then returned to serving the lively throng at the bar.

Away from the Tiki, the marina was unusually quiet in terms of sight and sound. I could even hear my A/C unit humming from on top of the wheelhouse as I approached. There was a second reason I omitted the truth to Diana. I couldn't shake the notion that she knew more about the day than she had or was letting on. I decided to say nothing about Tio, the Navy boat or Maria's kidnapping until I had spoken to Jeff.

"Assuming I can find him," I muttered.

I heard the sound of the shower as I stepped into my Sala. While Ramon got himself sorted, I walked straight down to my cabin to check my toothpick to see if anyone had tried to enter the boat. Much to my surprise, it was still there. I went back to the Sala, grabbed a beer from the fridge and sat on the couch to make sense of the last couple of days.

I tried Jeff on my cell phone but once again it just cut to voicemail.

"Shit," I said as I tossed it across the coffee table.

Where is that man?

My thoughts turned to what I'd do next once I extracted myself from the shitstorm I had gotten myself into. I remember my time in Nicaragua from a few years back when I spent some time with a friend who was a commercial lobster fisherman. He invited me out with him several times over a couple of months. It was a good experience, but I quickly filed that one under "Too Much Hard Work."

The place was a different matter. There was a nice little marina where he docked his boat and I really enjoyed the atmosphere. It was one of those small fishing towns with a decent economy thanks to the lobster industry, plus friendly people and great food.

"It would be a good place to ride out the winter months," I thought as I closed my eyes.

I was just about to drift off when Ramon appeared, having finished his shower and dressed. He must have noticed a distant look in my eye.

"What's up?"

"I tried to call Jeff and it's gone straight to voicemail again," I told him wearily.

"So, what do you wanna do?" he asked.

"I don't know there's not much we can do... until we find him anyway."

I reached in my bag and placed Tio's packet on the table. I quickly scribbled a note to keep track of what we'd used.

"Take some notes from there and go get us a burger or something from the Tiki. I am just going to shower myself.

"Will do," he answered.

He casually grabbed some money and disappeared out of the cabin. I wandered down to my room and decided to look at my emails first. Much to my disappointment, there wasn't anything of importance. The shower freshened my mind and my body, and I planned the next move. I knew there were chores to do, washing for a start, but that could wait for another day.

Once I'd finished in the shower, I dressed and crashed out on the bed to wait for Ramon to come back.

Chapter Twenty-Four

WHAT ENDED UP BEING some considerable time later, I woke to find Diana resting asleep next to me. I looked at my watch and saw it was almost 3 am. I assume Ramon had either not been able to wake me, not the first time, or simply not bothered.

My stomach growled loudly, and I eased myself out of bed and stepped into the Salon. I noticed Ramon was not on the sofa and assumed he'd made his way over to Tracy's catamaran. He'd left a to-go container in the microwave that contained a now-soggy burger inside. It didn't inspire me so I tossed in the trash and made some eggs instead.

I felt wide awake after I'd eaten and made use of the quiet time. I slipped down to my cabin and grabbed my laundry and walked up to the laundry room in the marina house that was for all to use.

The marina was totally silent now. The Tiki was closed, and all there was to light the way was the glow of the parking lot lights. I put my washing on and headed back to the *San Blas* in case Diana woke up. I went and checked my phone and emails again, then remembered the camera was still in my desk drawer..

I grabbed a fresh coffee, reattached it to the computer and put it on fast-forward so I could watch the images at an accelerated rate, and then I saw it. A dark figure stepped across the dock and onto the *San Blas*. My eyes widened as I leaned forward and pressed rewind, only to be infuriated when I saw who it was.

I grabbed my phone and dialed Ramon, who answered after a few rings. I could tell I woke him.

"Ramon, where are you?" I asked.

"With Tracy on the catamaran. What's up?"

"Can you get back to the boat ASAP, it looks like we have a situation?" I said urgently.

"Sure, be there in a few minutes," he added before the phone cut off.

He was breathless and covered in sweat when he arrived in the cabin a few minutes later.

"What's happening, man?"

"You didn't have to run," I smiled apologetically.

"Hey, if you've called me at 3:30 in the morning, it must be an emergency," he replied.

I leaned forward and pressed play on the camera footage. We both watched as the video showed a suspicious-looking Cantrelle as he looked around, and when he thought it was all clear, he climbed aboard the *San Blas* and tried to open the hatch with his penknife. Ramon's eyes were as wide as mine.

"Just who the fuck is this guy, Tomas? I thought you said he was one of Jeff's people?"

"He is, but maybe he's someone else's person as well. Either way, we're about to find out."

I grabbed my phone and called Cantrelle; he was obviously asleep as well.

"Listen, sorry to wake you, I got some news from Jeff. Can you come down to my boat so we can all talk straight away?" I lied.

He agreed and hung up. I told Ramon he'd be with us in a few minutes. He poured himself a coffee as I slipped into my room to grab my other 45. caliber pistol from my nightstand. I was careful not to wake Diana. She was best left where she was.

I returned to the Salon and grabbed a seat near the window so I could watch out for Cantrelle. We just waited there with our coffee. I hoped we were about to get some answers. Minutes later, I spotted him as he walked across the marina parking lot and toward the boat. Ramon moved to the door and clenched his fist in anticipation.

"Easy, brother, have a seat. Let's let this play out," I told him.

"Alright, but if I don't like what I hear or this asshole has anything to do with Maria's kidnapping, I'm going to bury the fucker," he snarled as he moved back to his chair.

Cantrelle walked in shortly after. Ramon sat on the sofa and I was perched on a chair on the other side of the Salon.

"Hey Cantrelle, thanks for coming over so quickly. Take a seat on the sofa," I gestured.

He slid the door shut and sat on the far end of the sofa.

"We have a few questions. I wonder if you could explain this..." I said grandly as I picked up the laptop and showed him the screen. Displayed was a still image of Cantrelle as he tried to force open the hatch on my boat. He looked about as stunned as Ramon. I leaned over the table and picked up my pistol, and pointed it directly at his head.

"Now, if you have some way to explain this, I suggest you divulge it quickly," I threatened.

He paused for a moment before replying, "Okay, wait a minute, Cap. There is an explanation."

Without warning, Ramon leapt up from the sofa and landed a powerful right hook on the side of Cantrelle's head. If it had been a cartoon, his head would've spun around. He shook his head and wiped blood from the corner of his mouth.

"Explain faster or you're going to be a permanent part of the reef out there, fucker," growled Ramon as he stood over him fist clenched ready to punch him again.

"He's FBI, now drop the fucking gun," yelled Diana from behind us.

I turned around and she was standing, legs apart, with a gun pointed right at me. I was stunned and Ramon's expression showed he was the same as he sat back on the sofa. My gun pointed at Cantrelle's head.

What in the absolute fuck is going on?

"You got some credentials there, Diana... or whoever the fuck you are?" I asked calmly. A small twinge of irritation filled me that I'd slept with her and didn't even see the clues that pointed to her being undercover. Fucking idiot. I should have known.

"Tomas, lower your weapon and we can talk about it," she replied equally at ease.

"Ladies first," I gestured with a nod.

"Okay, Okay, Tomas, I'm doing that," she responded as she lowered her weapon deliberately slow.

I made a slow arc with my arm and pointed the gun at her.

"Now, take a rest with your 'partner'," I gestured to her.

Ramon stood up and she moved toward the sofa with her hands in the air. I took the gun off her and moved further away so I could watch both of them.

Diana's eyes looked immensely sad as she peered up and said, "Please, Tomas, put the gun down and don't do anything you'll regret. We really can explain. We've got nothing to do with Maria's disappearance—I promise you! We can even help you with that."

Ramon opened his mouth to say something but I stopped him before he could start. I laid my gun on the side so I could still grab it quickly if necessary.

"Go head, explain," I demanded.

She looked over at Cantrelle and he gave the affirmative nod. She took a deep breath before she started.

"About seven months ago, the US agreed to work with the Mexican government on a joint task force to take down the cartels. The main target was Chapo Guzman, the leader of the Sinaloa Cartel.

"And, what exactly does this have to do with Cantrelle trying to break into my damn boat?!" I snapped.

"Give me a chance. We tried sending Mexican undercover operatives into their organization, but they disappeared, presumed killed, so we tried a different approach. We had info that Jeffryn was a level player on this end and we figured that would be an easier way to infiltrate the organization."

"I'm sorry, but you can't expect me to believe Jeff is a drug dealer!" I said in disbelief.

"We don't either, but this trip you guys made collecting the stolen diesel was a job for Miguel Fuentes, and he is a high-level player. Our place was a deep cover operation to infiltrate everything from this side. We already have people in place throughout the cartel thanks to this backdoor approach."

"Fine, but you still haven't explained what this has to do with me and my boat," I shouted in frustration.

"Honestly, you were an unknown that we were trying to make known," she said succinctly. "You showed up the other day and on your first night you were at Jeffryn's party talking to Miguel Fuentes and his brother. We ran background checks on you and that turned up nothing, so Cantrelle was told to find out more. Nothing more."

In other circumstances, I might have just tried to get out of the situation as quickly as possible.

I'd left all this type of shit behind. And now here you are getting dragged back in.

I'd have never gotten involved if I had even thought something, or someone, was off. I'd always been able to spot someone who wasn't what they said they were, and yet these two had totally slipped past my usually refined bullshit spotter.

There was a reason they found very little about me because I'd purposely made myself a ghost once I left that life behind. I thought it would protect me and as it turned out, it caused more focus than an unknown really ought to warrant. The reason that Ramon and I weren't disabling them and heading out to open water... Maria.

We may have had a lot of non-legal help on our side, but the FBI had serious resources. If we had both sides of the law working with us, the chances that we could rescue her increased. Ramon looked over and his expression told me he'd already worked out what I was thinking. We didn't have to like it, and in the words of Negan from *The Walking Dead,* they'd 'shit in our scrambled eggs,' but there was a deal already hinted at, one that would require us to eat it in return for getting Maria back safely. There was only one answer.

"Right, so what can you do to help?" I queried.

"Since your incident with the Mexican Navy, Miguel and Victor are on the run. We want to find him and see if we can get him to turn States Evidence against Guzman," she stated.

"Like Jeff, assuming you can find him. How exactly do you propose to do that?" I shrugged.

"Miguel knows that he is a dead man if he stays in Mexico. At first, we worked on the premise that the kidnapping of Maria was Miguel's way of getting leverage to get Jeffryn to use his family ship to move drugs, but it is actually an end game for Miguel. He planned to rob you and the cartels, then disappear... that is... until the Navy Captain tried to do the same. Despite that, you somehow made it out with the money."

"Money?" I questioned, "I have no idea what you are talking about."

She smiled, almost as if to show she knew I lied, but then continued. "The Mexican Navy already has the Captain and twelve others incarcerated and I guess they'll try them for treason. Don Miguel is on the run and he has already struck a deal with Jeffryn to get his sister back."

"What?! Do you actually know where Jeff is after all?" I fired back angrily.

"He's in our safe house now," she admitted, "and we have tried to keep the airwaves clear to avoid anything getting out."

I stood up with purpose. "I need to see him… now!"

"Hang on, let me make a phone call and see what I can sort out," she asked.

"Make all the fucking calls you need. Make it happen!"

I gestured to Ramon to follow me out to the deck. As soon as I closed the door behind us he spoke up with concern. "Tomas, do you honestly trust these people?"

"No," I shook my head, "not one bit, not yet anyway. I am going to go with them once they arrange this. I need you to stay here. Once we're gone, get on the phone to Magdaleno and see if Antonio managed to get hold of Javier. Hopefully, he got my message and is in the country."

The look of concern worsened on Ramon's face. "Do you really think you're gonna need that kind of action," he questioned.

I got why he was so worried. Javier wasn't exactly a loose cannon, but he was the sort of man who could wipe out a whole village and you'd never even see him. He could literally be the Ghost of Death.

"I hear you." I nodded. "But I ain't taking any chances with Maria's life on the line, not to mention our own."

"Alright man, just let me know when you hear something. I'll be here waiting."

We returned to the Salon, and Cantrelle extended his hand.

"I'm sorry, Tomas, it honestly wasn't about you at all."

The best I could offer was an untrusting scowl. I wasn't about to shake his hand after the way he'd lied and used us.

"Ramon, why don't you stay back in case any of our friends show up?" I suggested.

"Fair enough," he mumbled as Diana finished her phone call.

"Okay, let's go," she stated.

Diana walked off ahead with Cantrelle and I followed behind. She said nothing as I brought up the rear, and she still had a deeply sad look in her eyes. I just glanced at her as I walked past. Nobody said anything as we trod purposely down the dock toward the parking lot. I got the impression Diana wanted to say something, just not in front of Cantrelle.

My mind spanned with confusion over Diana. I had enjoyed our time together and genuinely thought we hit it off. She had been able to both surprise and enamor me during our time together, but now I had no idea if any of it was real. Even if she protested she'd been genuine about everything, I couldn't possibly believe her after such a betrayal? I knew that my silence likely caused her pain, but it was better that right now than me allowing my emotions to take control, especially with so much on the line.

When we reached the truck, I jumped in the back seat and closed the door forcefully behind me. Diana looked at me through the window, then slowly walked around and got in the passenger side. It took us only twenty minutes to drive to the safe house and we did it in stony silence. It turned out to be a condo near the ferry dock.

The parking lot was full, but I didn't notice anything suspicious or that I didn't like. We got out the truck and as I walked around the back, Diana grabbed me by the arm. I at least turned to look at her, but I had nothing to say.

"I want you to know what's happened between us, that is real, on my side anyway. For what it's worth, I am sorry. I was only doing my job."

That last part enraged me slightly, but I took a deep breath and paused before I responded.

"Right now, I need to see Jeff. We can talk about this later," I said sternly.

I didn't bother to wait for a response. There was nothing she could say that would change how deceived and untrusting I felt toward her at that moment. The two of them led me to a service elevator that we took up to the eleventh floor. It wasn't the top, but close enough. Always something to keep in mind in dangerous circumstances. I proceeded to follow them to a room across the hall.

The first thing I saw when we entered was an array of computer screens and laptops with two men sitting at the makeshift console. On various different feeds, they watched cameras that showed the elevator, the hallway, even the parking lot below and the ferry dock.

I was ushered into another room and there we found Jeff sitting with a couple of other men. My friend was sitting by himself at the window while the others looked at maps scattered over the breakfast bar on the other side of the room. Jeff jumped out of his chair as soon as he saw me.

"Tomas!" he shouted brightly, "My friend, it is so good to see you!"

He gave me a big hug.

"Jeff, what the fuck is going on? Are they holding you here?"

"No, it's not like that," he replied with a shake of his head. "Diana approached me yesterday and told me everything. I need their help to get Maria back."

"Does anyone even know where she is being held?" I added quickly.

Before he even had a chance to answer, Diana stepped into the conversation and handed me a photo. It showed two guys getting out of a black SUV with Maria.

"We picked this up from a surveillance camera we have on the other side of the ferry," she explained as she walked to a map on a board. "We used satellite surveillance to follow them and had them travelling south into this area but then we lost them shortly after. Based on the time of the ransom call coming in some ten to fifteen minutes later, we believe she is in a five-mile radius of that point."

I studied the map for a moment.

"There's a lot of properties and buildings in that area. That's a big radius," I said with worry.

"It is, but the guys in the other room aren't just watching camera feeds. They are also looking for any connections to Miguel in that area—anything he owns, frequents, has previously been involved with. We're turning over every stone."

I stood and looked at the map. "Can you excuse us?" I asked firmly, "I need to talk to Jeff privately."

"Sure, you can go out on the balcony. I will go and check on the search," replied Diana.

"We'll go get some cans from the soda machine downstairs, if it's all the same. Butch and Sundance here can come if they stay back," I argued.

There wasn't a spot in that room not bugged. I thought we'd have a fifty-fifty chance outside by the pool area. It was still dark and you could see the lights shimmer off the water in the distance as we walked along the walkway. We stood by the machine with our two shadows someway back.

"Jeff, I'm sorry this is all happening, man," I said as I put my hand on his shoulder. "We have most of the team on it. Ramon is on my boat calling his contact... and I've put a call into Javier."

He just looked back solemnly, a single tear running down his cheek, then his face turned to anger.

"It wasn't supposed to go down like this. Tomas, if they hurt my baby sister, Javier won't be enough. I'll burn everything to the ground," he spat venomously.

"You and Maria are family. We're gonna get her back. Miguel just wants the money, killing her isn't going to get him any closer to getting it, and he can't disappear without it."

Jeff nodded in agreement. He knew as well as I did that Miguel wouldn't throw away his only leverage. I pulled out my phone and one of Diana's men jogged forward and told me we were under "dark conditions" and no cell calls were allowed.

"This is necessary, I assure you."

He radioed up and apparently Diana approved it, then stepped into the background again. I pulled up China's number and reached out to her.

"Hey China, you got any news?" I asked.

"Oh, do I. Tell the FBI goons you're with that Don Moguel has a shell company called PetroPlus Ltd, and it owns an apartment complex on the west side of Cancun called LaBrisa."

I went silent for a minute. I wasn't sure what impressed me more... the fact she knew where I was, that she knew who I was with and that China knew what they were looking for.

"Damn... are you sure?" I asked, just to make sure she had everything right. Even though I already knew deep down she did. She wouldn't say something if she wasn't sure.

"Seriously... yes, I'm sure. An inside connection has reached out and told me that's where Maria is being held."

"You got an address?" I asked, barely needing to.

"Yeah, I'll text it to you."

"Let me know when you get Maria back," she replied and hung up.

"What'd she say? It looks like something is wrong." Jeff interrupted, as I stared at my phone.

"She said she thinks she has info about where Maria is being held—it's a place owned by one of Miguel's shell companies called LaBrisa, an apartment complex."

Jeff's eyes got wide. "I know the place let's go get her and then we can squash that fucker."

We went back up to the eleventh floor, and I called Cantrelle and Diana over. I showed them the address that China had sent over and explained its relevance. She grabbed my phone, without asking, and jogged over to the geeks at the computers to check it out.

"How well do you trust this intel and the person providing it?" questioned Cantrelle.

"The person, unquestionably, the info, I don't know where it came from but if I know her like I do, at least ninety percent."

"Good enough for me," he answered enthusiastically. He walked over to the sliding door and made some radio calls. Several minutes later a group of men walked in dressed in black carrying large bags.

They proceeded to unpack and had everything from night vision and sniper rifles to full-on tactical assault machine guns.

Diana came back from the console and confirmed to Cantrelle that it was all systems go. She disappeared into another room and came back with a bullet-proof vest and a black jacket.

"Maria's important to both of us. We want to come."

"Absolutely not," she spat out with a scoff as she shook her head. "It's too dangerous."

"I wasn't asking you."

She paused, turning to me with a sigh. "Jeff is under protection. It's best if you stay here."

"Like I said... We're going. Now put your personal feelings aside, and make it happen."

Her lips parted before she clenched her jaw and shook her head. I'd hit a sore spot, but honestly, she fucking lied to me and used me. So she really doesn't have a leg to stand on. Especially since they wouldn't even have the information had my contact not gotten it for them.

Without another word, we headed down toward the parking lot and jumped into various vehicles, Diana ended up with me. She was about to take the wheel as Jeff finally spoke up, Diana stopping in her tracks. "I know that place. It's a gated community. I can get us in undetected."

"Is that right?" She asked, glancing at him. "Alright then. You drive."

She tossed him the keys and let him take the driver seat. The urge to get to Maria only intensified as I desperately needed to make sure she was okay.

CHAPTER TWENTY-FIVE

WE DROVE IN TWO partially-split convoys through Central Cancun, then turned off the main freeway and toward the outskirts of town. The decision was made to drive quite fast through the residential streets, partly because Jeff wanted to get there as quickly as possible, and partly to leave as little time as possible for people to tip them off. It was early enough so the streets were quite deserted and it was still quite dark, both working in our favor.

We passed a couple of signs that read Waterfall And Parking, and I leaned forward and asked Jeff, "Where are we heading?"

He pointed out the window. "The apartment complex is on the other side of these hills. There's a partially hidden area that will conceal the trucks. Cantrelle and his man can then hike it through the woods and come out right in their backyard."

It was then Diana's turn to pose a question, "Seriously, how well do you know this area?"

"Better than I should," he grinned slightly manically. "I grew pot all over these hills when I was a teenager."

The pride he had saying that to an FBI agent might as well have been gleaming out in pink neon above the truck. It would have been rude not to smirk. Jeff dropped the lights as we pulled into a parking lot and the other trucks did the same. We then took a rickety track between some concession stands at the back. You could also make out a loud waterfall not too far away, even if you couldn't see it because it was dark.

At the end of the track, he took us about a hundred yards through some tall grass and onto an even worse back road. The trucks bounced up and down in the dips and potholes. At the end, it opened out into a small clearing just big enough for all the vehicles. It was pitch black, bar a sliver of moonlight left before dawn erased it. Everyone congregated at our truck and waited for instructions.

Jeff slammed the truck in park and said. "The apartments are directly over this hill, about three-hundred yards." He pointed out into the darkness. "If you go straight in this direction, you will run into an old logging road and that will take you up the hill. It's pretty overgrown but you'll know it when you see it."

Everyone nodded they followed so far.

"When you make it to the top, you'll see the rear of the apartments at the bottom of it. There are three floors and four apartments per floor. From there, I can't help you but my guess would be the middle floor, hard to approach but close enough to the ground to escape."

"And you're sure it's the right complex?" checked Cantrelle.

"It's the only apartment on this side of town," assured Jeff.

Diana reached into a case and started handing round ear buds to everyone. We knew how they worked, but I had to remind myself not to say anything unnecessary as they were voice-activated. A comms check was carried out and everyone signaled they could hear. Cantrelle and his men dropped their night-vision goggles down and snuck off into the bushes to make their way up the hill.

"Base, team one," came Cantrelle over the earpieces. "I'm getting static from the waterfall; turn off your mics unless you need them."

"Roger, team one," confirmed Diana, who then unclipped the mics from our shirts.

We could still listen and we heard the team breathing as they humped it up the hill. In little more than a few minutes, they updated that they'd found the road. I was impressed they'd made up the hill so quickly, but that is what Navy SEALs do. There was more dead air for a few minutes, then Cantrelle updated again.

"Base, team leader one, we have a body at the east end of the complex.

My heart dropped like a broken ship over the Mariana Trench.

"*God, please no,*" I thought, as I suspected Jeff did too.

"No identity possible, but the victim appears to be male," he updated to my relief.

We just waited quietly as the updates came in.

"Team one advancing on the west side of the house. Team two covers the east side, team three covers the north. Team four, overwatch, hold position out front."

The ensuing silence lasted just a few minutes, but it felt like an eternity.

"Team one, ready to breach the west side…" confirmed Cantrelle.

"Team two, ready east side…" followed a colleague.

"Team three ready north side…" updated a third.

"Go, go, go," yelled Cantrelle.

The sound of explosions in our ears were so loud all three of us flinched. The teams then went breathing hard guessing they were going from room to room, usually followed by a location and a loud "Clear" as they rolled through the building. My heart pounded and my mouth dried almost instantly. Each notification left fewer and fewer rooms where they might find Maria. We heard gunshots in our ears and, finally, we heard the words we had waited for from one of the teams on the second floor.

"Eyes on, eyes on… we have the girl, we have the girl. Two perps shot and killed. The girl is alive, repeat, the hostage is alive."

"Overwatch, we are extracting out the rear," Cantrelle confirmed.

The worry just evaporated from Jeff, and I felt much the same. They continued to scour the building and eventually took out eight of Don Miguel's men. Whilst his men swept for stragglers and any remaining hostiles, Cantrelle's team escorted her from the complex and back over the hill.

We just sat there and we could hear her voice whispering in the background but not loud enough to make out. Eventually, the sound of low voices and footsteps came from the woods. Jeff and I both rushed forward to where they were expected to appear.

"Maria," he screamed as he ran toward her.

Night was fading into the dawn, and Diana and I watched as the two of them hugged like they hadn't seen each other in years. He lifted her feet off the ground and almost swung her around. She cried and held him tight.

"I knew you would come, Jeffryn," she exclaimed.

It was a moving image, one that brought a tear to my eye.

Diana picked up a bottle of water and took a long swig before she splashed some water on her face. She walked over to Jeff and Maria.

"Everyone, I don't want to break up the family reunion, but the other teams will be here in a moment. It is almost daylight and we need to get back to the safe house."

I ushered both of them to the truck and opened the back door for the two of them before I climbed in the front with Diana. She pulled away just as the other teams arrived back at the clearing and started to drive along the track in darkness. She must have memorized the way and needed no help from Jeff. I looked over my shoulder and Maria was quiet and had rested her head on Jeff's shoulder with her arms wrapped around him.

"The outdoor sentries were already dead before we breached and took out the rest." Cantrelle said to Diana, causing her to nod.

"Okay, we will deal with that later. Let's get out of here."

We appeared through the long grass and into the parking lot. There were a handful of vendors opening their stands as we appeared through the long grass and made our way back to the main road. Most of them looked at us but they didn't seem to give us a second thought.

As we drove along, Jeff reached over and gave my shoulder a squeeze. No words were necessary, but he said them anyway.

"I owe you, my friend, more than you can know."

I laid my hand on his and replied, "We're family, you'd have done the same if the tables were turned."

The sun started to rise as we traveled along the roads for about twenty minutes. Diana confirmed to Jeff and Maria that they were being taken to the safe house for debriefing. I honestly didn't care about any of that during that moment. I was just euphoric that Maria was safe and sound.

"Jeff, please, I want to go home! I want to go home!" shrieked Maria.

Jeff turned to Diana and told her firmly, "I will be taking my sister home; we can meet after."

Diana was about to say something when she looked at me and I shook my head.

"Okay," she sighed," Jeffryn, take care of your sister at home, for the time being, but I will need to debrief you guys today!"

Jeff said nothing, he just held his sister in his arms and looked out the window.

The four of us remained quiet for the rest of the drive through town until we arrived at the ferry. Maria was almost asleep on Jeff's shoulder as Diana and I got out. She suggested we go for a coffee and stretch our legs. I looked over at Jeff and he nodded his approval to leave them for five minutes.

The sun had already lifted its head above the horizon as we made our way to the concession stand. The early morning and late afternoon ferry journeys were always pleasant when the sun provided a breathtaking backdrop. About halfway there, Diana hooked her arm through mine.

"I hope you know I am genuinely sorry for deceiving you. Please believe me, my feelings for you are real."

I didn't know how I felt, about her or what she'd done, but I tried to respond positively.

"I understand doing your duty and your job, probably more than most, but I now have no idea what parts of our relationship were you doing your job... and what parts were your real feelings."

Even I was moved by the glassy eyes that looked up at me. "I liked you right from the start."

"I like you a lot as well, Diana, and I already consider us close. However, you only know a small part about me and I clearly know even less about you," I admitted. "Let's remain friends for a while and see where it takes us, if anywhere."

She nodded meekly but remained entwined in my arm until we reached the stand. We ordered a pair of coffees and a doughnut each, then made our way over to a picnic table situated between the stand and the pilothouse. The two of us sat there quietly eating as we both looked out over the water. It now had a deep orange glow from the sun that was just heating up.

"You know, when I first met you, I wasn't sure if you were a good guy or a bad guy, mostly because of the company I saw you with. You changed my opinion on our boat ride together, by the passionate way your eyes lit up when you spoke about your boat and life, and the way you were on the dive. I knew you were genuine," she told me.

I was looking down at my coffee, and I heard a deep sigh from Diana. I looked up to see her sad face, and I had absolutely no idea how to respond.

"You astounded me by the way you risked your life to help a friend and everything you have done for your friends. Men like you are few and far between these days."

I had to say something. It would have been cruel not to.

"I think you are an awesome woman, Diana, and I know you mean what you say. Can we just aim for friendship right now? You obviously have a great career in the FBI and you're clearly very good at it, but that is a very different life to the one I am aiming for."

She looked slightly relieved.

"Think I'm good at it, huh?" she teased.

"I do. We can stay in touch. I've been thinking about spending the winter in Nicaragua, if you fancy a trip to visit?" I suggested.

"I admire your life, where you can do something like that," she told me.

"Not too bad, is it?" I smiled.

I leaned over and looked toward the bow. The ferry was about to make its landing on the far side, so I suggested we go back to the truck. There were a large number of vehicles in front of us that loaded first, and most of the occupants had hotel uniforms on and were making their morning commute.

The gate opened and the cars and trucks filed down the ramp and up the dock. We took the first turn and returned to the safe house located nearby. When we pulled into the parking lot, we were greeted by Jeff's security team that had called straight after Maria had her panic attack.

"I am going with Jeff and Maria back to her place," I leaned over and said to Diana, "I will call you when she is ready to cope with questions and visitors."

"Alright, but Tomas, please make it today," she urged.

"I'll make no promises. She has been through a lot," I replied.

We came to a stop and Jeff gave Maria a delicate nudge. She woke quite quickly but was still groggy, probably a lack of sleep during her ordeal. Jeff helped her into the Land Rover and got in the back with her. I sprang into the front with the driver.

"When we get back, drop me at the marina road so you can get back to the house quicker," I told the driver.

He tried to protest that they'd drop me at the marina, but I insisted I fancied the walk, which I did. When we arrived at the marina road, they did exactly as I asked and dropped me off. It was only about three hundred yards to the boat launch and Tiki bar. I wanted a few moments of fresh air to clear my mind. I also realized Ramon was at the boat and he would have countless questions about what happened. All I had told him so far was that she was safe via a text. By jumping out at the marina road, I had time to process stuff.

As I walked down the road, I could see the whole marina stretching out into the Gulf in front of me. The sun was well over the horizon now and lit up the entire scene. People were already out setting up their umbrellas on the beach as kids splashed around in the calm water. The marina itself was already bubbling with life.

I took my time and strolled at a leisurely pace. I avoided the parking lot and went straight down to the boat launch at the end of the road and then up the beach to the dock where the *San Blas* was moored. As soon as I stepped on the boat, Ramon's head appeared from behind the door.

"Hey, man, how's it all gone since you got Maria back? Is she okay?" he asked quickly.

"She's alive, she's alright," I told him. "A few bruises and she's taken a beating mentally, but there's no long-lasting physical damage."

He pumped both fists on my shoulders and said, "Thank God, man. I was pacing until I got your text. I have tried to track Javier down since you left, but no one knows how to find him. Until we're free of this shit storm, I'll keep trying."

I nodded and agreed.

"So, what now, man?" he questioned.

I looked over at him with tired, bloodshot eyes. "I don't know about you, but I need some sleep. That was one hell of a night. If you don't mind me suggesting, why don't you amuse yourself with Tracy or one of your other female acquaintances while I get myself some shut-eye? I'll fill you in later this afternoon."

"Sounds like a good idea, you do look like shit, my friend," he joked.

He went back inside and grabbed his stuff as I sat on the transom bench and looked out over the marina. After such a crazy few days, it was the sort of calm I needed. I watched him wander over to the catamaran and dragged my tired body inside. If the marina was the essence of calm, the inside of my boat was the definition of slumber.

One may have thought there had been a party going on while I was away. There were dirty dishes in the sinks, glasses scattered about, empty beer cans and bottles and even the remainder of a takeaway from the Tiki. I just shook my head and walked straight past it to my cabin, slumping down on my bed and waited for the water to heat up. I must have fallen asleep shortly after.

It was my phone that dragged my subconscious mind back to the waking world. I looked at the caller ID and it was Diana, so I answered.

"Oh, you're alive then," she said with sarcasm.

I looked down and realized I was still in the same clothes.

"Ah, shit, my water tank will be empty. I fell asleep and left the system on for a shower. Part of the joys of living on a boat," I half muttered to myself. "I am sorry, I haven't spoken to Jeff yet. Give me ten minutes and I'll get a hold of him."

"It's okay," she cut in quickly, "I tried calling you several times. Jeff spoke to me and said she'd calmed down enough for us to talk to her in a limited capacity. We have just finished there and are on the way to the morgue. The body that was discovered at the apartments is apparently that of Don Miguel. His brother is probably fish food in the Gulf. We're then going through some computers and cell phones that we retrieved from the scene and other bodies."

"I appreciate the update, Diana, and please don't be offended, but my involvement and need to know is over. Come visit as a friend, but please leave work at the door."

I was metaphorically tired and ready for the last few days to end.

"I'm sorry, Tomas, I just thought you would like to know. Put you and your friends at ease. I will catch you later," she added before we said our goodbyes.

I rolled down my call list and saw three missed calls from China. I must have been out like a light. I flicked to her number and gave her a call.

"Nice of you to call back, mister." She said the moment she answered.

"Sorry, I crashed right out. We got Maria back early this morning, but I guess you knew that already?"

"I did and that's great news. I am happy my information worked out for all of you. I assumed you'd be asleep. By the way, you'll have to tell me how you manage sleeping like that one day."

"Ah, trade secret," I teased.

"I wanted to let you know that Jeffryn called me this afternoon and invited me to a party at his house. A big celebration in your honor and for Maria's safe return. If you're up for it,

I thought I would arrive early and come down to your boat to see you... seeing as you never find the time to come see me," she ribbed.

My heart suddenly sped up, and I felt a knot in my stomach.

"When will you be here?" I asked slightly nervously.

"Funny that, I am already here. I just landed at the airport and Jeffryn is on his way to pick me up. I had to call him, seeing as you weren't picking up."

"Are you hungry?" I asked.

"I am. I didn't get a chance to eat when I left."

"I'll thaw something out now and we can have dinner on the boat," I suggested.

"Perfect, I can't wait to see you."

Chapter Twenty-Six

I ran outside and filled my freshwater tank. I tried not to panic, but my heart was in my throat. It had been a while since we saw each other. I flew back inside and went on a cleaning blitz, to the extent I chucked the dirty plates away rather than waste time washing them. I was like Mrs. Doubtfire on speed. When everything looked good, I quickly gave everything outside a quick wash down as I thought about what meal I could bedazzle her with?

I settled on my seafood soup. I knew I had all the ingredients for it and I set about whipping it up. Its proper name was Sopa de Marsico's with Yuca and it was one of China's favorites. Made up of lobster, shrimp fish and Yuka cooked in coconut milk, she actually taught me how to make it when we were together. Satisfied everything was as it should be, I dove in the shower and got changed as it simmered.

It needed the right drink, and I went to my locked drinks cabinet and grabbed a bottle of Domaine Ramonet Chardonnay. It was a

$1300 bottle of wine that was given to me as a gift. I stored it in a hard box with lots of padding, just waiting for the right moment.

"Oh, this definitely qualifies!" I told myself.

Everything was ready. I put on some music and settled my nerves with a bottle of Corona from the refrigerator. My mind was all over the place as I sat on the deck in between tending to the soup. Some might have described me like a teenager on his first date.

China always had a powerful effect on me. We may have kept in contact by phone and email, but I hadn't been able to bring myself to get together with her. That was why it had been over a year. Every man has the ideal woman in his mind, in totality looks, body and mind, personality etc and she was mine.

She was thirteen years younger than me, but wise beyond her years. It was why we got along so well. She had a personality that fit any situation, from chilling on the beach with friends, taking charge in business negotiations or donning a gown to be the belle of the ball. It really stung when she told me "in another life" when I asked her to marry me. It still did! I'll never understand what that meant, but I knew she still cared for me.

The only downside, the lone one, was the secret side to her—the middle of the night phone calls, the out-of-town trips that lasted weeks but where she never went anywhere of note. I originally put it down to family responsibilities that she was embarrassed about or didn't want me to know about.

Then one day, I saw an encrypted Sat-phone in her office drawer with a code book when I went looking for something she needed. It was military hardware because I'd used the same model when I worked for a military sealift company in the Persian Gulf. That made me suspect CIA, NSA, or some other acronym. She has always had really good intel about anything.

I'd been going to-and-fro for about forty-five minutes when Jeff's Cheyanne turned down the marina road. I waited until they turned into the parking lot before I met them at the end of the dock. China smiled brightly at me from behind the windscreen when she first saw me. She flew out of the vehicle like a cyclone and ran over to me. She threw her arms wide, jumped up at me and clung on with her legs and arms.

"Tomas," she squealed in delight as I held onto her tightly as she kissed my cheek. I could smell her hair and she had on the same unmistakable perfume—Happy Heart—and mine certainly was. I couldn't possibly forget that smell... ever.

"China," I grinned inanely, "it is sooo good to see you."

"And you too," she fired back, followed by more kisses.

Jeff just stood there quietly and let us appreciate the moment.

She eventually released her grip and dropped her feet to the ground. That smile was enough to reduce me to a wreck all on its own.

"So, let's see this boat of yours," she said with enthusiasm.

"Let's do it. Do you have any bags?" I checked.

"Jeff has kindly said he'll take them up to the house. We can go up there after dinner," she detailed.

"Sounds like a plan. Jeff, we'll be there about 10 pm," I proposed as I looked at my watch.

"Okay, see you then," he replied without breaking his smile.

He climbed back in the Cheyanne and left. China grabbed hold of my arm tightly as we walked in-step down the dock to the *San*

Blas. It was about two hours until sunset, and the sun was still well above the horizon.

"Oh, wow, Tomas, she is beautiful," exclaimed China when she first set eyes on my other baby. "The photos don't do her justice."

"Glad you like her. She's still a work in progress, but we'll get there," I told her.

I helped her onto the rear deck and she instantly inhaled the smell of the soup as it wafted through the door.

"And what is that I smell?" she asked as she gravitated toward the aroma.

"You need to ask?" I winked. "It's Sopa de Marsico's!"

She strolled through the door, walked over and lifted the lid to exclaim, "Oh, wow. That smells delicious!"

"It should be, it's your recipe," I truthfully admitted.

She gazed around the cabin, pausing to slowly look at everything.

"May I?" she pointed toward my cabin and asked.

"Of course, feel free," I smiled.

"It's more spacious than it looks from the outside," she said, impressed. "Its absolutely beautiful and you fully deserve it Tomas."

China's eyes sparkled as she strolled around the boat.

"Do you fancy a quick cruise?" I asked on the spur of the moment.

"Oh, hell yes," came the enthusiastic reply.

We stepped back into the Salon and she noticed the bottle of wine neatly rested in a chill bucket. China lifted it toward her face and looked at the label. I acted like I hadn't noticed and was a touch disappointed when she didn't show any reaction. China knew her wine and I couldn't help myself.

"It's not every day I can break out a bottle of wine that costs more than a grand. In truth, it is my first and I suspect my last," I joked. "Can I get you a drink?"

"It's some bottle," she grinned, "just water for now. I will save myself for a thousand dollar bottle of wine. You must be doing well to be drinking wine this expensive."

"Cards on the table," I added with a shake of the head, "that was actually a gift from an associate I helped out. I have genuinely been saving it for a special occasion." China sauntered over and gave me a kiss on the cheek.

"I think this qualifies," she whispered.

I handed her the bottle of water and checked the soup. It was ready and I put it to the side for later.

"She might be a little loud but it'll be quieter once I close the door," I told her as I grabbed my boat keys. I walked over to the controls and fired her up. The engines roared into life, and I looked back at her and raised my eyebrows a few times with a grin.

"You are such a guy sometimes," she chuckled.

"Have a seat. I'll throw the lines off," I told her.

The strangest thing happened when I went back to throw the lines. I was with China but Diana popped into my head. She was hurt that I was upset with her, the truth is I never thought we had a real chance at being together, especially after I found out about her being FBI. She could have busted me as well if things hadn't worked out the way they did? I looked back at China, who was sitting on the couch waiting for me.

They were tough to compare. Diana was very much the Tom-Boy type while China was more the ballroom type. Her idea of roughing it was bad room service at the Hilton. I refused to let it ruin the moment and dismissed the thoughts of Diana. I threw the lines onto the dock and walked back inside.

The engine noise reduced dramatically when I closed the door. China got up and wandered over to sit next to me at the console. I eased the engines into gear, and she pushed herself closer to me as we slowly moved away.

"It means the world to be here with you again," she told me as she moved a hand to my leg.

"Same here, darlin'," I said softly as I looked over.

Within a few minutes, we were idling through the jetties. I noticed a bit of wind from the southwest had picked up once we left the marina. I wanted to avoid any choppy water.

"It might get a touch bumpy for a minute, but we'll go around the east end of the island and it'll be calm as glass over there," I explained.

"Aye, Aye, Captain," she teased with a grin.

I made my turn outside the jetty and waves were quite small, less than two-feet high. I guided us east and told her we'd be on the east side of the island in five minutes. As hard as I tried to resist, I couldn't help but show off a little. I gave her a wink and threw the throttles forward. The boat gave a deep rumble and both of us pushed back in our seats.

"Woohoo," she cheered. "How fast are we going?"

I checked the GPS and it showed 46 knots.

"Nearly fifty, but watch this..."

I pushed the leaver further forward, and she increased her pace. The bow slowly bounced up and down along the waves, creating a large wake behind. The Salon was located in the aft center, so the movement was less pronounced. We both grinned and lapped up the rush.

Looking out of the window, I saw the condos flashing by. I pointed out the beach to her where everyone was enjoying themselves. I don't know what was more exhilarating; the joy of cruising along or doing it with China next to me. I didn't expect to see her anytime soon and I thought of her a lot.

A few minutes later, I made our turn toward the east section of the island, easing the throttle back but we were still moving along nicely. Once I completed the turn, the water quickly became still and reflective, the only disruption being the *San Blas*.

"It's so beautiful here," she said in awe.

"It sure is something," I replied as I dropped the engines to idle. "Here, I need you to take over for a moment so I make sure we get past the coral heads."

In truth, I didn't really, I just wanted to give her a thrill. I put her in my spot and placed her hands on the wheel. I then walked out to the bow and found the break in the reef I was looking for.

"That way, just a small nudge on the gas. Deep down, I was almost certain she knew how to drive a boat. China navigated us through nicely and I couldn't help but smile when I looked back. Once we were through, I made my way back to the console.

"Wanna keep the wheel?" I asked.

"Nice try, but I'm here on vacation. This is your boat, Captain," she sniggered.

I took control again and looked over with a loving smile. For me, this was heaven.

"Watch where you're going, mister," she mock-ordered.

I ran the boat all the way up close to the beach, and we ended up in the same spot where I'd spent the night on Tracy's catamaran a few nights earlier. I trundled us up to about fifty feet from the beach and threw the anchor out from the aft compartment. We slow-lined until we were some thirty feet from the beach before I dropped the main one. As soon as they dug in, I turned the engines off.

"Pour us both a glass of wine, while I set things up back here," I suggested.

I went back and grabbed a couple of lawn chairs from the compartment and set them up with the tray from the Salon, arranging everything like it was a romantic table for two on the aft deck. I even went as far as some music, although rather than some Classical background music, I opted for a bit of Reggae. I turned the volume low enough where we could have a conversation.

When China came through and handed me a glass, I had just finished.

"To the day all turning out okay and to finally being reunited with you," I toasted.

"To your dream coming true and your fabulous boat," she added as we chinked glasses.

I pulled a chair out for her, then went back to putting the finishing touches to the soup. We ended up with the setting sun behind, thanks to the direction of the current, and it sat there like the perfect theater backdrop. We sat and looked over the water and enjoyed the moment of calm as the music provided a chilled soundtrack.

"It's easy to see why you fell in love with this lifestyle," she admitted.

"The days that make it worth it far outnumber the days that don't." I replied.

As we talked about the good times we shared, I suddenly noticed a tear run down her cheek.

"China, what's up?" I asked concerned as more began to appear.

I rose from my chair and leaned forward so I could give her a hug. She eventually pulled her tearful eye from my shoulder.

"Just time with you has brought up the past memories. You know, when you asked me to leave with you, I hope you know I wanted to, didn't you? More than anything in the world, but I couldn't. There are things about my life that I just can't say and I think you always knew that."

"Oh, China, I know. I truly do. It was clear that you were part of something that you couldn't talk about. I have always respected you for that and hoped that maybe one day you would be able to tell me, at least some parts. However, if you have to kill me after you do so, I'll pass if it's all the same"

That last little joke seemed to lift her spirits and she relaxed slightly.

"Trust you to make a joke," she smiled and wiped away her tears. "Sorry, didn't mean to ruin the mood."

"You didn't ruin anything. It means a lot to me for you to tell me that. Food's almost ready, are you hungry?" I asked as I kissed her forehead.

She nodded, so I went back inside where the soup was now simmering. I prepared a couple of bowls for us, with some corn tortillas on the side, and placed them on the table.

"Wow, that looks delicious," purred China.

I sat down and we tucked in. Throughout the meal, we chatted about recent times. I told her about my journey to the States to buy the boat and the modifications that I'd made. In turn, she explained how her family had recently purchased land in Roatan Honduras. She had been sending her family money for years and they used it to purchase the land. She looked so happy as she extolled how the family dream had come true.

The sky above us slowly turned to dark blue and black as we sat there and talked. Once we'd finished, she slid her chair over to me and we sat there with our feet propped up on the transom. I was lost for words at how much I enjoyed being in her company again and hearing that beautiful voice. After what I had experienced the last few days, it felt wonderful to slow down and actually relax. To pause and appreciate the moment.

We remained like that until the wine ran out. China stood and grabbed my hand.

"Shall we go inside?" she suggested.

"Why not?" I smiled before I downed the rest of my glass.

She led me down to my cabin and lowered herself slowly onto the bed. I eased off my shirt and removed my trousers when my cell phone rang.

You have got to be fucking kidding me.

I let out an audible "shit" at which China rolled back her head and laughed.

"I bet it's Ramon, woman trouble again!" she sniggered.

"If it is, I'm gonna cut it off so it's no longer a problem," I muttered, and that only made her laugh harder.

I picked it up and the ID showed it was Jeff.

"You'd better answer it," she said earnestly.

"I swiped to answer and greeted him with, "Jeff, my friend, your timing... this had better be fucking important."

My slightly mock irritation was greeted with howls of laughter from both China and Jeff on the phone.

"Sorry, bro, bad timing? I just called to see what time you want me to pick you both up?"

I felt a bit naughty so I replied, "You don't need to. We're going to stay on the boat tonight away from the marina.

China jumped into a sitting position and declared with a smirk, "No, Tomas, we're going to Jeff's as expected. Now be a good boy! Tell him to pick us up in a couple of hours. That should give me time to make you presentable."

"You heard the boss," I submitted.

"Presentable, huh, Gringo," hinted Jeff. "See you in a..."

I hung up, pressed off and tossed the phone on the side.

"Did you just turn your phone off," she laughed.

"Yep!"

China bounced to her feet, her lips crashed against mine before she pulled away with a smile. "Let's get back to it, shall we?"

China's hands drifted down, her fingertips brushed just above the waistband. It was a deliberate touch—provocative—and sent ripples through me, wanting more. Her smirk grew wider, meeting my gaze where her dark eyes were ablaze with challenge.

"You're still overdressed," she said softly, her voice dripping with playful reproach.

She hooked her fingers into my waistband and gave a tug just enough to set my pulse racing.

The soft light of the cabin gave her complexion an erotic glow. I closed the distance between us, my hands bracing on either side of her hips as I leaned into her, my lips brushing against her neck. I felt her quiver as her body arced in closer as though she couldn't bear an inch of space between us.

"You're trouble," I whispered, my lips grazing the shell of her ear.

She laughed, the sound low and wicked. "You like trouble."

Her body collided with mine; curves molded perfectly into my own as the coolness first kissed my skin. Her lips found mine again, but this time there was no tenderness in her kiss. It was scalding, devouring, leaving no space for my hesitation. My hands slid down to her thighs to lift her easily as she wrapped her legs around my waist.

She fit against me, like she was made to be there. And something about that sent a swell of heat through me. Quickly I dropped us both onto the bed. Her laughter, soft and breathless, filled the cabin as she leaned back slightly, her hands resting on my shoulders.

"Still think I'm trouble?" she asked, her voice barely more than a whisper.

"The best kind," I whispered.

Chapter Twenty-Seven

A couple of hours later, we made our way into the marina where Jeff's SUV was already parked at the end of the pier. Once the boat was secure, he boarded, and we both walked into the cabin.

"Where's China?" asked Jeff as he looked around.

"She's getting ready, she should be almost done," I replied as he took a seat on the couch, and I grabbed the computer chair across from him. He just smiled as he looked over at me.

"Sooo," he clicked his tongue, "did you two pick up where you left off?"

"It's been nice to see her again, and it's been a long time. I'm not saying anything else," I answered with a knowing glance of what he was digging for.

"I'm going to put the two of you up at my house tonight. After you lock up, I am going to need the keys to your boat, Gringo," he announced.

"Say what? Errr, no," I smiled and shook my head. "My boat doesn't go anywhere without me."

Jeff laughed out loud. "Oh, trust me, my friend. I am just going to have Jose fill her up with fuel for you as a show of my appreciation for all that you have done.

"Okay," I relented with hesitation, "but it's really not necessary. Just promise you won't let anything happen to my baby."

"Don't worry. I'll wait for the two in the truck," he added as he got up and left the cabin.

I went down to my room to find China finishing up as she placed her earring in her ear.

"Jeff's here," I told her, "Shall we?"

"Let's go, sir," she replied, playing along.

We jumped in Jeff's SUV and twenty minutes later, we slow-rolled through the gates of his place. I was with China in the back seat and her jaw almost dropped when she saw his house.

"Jesus, Jeff, is this all *your* place?!" she asked in shock.

"It's just my humble abode," he joked.

"Humble, more like the fucking White House," I jumped in, never one to miss a chance for a swift joke, and we both laughed.

"Okay, maybe a bit more than humble," he laughed.

He parked right out front and led us through the two huge, hand-carved double doors. China looked up at the giant marlin etched into the woodwork.

"That is magnificent," she told him.

"Yeah, I've always liked that part as well," I added.

Jeff didn't utter a word as we walked through the giant foyer and into the sunken living room. She continued to marvel at his place and I could tell Jeff was enjoying the attention, and it made me momentarily jealous. We continued on out to the pool deck and it looked even more beautiful than it had the last time he'd hosted a shin-dig the other night.

He took us over to the pool bar and asked, "Either of you want a drink?"

China and I looked at each in unison, "Yes, please."

She pointed to the margarita dispenser.

"A margarita for the lady, and for the gentleman...?" he continued.

I gave him a knowing look, and he smiled back as soon as he recognized it.

"One Johnnie Walker Blue, coming up."

We grabbed our drinks and China took a few steps away from us as she looked around the estate.

"Where's Maria?" she questioned.

"She's gone back to her place with some of my security team. She's still quite freaked out about the kidnapping," he replied as he continued what he was doing.

"I thought you were going to have her stay here for a bit?" I asked, a little worried about her leaving the security of her brother.

"I tried, but she needed her own surroundings to help settle her. I wasn't keen but even Diana agreed it might help once she'd finished debriefing her."

China gave him a playful slap on the arm.

"I imagine she is," she added. "It's alright for you men to be in the thick of it, but I doubt she ever expected to be kidnapped by cartel members."

"I'm just kidding," Jeff confessed. "I pleaded with her to stay here. She's upstairs. She asked you to go and see her when you arrived. I think she wants to thank you for your part."

I felt a moment of awkwardness as it dawned on me that I had been with Maria just a couple of nights earlier.

"Of course I can." she agreed.

We both watched China walk through the house and disappear through the doorway towards the stairs. Jeff reached down behind the bar and pulled out a pair of Cuban cigars with a smile on his face.

"A celebratory gift, my friend. Let's go burn one."

I took one from his hand, picked up my drink, and followed along behind him. We strolled over to some tables and sat at one by the railings that looked out over the garden. It was lit with floodlights and when you looked up, you could see a half moon sitting above us. It provided enough light that you could see over the bluff and out to the Gulf. The palm trees all had different colored lights that provided an array of color across the grounds. I could also see the edge of the path that Maria and I took the night of the party.

Jeff handed me a lighter, and I lit my cigar and leaned back. I took a deep puff on it and felt the warm smoke fill my mouth before I exhaled. The mixed taste of the cigar and Johnnie Walker was delightful. The two of us sat and enjoyed the moment, both looking out across the grounds and to the Gulf.

He then turned to me and asked, "We never got a chance to talk about it. What went down with the job?"

I inhaled deeply on my cigar and replied, "Brother, it was a set-up right from the start, but we were prepared. I can't deny I had my doubts, so I had China look into that idiot Don Miguel. Don't ask me how, but she knew he was planning to rip us off and kill us... so we took a different approach." I took another drag on my cigar and continued, "So Ramon and I made a plan of our own.

"I'm sorry, man, I really thought he was on the level this time after the last botched deal."

"I can give you all the details, but it'll take a while," I finished with a wink.

"And the money?" he retorted sarcastically.

"I've already given the guys their cut before the meet, and the rest either got taken by those bastards in the Mexican Navy or the goons on the barge. I can't be sure."

His smile got bigger as he asked again, "You're telling me you lost the money?"

With just the right amount of sarcasm, I replied, "I mean, there was so much gunfire and confusion, who knows what happened to it."

I puffed on my cigar and sat back. He grinned and shook his head. He knew I was lying, but he also knows that he would have done the same thing had he been in my shoes.

"Roger that, Gringo, Roger that."

We started to chat about the old days, and I thought about Tio. It was time for some serious conversation for a moment.

"Jeff, did you know Tio had cancer?" I asked.

His smile evaporated instantly. "Yeah, he told me. We were both hopeful he would have more time. I would have told you but he swore me to secrecy and that he'd let everyone know when he was ready."

My eyes welled up and an unpleasant lump appeared in my throat.

"You know he's gone?" I checked.

"I do, going out saving all your asses as I heard it from Cantrelle."

We both fought to hold back the tears.

"He did, man, he really did," I added.

"Don't worry," he said as he put a hand on my shoulder. "We will take care of his family."

I wiped the tears from my eyes and raised my glass.

"To Tio!"

"To Tio," he repeated as our glasses chimed.

We continued to catch up for another couple of hours; at one point we moved from the table to the lounge chairs near the pool. The shimmering blue light from the water provided a nice ambience. China was still inside with Maria and part of me wondered what the two of them could be talking about for such a long time. I hoped my name was out of the conversation.

We'd had several drinks and I felt like I could pass out at any moment from exhaustion. I looked at my watch and it was already 2 am. I stood and gave Jeff's chair a kick as he too had just dozed off.

"Which room is mine, brother,"

He stood and wobbled just slightly from all the alcohol.

"Just follow me," he told me with a slight slur and began to stumble toward the living room.

As I followed behind, my boots felt like they were full of lead. All of my muscles ached and the scratches on my arm from the shells under the bridge made it look like I'd lost a fight with a tiger. We passed through the sunken lounge to a large staircase at the far end.

"Up the stairs, second door on the left," he guided me.

He gave me a thumbs up, then walked past the stairs to another hallway further on.

"Roger that, bro, see you in the morning," I added as I climbed upward.

He didn't say anything as he raised his hand in acknowledgement and staggered away from me. The stairs felt like they took a Herculean effort to climb. Like a man desperate for the prize, I needed a bed. As soon as I found my room, I flopped on the bed and passed out almost immediately.

The next morning, I awoke, head throbbing and the sun too bright as it peered through the side of the curtains in the room. However, as I rolled over I found China fast asleep next to me. I hadn't been sure if we'd share the same room or not, and realized she must have joined me long after I'd crashed.

It was only half seven, and I contemplated waking her, but she obviously came in late so I let her sleep. I crawled off the bed, and silently made my way to the bathroom for a shower.

Like the rest of the house, the shower was huge and big enough to hold a queen-sized bed. It had black ceramic tiles with a gold design inlaid onto each piece. I suspected it probably wasn't real, but with Jeff, you never knew for sure.

The water rained on my battered body and I thought about how I was ready for a return to my quiet life once again; I could just jump on my boat and sail away. I occasionally felt lonely there by myself, but not often because I genuinely enjoyed being alone with my own thoughts.

Being alone at sea was a great time to sit silently in contemplation, to reflect on the important things in life. I sometimes thought of my voyages as soul-searching expeditions, where only I knew what revelations were revealed and what was found. It was a lifestyle that didn't suit everyone, but it perfectly suited me.

As I finished my shower, it suddenly dawned on me that I'd left my bag with our change of clothes in Jeff's truck.

Shit. I'm going to have to go get it.

I wasn't usually the type of person to walk around someone else's home half naked, but right now I really didn't have a choice. I wrapped a towel around my waist and snuck out of the room and down the stairs to the front door. The brightness of the sun caused me to squint as soon as I stepped outside.

"Fuck, why is it so bright?" After a moment, my eyes adjusted and I made my way over towards the vehicle.

"Buenos Días, Senior Tomas."

I adjusted my hand to see one of Jeff's security guards standing off to the side of me. Of course someone would be out here to see me like this. I returned their greeting and sheepishly asked if they could grab my duffel bag from the rear seat.

"Of course, Senior Tomas. Wait right there."

He retrieved my bag, making his way towards me with a smile. "Do you need anything else?"

"No, that's it. Thanks." Turning, I made my way back inside and was just closing the door when my name being called startled me from behind.

"Senior Tomas."

I spun my head round to see an elderly woman in a maid uniform. I had one hand on the door handle and one on the bag, and neither on my towel. Without any warning, the top untucked and the towel fell to the floor. Some might have just brazen it out, but I was too tired for that. I am not sure which one of us had the bigger eyes. I quickly covered my modesty with the bag. Embarrassed that this little old lady just got a morning view I'm sure she wasn't expecting.

"Would you like some coffee?" she asked and tried hard not to smirk.

"Errm, yes...," I stammered as I reached down to grab the towel. "That would be great.

I also had to stifle a nervous laugh as I also fumbled around for the towel and quickly put it back in place.

"Very good," she answered.

The maid then walked off, and I overheard her chuckle as she walked back to the kitchen. I ascended the stairs quickly and returned to the room. Amusement and embarrassment filled me at what had happened as I chuckled it off and rustled through my bag to find my toothbrush.

"Just what are you laughing at, mister?" A sweet voice called from behind me.

It was China. She also made me jump and as I stepped back in shock, I clattered into the towel rack and knocked it over.

"Fuck's sake," I mumbled. "What the hell is wrong with me today?"

"You okay?" She laughed, shaking her head.

"Yeah, people just keep popping out from everywhere in this house."

She looked at me confused, and I told her about the last few minutes. She was silent for a moment, before she erupted in laughter. "Are you serious?"

"In my defense, I'm not exactly used to a bunch of people in the morning."

Once she'd composed herself again, she leaned in and gave me a kiss on the cheek.

"Would you go ask your girlfriend for some coffee?" she teased mercilessly.

"Appreciate the understanding," I fired back in mock irritation.

I walked downstairs to the kitchen once I was dressed. The maid I'd previously encountered was at the stove talking to a younger female in Spanish. I greeted them both as I entered the room.

"Buenos días," they replied, the younger staff member smirking slightly as she looked at me.

I felt a little embarrassed about my naked escapade, so I introduced myself—I had totally forgotten the older lady had addressed me by name earlier. The older lady introduced herself as Rosa, and the younger woman as her daughter Andrea.

"Nice to meet you."

"Nice to see you too," replied Rosa with a wink.

Her daughter tried hard to suppress her laughter but soon rushed out the room with her hand across her face. Her mother had obviously told her about what had happened. And all I could do was smile serenely as I asked for two cups of coffee.

Is the day over yet?

With coffees in hand, I returned to my room and China. The sound of the shower running echoed through the room, instead of bothering her I laid on the bed and grabbed the TV remote. I thought I'd take the opportunity to catch up on some news. Toying with the idea of getting satellite TV for the boat, but I'd hardly use it, and besides, I had a large stash of movies and a DVD player.

The first item on the news was a school shooting. Not the sort of thing you wanted to start your day with, so I clicked the TV off and put the remote back on the side.

"And that is why I didn't get satellite TV—it's all too depressing," I justified to myself.

I wandered over to the drapes and pulled the cord to open them. They revealed a large glass door and a private outdoor patio that overlooked the front lawn. It wasn't as impressive as the back, but still a glorious view. There were several large rose gardens surrounded by a perfectly cut lawn.

"Very nice, Jeff," I said out loud as I opened it and stepped out into the morning sun once more. "Very nice indeed."

I took a seat at the small table and sipped on my coffee as I gazed upon the grounds. Wondering what life like this would be like, if I had chosen a life like Jeff's. If I had gotten more into what he had. Would I be in jail? Or better yet, would I even be alive. China appeared through the door a few minutes later dressed in a white fluffy robe.

"Oh, that coffee smells good," she grinned.

"Yours is just inside."

She disappeared, came back with her cup and took the seat opposite me. I glanced over and just seeing her there took my breath away. Her hair was still damp and her brown eyes sparkled in the morning sunshine. She was a woman who didn't need make-up to look amazing.

We chatted and caught up a bit while we drank our coffee. The sun soon shone directly in our eyes from ahead, so China suggested we go inside. She also mentioned that Maria was heading back to her place this morning and had offered to cook us breakfast.

"Give me two minutes and we can head over there," she said as she grabbed her clothes from the bag and went to the bathroom. I waited one minute and followed her. She saw me as soon as I stepped through the door. A smile widened on her face as she raised an eyebrow.

"You are such a man," she giggled as she dropped her robe to the floor.

Chapter Twenty-Eight

THE TWO OF US walked across the main lawn and out the back and down the path that led toward where Maria was staying. I felt pretty awkward and found myself in a situation I'd never expected. I had a relationship with both of them, and in some ways, rekindled it with both of them. Some would argue it was a friends *with benefits* situation, but it didn't make it any less tense to be with both in the same room.

It wasn't as if they didn't know about each other. It was one of those situations where things are known, but questions are never asked. Maria and I were a subject that was the same for China and myself as the "other" parts of her life. At the end of the day, everyone knew that China was the one I could never let go.

We reached the porch, and I saw Maria in the kitchen through the sliding glass door and waved. To look at her, you'd never know what she'd recently been through.

"Good morning," she greeted us.

Maria stopped what she was doing and came over to give me a hug.

"Did you get any sleep?" I blushed with a little smile. "I did." She smiled back at me as she let go of her hug. "Jeffryn and Ramon are upstairs and breakfast will be ready soon."

I wondered why I hadn't seen Jeff, and now I knew. As for Ramon, a freshly cooked breakfast would never be turned down. I looked over to China and she subtly motioned with her hand.

"You go ahead, I'm going to help Maria," she told me.

The two of them together, alone again, wasn't something that left me all that comfortable, but I'd made my bed and had to lie in, metaphorically and in some ways, literally. I nodded and walked upstairs, but the sound of giggling as soon as I left did nothing to ease my discomfort.

I found Jeff and Ramon sitting on the balcony upstairs. Ramon looked his usual hungover self with his head laid back on the chair as if he were looking at the sky. Jeff was on his cell phone chatting on the other side of the table. I sat down next to Ramon and nudged him with my elbow.

"What time did you get in last night?" I teased.

"I didn't," he replied hoarsely. "Jeff's people let me crash at the boat house."

"Why didn't you go back to the boat?" I asked.

My alarm raised higher when Jeff looked over and shook his head.

"Ramon," I said as I sat forward, "is there a problem with the boat?"

Jeff smiled again and answered for him. "Relax, Gringo, she is fine. As promised, I had the guys take her over to the fuel dock and fill her up. The boat house meant Ramon, didn't have to be disturbed."

A sense of relief washed over me and I could once again enjoy the state of Ramon due to his own "overdoing it" self. I poured myself a glass of pineapple juice from the pitcher on the table and took a mouthful, instantly regretting it. I immediately felt the warm burn of spiced rum as it trickled down my throat.

"Honestly, do you guys ever drink anything without alcohol in it?"

"I do my best to avoid it if possible," groaned Ramon. "On this occasion, it is more hair of the dog than enjoyment."

He shuffled uncomfortably in his chair and let out a deep breath.

"Sometimes, you both astound even me," I declared as I pushed the rest of the glass away. "Once Captain Happy here gets some food in him, what is the plan for the day?" I asked Jeff.

"I thought we could finish this delightful breakfast that Maria is cooking up, then we can head down to the port."

"Has anyone heard from Diana, Cantrelle, or any of our merry FBI friends?" I queried. Curious as to what happened to all of them after our rendezvous.

Ramon finally moved; he sat up, pushed his sunglasses down his nose and peered over them.

"She was looking for you last night, I think. She pulled up in the tiki parking lot and left as soon as she saw your boat wasn't there. I might be mistaken, but I thought I saw her arrive a second time, but she left as soon as she saw you pulling in with China on board. I guess she gave up once she saw you had company."

I'd had to juggle two women in the same location before when I was younger and more foolish, but never three.

"Are you dating our little FBI lady?" Jeff teased, with a laugh.

"Nah, other than the fact she's a Fed, Diana is pretty cool. I simply enjoyed hanging out with her."

He was about to say something else and stopped when he saw China come down the stairs.

"Breakfast is ready, now go wash up... especially you, Ramon. There's no telling where those hands have been!"

Jeff and I roared with laughter as we got up and moved toward the stairs. Everyone loved Ramon and we'd all do anything in the world for him. We have all bailed him out at one time or another, but he has repaid those favors many times over with his high powered contacts. However, he was often the butt of jokes simply due to his outrageous antics.

We all moved to the dining room and sat around a large table. We talked about the old times and shared a lot of laughter. It was great to be together again after almost two years. It was a great feeling. Most of the stories were about Ramon and the scrapes he'd got himself into, but he enjoyed it as much as anyone, especially when he was the center of attention.

"Hey Jeff, I think we're going to go ahead and gather our things and head to the port, buddy."

"Okay. I'm heading that way now. Maria, can bring you guys down when you're ready," he confirmed. "We're having a BBQ in your honor at the Tiki."

"Thats not necessary brother, it wasn't just me," I told him.

"Relax, it was a collective idea and some of our other friends will be there," he added.

"Okay, just don't make it all about me," I pleaded. "Let's make it about getting Maria home safe."

Everyone added, "Amen" as we all held our glasses up.

A few minutes later, Ramon decided he would head down with Jeff and keep him company, and we would follow a short while later with Maria.

As China and I walked along her garden and toward the path, I couldn't help but be curious on what she had planned next. "How long are you going to stay on the island?"

"Tryin' to get rid of me already," she teased.

"No, I just wondered how long you intend to grace me with your presence," I replied with a grin.

"That is the right answer. I have a flight tomorrow afternoon."

"Any chance you could change your plans, maybe fly out of Progreso the day after?" I inquired.

"Maybe, I'd need to make a couple of calls," she answered. "And just how do I get to Progreso?"

"I was thinking we could take my boat over. Ramon and I need to meet in Frontera to take care of a few things before I head back to the States."

"A few things...?" she said with a raised eyebrow.

"Nothing for you to worry about," I assured her.

"Be careful, you idiot. My contacts have said there are a lot of people quite angry over this whole incident."

"I hear you, but you said they thought we were still on the run; what's the chances they will be looking for us in Frontera?" I asked.

"Slim, but this is Mexico and Don Miguel still has people loyal to him, people who are angry!"

"Roger that. We may have to change plans if so, but either way, I'd love for you to come with me to Progreso?"

"Okay," she relented. "Let me make some calls."

As we walked into my room, I sensed that the mention of Paraiso had created a slightly awkward air. I never really explained to her why I had to leave when I did. Sure, I asked her to be with me and went as far as a marriage proposal, but there was a lot of "why" that we never discussed, on both sides. She had her reasons for staying, I had mine for leaving. I knew why I couldn't share the details, but I was never sure why she couldn't share hers. I could only conclude she had similar, deep-seated aspects like me.

We shared a similar circle of friends, and it had surprised me neither of us ever found out more about the other. She knew I had an exit strategy and that I "knew" people from my involvement with them. She was likely involved with the same people, but I'd come to realize that her life would be in danger if anyone knew of our relationship. It closed the circle too tight for some people's liking.

I was certain she knew the people I worked for lost a significant amount of money. I paid back around half to the worst people, but there was no way I'd clear my debt with the others and leave with nothing. It's never good when powerful people think you have betrayed them.

She grabbed her phone from her bag and kissed me enroute to the balcony. I'd just finished collecting all my stuff from the bathroom when she came back in.

"It's all good. I was able to rebook my flight out of Progreso."

"Perfect," I answered as I clapped my hands together. I grabbed the rest of our stuff and tossed it in our bags.

"Shall we" I said as I zipped the bag and pulled it off the bed.

When we made it outside we saw that Jeff had left the Range Rover for us so we piled in.

We joked, laughed and chatted, but both of us steered clear of anything that could bring the mood down. I think we both wanted to enjoy the time we had to the fullest.

The mood was so good that China started singing to the radio as we drove to the marina. I hadn't heard her do that in a long time. She always had an amazing voice and could have been a singer had she really wanted that career. It filled me with ecstasy to see her like that again. When we lived together, we'd often take day trips to Villahermosa and she would sing almost the entire journey.

The port came into view as we came over the hill. The Tiki parking lot was already full.

I looked over to the fuel depot to look for the *San Blas*, but there were some large sand-blasting curtains in the way. They were large tarps on big, portable pipe frames that were used to keep sand contained within an area when blasting. I assumed they were there to be picked up because no one would be blasting around million-dollar yachts.

I rolled the SUV into Jeff's reserved spot by the back door. The sound of pinging and dinging of steel drums came from the tiki as we made our way toward the front. It didn't take long to find Jeff, he stood at the bar with Ramon and the rest of the guys enjoying himself as always. The moment he spotted us, he leapt over and welcomed us before he passed the two of us a beer each from a bucket on the bar.

I looked at my watch. "It's only 11:00am ," I reminded him with a laugh before taking the drink. "Ah, what the hell."

The rest of the crew gathered round and greeted us with hugs and handshakes. I recognized almost everyone, but there were a couple of strangers I couldn't place. Across the tiki were other customers quietly enjoying some food and the band. It felt just a little odd to have everyone staring at us, especially when a band was playing away. Jeff seemed extra excited, and he walked through the throng of people to the stage. They stopped playing, as he took the microphone out of the stand.

"Friends, colleagues, ladies and gentlemen," he started.

He paused and waved at me to join him. I was a little confused, a little apprehensive and a little reluctant, but China gave me a gentle shove in the right direction. My face felt like it had been facing the hot reflection of the sun off water. I had no idea why the big deal was all about me—we all played a part—but I decided to go with it.

I lifted myself onto the stage and Jeff gave me a massive hug. The audience clapped, cheered and whistled.

"This is Tomas, or better known as *The Captain*. My friend, my family. As many of you know, he is both famous and notorious..."

Everyone laughed at the comment.

"Not everyone here knows Tomas, but you all know Maria, my sister," he continued as he touched his chest. "Many of you know what she went through this week. This man, this man..."

He put his hand on my shoulder.

"...he left a certain lifestyle a long time ago, for good reasons, but when I called him to tell him Maria had been taken..."

I felt a tear just begin to form in my eye as he patted me on the shoulder and cleared his throat.

"...this man didn't pause! He didn't hesitate! 'I'm all in, my brother,' he said, 'whatever it takes.'

The cheers and applause resumed loudly.

"Tomas, he got the crew together. You guys answered the call, my other brothers," he added with a point at the bar. "Ramon, his second, raise your glass, my friend."

He didn't need to be asked twice, and he milked the adulation for all it was worth—of course.

"Magdelano, Shirma, Izquierdo, hold up your beers, let us all thank you for what you have done."

Then came the moment I dreaded.

"One man is not here with us, not physically, anyway. He fought a long battle with cancer that he'd almost lost, and yet, he still wanted one last adventure. He decided it wasn't the disease that would kill him for nothing. It was important to him that he go out a hero, and he did so, saving the lives of his closest friends. Everyone knows a great first mate is the thing that glues a crew together. He was a mentor to crewmates, a confident to his superiors, and a fucking good sailor. There will never be another Jorge Munoz. Cheers, Tio!"

The toughest men I knew wiped tears from their eyes as they saluted their fallen friend Tio.

"If it wasn't for all of you, I wouldn't have got my sister back. And last but not least, China. It is great to see you again and my never-ending gratitude. To Tomas, to all of you, *thank you*, and let's get this fuckin' party started," he yelled.

The band struck up again and we made our way back to the group by the bar. It was like a group of old veterans had gotten together. We told stories of the old days, the ones we could, and we all caught up properly as there had been little time for that. Maria arrived a little while later and got a huge round of applause. I felt a touch nostalgic to have everyone back together. The last time it happened was my 30th birthday party—what a night that was. Waiters brought around plates of lobster and crab claws, and yet it still felt a little odd without Diana.

I just sat there and listened to the laughter surrounding us. I particularly enjoyed Ramon and China verbally sparring. They were always good friends, right from the start when we first met, and they took great pleasure trying to get one over the other.

At one point, she tilted her head back and whispered, "How does it feel to have all the boys back together?"

"Not too bad." I smiled.

We stayed there a good portion of the afternoon and carried on as the sun neared the horizon leaving a couple hours before sunset. The guys tore through another round of food and about an hour after dinner, we were all on our way to a well-earned drunken buzz.

"Why don't we stretch our legs," I suggested to China, "we can check on the boat and get our stuff from the truck?"

"Sure, give me a moment... and just stay here," she answered.

I didn't get a chance to give an answer before she walked around the table and whispered something in Jeff's ear. I just smiled at them, partly confused, although I was also listening to Ramon who was talking about some girl he met.

Jeff stood up and whistled at the band to stop once again.

"Friends, can you grab your drinks and make your way to the Marina House," he asked.

What the actual fuck is going on?

China walked back to me and Maria appeared on the other side. They wrapped their arms around each of mine and grinned at me with massive smiles.

"Let's go, Captain," they suggested in unison.

I guessed there was some sort of surprise to come, but I genuinely had no idea what it was.

Chapter Twenty-Nine

As we started our walk to the fuel dock, I realized I couldn't see my boat due to the angle and the sand curtains. I panicked and all sorts of stuff ran through my head. I know it couldn't be anything bad but you can't help but worry in times like this.

"Please, please tell me they haven't done something—I'll hate—to my boat?" I stressed, praying to god that my boat was okay.

Jeff was in front with the crew, and I continued to be shepherded along by China and Maria.

"Okay, you've had your fun. What the hell is going on?"

"You'll see!" China told me with a tight grip on my arm that showed me she was excited about something.

What made it all the stranger was that almost everyone from the tiki, a large mob of people, had joined us and walked behind. I didn't even know most of them. What I did know was that it had to have something to do with my boat. And my nerves grew the closer we got.

That dramatically increased when I looked over to the dry boat storage area and saw another group of men walking toward the same place we were headed to. We all arrived almost simultaneously.

When we got to within twenty yards of the curtain, Jeff said, "Okay, I need all the crew here behind Tomas!"

Maria and China continued to hold my locked arms tight. With everyone assembled where he wanted them, Jeff was ready.

"Tomas, the crew and I got together to do something special for you. Not just for what you have done this past week or so, but for all the things you have done over the years. You have been a fearless leader, a friend and brother. You have sacrificed for us, bleed with us and touched each of our lives. We have all chipped in to repay a fraction of what you have done for us."

He motioned to the crew that walked over from the dry boat area to pull back the curtains. Slowly they parted, and what came into view left me stunned. My jaw dropped open, as I pulled my hands to my mouth.

"Surprise!" Everyone yelled.

There was an unbelievable, two-tier tuna tower with a flybridge sitting atop my boat.

"Oh, my god, just... how?!" I said as everyone roared and applauded.

I was so stunned my hands began to shake. China and Maria were also teary eyed in the moment and they released my arms so I could give them both a hug. The entire crew, with Jeff, then stepped over and embraced me. I was totally overwhelmed with emotion and it was the most amazing feeling in the world that those closest to me would do such a thing for me.

I walked toward the boat like a kid who'd just been given his first bike for Christmas. I couldn't say anything. I was still processing what they'd done for me. It was at that point that I noticed Jeff's boat over to the side, minus a tower.

"Holy shit," I said with my hands on my cheeks as I turned and looked at Jeff. He stood there like the proud parent who'd just given their kid that bicycle they've always wanted.

"Don't worry," he laughed, "your crew paid me for it. There just wasn't enough time to build a new one for your boat."

Everyone laughed at my stunned disbelief and cheered again. I just looked around at them, my family. I had a lump the size of a golf ball in my throat when I tried to address them. They bought me a few moments when chants of "speech" rang out.

"What can I say, just... fuck, you have me speechless. There are so many years we have spent together, through good times and bad, and now even our families are family. We have stuck together and bailed each other out so many times... of course, Ramon more than anyone."

He raised his hand and gave a defiant wave as we all laughed.

"However, I never expected something like this. A captain isn't worth his salt without a great crew, and I have been blessed with the best crew I have ever had the privilege to work with. Thank you," I finished with my hands together, followed by a bow.

The claps and whistles erupted, and even those I didn't know shook my hand. It seemed it had been a marina-wide mission instigated by Jeff. They were most thrilled they'd pulled it off without me ever realizing. Jeff came over to my side.

"There's one more thing, follow me," he told me.

He led me down onto the back deck of the boat and reached for the deck hatch. We both pulled it aside and when I looked down, there was a brand new four-cylinder Yanmar diesel generator where my rusted, patched up piece of crap used to be.

"Jeff, this is too much, brother," I said as I felt a tear roll down my cheek. I threw my arm around him again as we stared at the engine.

"I take it you like it?" he smiled.

"You fucking kidding me man, this is unbelievable. Thank you, Jeff," I stammered, still reeling from the entire thing.

I looked over and saw China and Maria as they stared back at us with grins and hi-fives. I savored the moment, so it was engraved on my mind.

"Excuse the mess, we only just finished in time," said Ramon after he jumped aboard.

"I can't believe you all pulled this off in so little time," I added.

"It wasn't just us," confessed Jeff, "I doubled-up the yard crew with a few contractors."

I looked up at the tower, the sun casting a dark shadow across the deck, the polished aluminum glimmering in the sun.

"It's just amazing, I have nothing else to say but thank you. You all know what this means to me, and for it to come from all of you, makes it twice as special."

I pulled myself together enough to close the hatch. The majority of the others made their way back to the tiki. I looked out at all my friends that remained on the dock.

"Everyone on board, let's go for a ride," I yelled.

Ramon helped the ladies, and the rest of the crew aboard while I went into the cabin with Jeff. Nothing looked any different apart from the controls.

"This is new." I grinned.

"They are electronic, we got rid of those ol' dinosaur cables of yours. This is smoother, more dependable and easier to connect to the flybridge. I hope our modifications meet with approval?"

"That's an understatement." I laughed. "Let's fire her up."

I turned the key and the *San Blas* roared into life. The guys all cheered and the ladies just shook their heads at us. I walked out on deck, and over to Shirma and Izquierdo that were sitting on the transom bench.

"I know you both played a major part in all this, thank you so much from the bottom of my heart," I told them.

"No problem, Capi," they replied together.

"Throw off the lines, then come join us up on the bridge for a beer," I suggested.

"You got it," they answered as they got up.

I climbed the ladder to the bridge. As I stood there, it felt like I was on Jeff's boat. Walking closer to the console, I looked down and saw Maria and China chatting away near the bow. I switched the throttles to the flybridge and they slipped into gear effortlessly; Jeff was right, it really was nothing like cables.

I looked down and yelled, "Okay, Shirma, let's go."

The two of them expertly flipped the lines of the cleats before Shirma hollered back, "All lines aboard, Capi."

I clicked the engines into gear and spun the wheel. She slowly pulled away from the deck and I must have looked like a grinning idiot who was driving his first car. I eased us some twenty-feet from the dock, then clicked both engines ahead.

I idled the *San Blas* out into the marina basin, my eyes noting the fuel gauges were full before turning to Jeff. "I might have had her topped off as well."

"You're a good man." I replied, as he smiled wider.

"I know."

Taking the boat away from the other vessels that were moored in the marina, I increased the throttle, my baby cruised along and sounded better than she ever had. I aimed her for the jetties and spotted a slight swell offshore as we headed out.

"Everyone hold on," I shouted as I pushed the throttles to the stop and heard the turbos as they started to whistle as the RPMs came up. We accelerated so quickly that Jeff's hat blew off before he could catch it.

No point letting up. I chuckled to myself.

The guys were looking over the sides as we powered along the water. I looked about and saw my favorite two women holding onto the rails behind me. Their hair flew in the wind and they had a look that showed they loved it.

I looked at Jeff sitting next to me. "64 knots," I celebrated, "bet your beautiful beast won't do that."

He just smiled watching the bow lift over the swells. I let her rip for about five minutes before easing back to cruising speed. "I don't usually run her that long, but I thought I would enjoy a little of that free fuel you kindly gave me." I cruised for another twenty minutes and circled back to the marina.

I looked at the shiny new additions to my boat and still couldn't believe it. The dream of the tower I had in my mind for the *San*

Blas was nothing compared to reality. She looked so great that I gave myself a bit of praise for spending the money and labor I had on the inside so it looked as good as she did on the outside.

"I'm glad I could do this for you, Tomas. You have always been there for me, my brother. I'm going to go get us a beer."

I no sooner tied the boat up and a dark shadow loomed over me as Romon's deep voice spoke. "Someone here to see you cap." I turned to see Javier smiling slightly. My own smile spread across my lips as I gave him a hug. "I fucking knew it."

"Knew what?"

"That it was you that took out those sentries at the apartment," I replied as I shook my head.

"Yeah, well, we were just getting ready to breach when we heard your people coming through the woods so we retreated and let them handle the rest."

"But how did you know where?" I asked, slightly confused.

"I had my people following you since you picked up Ramon at the airport," he admitted quickly. "I have done some work in the past for Don Miguel's people. So, I found out through some contacts where she was being held and had my people get the information to China because I knew you would contact her."

Speechless at his words, I couldn't keep the smile from my face. "I can't thank you enough, brother."

"You're like a kid in a sweet store." Ramon smirked. "Sorry to bring you down to earth but we still need to go get our money."

Javier puts his hand on my shoulder, interrupting the conversation. "Looks like you guys have work to do and I have a job to get back to. You know how to get a hold of me if you need me." I was sorry to see him leaving so soon

As he climbed down the stairs I tapped Ramon. "Let's talk a minute before we go back to the party." He nodded and we took a seat on the sofa that wrapped around my new console.

"We need to discuss the next steps." "I assume you are talking about our cut." I nodded and replied in a low voice. "I know there is extra heat due to our little endeavor but they are looking for a couple Americans.

I was going to suggest we rent you a car tomorrow, you can pick up our money, and meet China me at the day dock in Progresso, I will give you an extra 10k from my cut for the trouble." He shook his hand dismissingly. "Don't worry Tomas, I can't fly home with 400k" he giggled. "Yeah right, I didn't really think about that part." I patted him on the shoulder as I stood up. "Shall we get back to the party?"

The Latin Run is a fiction novel but the characters and many of the stories within are based on actual events. I leave it to the reader to decide what to believe.